KU-201-941

LOVE THROUGH A STRANGER'S EYES

Chance Donovan returns home with a new face, new identity, a burning desire for revenge and good timing. His wife, Emily, is about to marry his best friend, the man Chance suspects is behind his nightmare imprisonment for the past few years. The minute Emily catches the ragged stranger stealing food from her lighthouse kitchen, she feels a strong attraction to him. Resisting the urge to send him packing, she decides to hire him. But will she break through the painful walls surrounding this quiet man? And why does his welcome touch make her forget the man she's about to marry?

Books by Jan Springer
Published by The House of Ulverscroft:

PEPPERMINT CREEK INN
AS BIG AS THE SKY

SPECIAL MESSAGE TO READERS

This book is published under the auspices of

THE ULVERSCROFT FOUNDATION

(registered charity No. 264873 UK)

Established in 1972 to provide funds for research, diagnosis and treatment of eye diseases. Examples of contributions made are: —

A Children's Assessment Unit at Moorfield's Hospital, London.

•

Twin operating theatres at the Western Ophthalmic Hospital, London.

•

A Chair of Ophthalmology at the Royal Australian College of Ophthalmologists.

•

The Ulverscroft Children's Eye Unit at the Great Ormond Street Hospital For Sick Children, London.

You can help further the work of the Foundation by making a donation or leaving a legacy. Every contribution, no matter how small, is received with gratitude. Please write for details to:

**THE ULVERSCROFT FOUNDATION,
The Green, Bradgate Road, Anstey,
Leicester LE7 7FU, England.
Telephone: (0116) 236 4325**

**In Australia write to:
THE ULVERSCROFT FOUNDATION,
c/o The Royal Australian and New Zealand
College of Ophthalmologists,
94-98 Chalmers Street, Surry Hills,
N.S.W. 2010, Australia**

Jan lives in Ontario, Canada. She enjoys writing her novels in a secluded cabin nestled in a stand of pine trees overlooking a picturesque lake. Hobbies include kayaking, ghost town hunting, vegetable gardening, cross-country skiing, nature walks and reading. Other books by Jan are *Peppermint Creek Inn* and *As Big As The Sky*.

JAN SPRINGER

—————◆—————

LOVE THROUGH A STRANGER'S EYES

Complete and Unabridged

ULVERSCROFT
Leicester

First published in the
United States of America

First Large Print Edition
published 2004

Names, characters and incidents depicted in this
book are products of the author's imagination or are
used fictitiously. Any resemblance to actual events,
locales, organizations, or persons, living or dead,
is entirely coincidental and beyond the intent
of the author or the publisher.

Copyright © 2002 by Janet Luchinger
All rights reserved

British Library CIP Data

Springer, Jan
    Love through a stranger's eyes.—Large print ed.—
Ulverscroft large print series: romance
1. Romantic suspense novels
2. Large type books
I. Title
813.6 [F]

ISBN 1–84395–447–8

Published by
F. A. Thorpe (Publishing)
Anstey, Leicestershire
Set by Words & Graphics Ltd.
Anstey, Leicestershire
Printed and bound in Great Britain by
T. J. International Ltd., Padstow, Cornwall

This book is printed on acid-free paper

Made with love for
Joey, Charlie, Uncle Sergio,
Grandma Berta and Aunt Lisetta.
We will cherish your memories forever.

1

Emily Montgomery McCullen peered through the darkness to the illuminated bedroom clock and smiled nervously.

Midnight. Halloween. The Witching Hour.

Time to put the romance formula to the test.

An involuntary shiver of apprehension scrambled up her spine and she returned her attention to the mirror. The pathetic sparkle of hope flashing in her hazel eyes brought a harsh chuckle from her lips.

Twenty-eight years old and she still believed in tales of romance. She should have her head examined. Her one true knight in shining armor was dead and no amount of wishful thinking or superstitious nonsense could change the fact she was destined not to have another wild romance in this lifetime.

Besides, who needed romance? She was getting married in a couple of weeks and soon she would have the kids she'd always wanted. At least that part of her dream could come true. And yet . . .

Since she was a small girl, she'd heard her uncle Jeb speak of the Halloween romance formula. If a girl of marrying age was bold enough, all she had to do was wait for the Halloween Witching Hour, sit in front of a mirror, brush her hair and at the same time eat an apple. If the image of a coffin appeared over her shoulder, she would not live another year. If the image of a man appeared, he would be her future husband.

Emily forced herself to pick up the cool apple with one hand and her mother's smooth ivory-handled brush in the other hand.

Okay, so she was being silly. So what? Who would it hurt? No one knew what she was doing tonight. No one had to know she'd totally flipped out.

With a shaky hand she drew the brush through her shoulder-length blond hair. At the same time she took a giant bite out of her apple, and kept her eyes glued to the mirror. To her disappointment nothing happened.

Oh well, at least the apple tasted good and her hair would get a nice brushing. She closed her eyes, sank back against the chair, and continued to nibble on the sweet treat.

Everything was unusually quiet tonight. No waves pounded against the steep cliff outside her Shipwreck Island lighthouse and the wind didn't so much as whisper against her windowpanes.

The only sounds she heard were the brush skimming through her thick curls, the crush of her teeth against her delicious victim and the faint tick of the clock.

She found herself relaxing under the slow ministrations of her brush strokes and began thinking of her future. Skip Cole was a nice enough fellow. Good father material. Only one problem though, he wanted her to leave her snug Canadian island and move back to New York City to live with him in his penthouse.

She hated the big city lights, noise and crowded streets. If she had to give up her dream of living in this cozy lighthouse for her other dream of having children come true, then she'd just have to compromise and leave her home.

Emily finished her apple, ran a final sweep through her hair and tried to ignore the lonely ache clutching her heart. When she opened her eyes, she gasped in disbelief. In the mirror, over her shoulder, hovered an image of her dead husband, smiling that wonderful crooked grin of his.

Her heart crashed painfully against her chest and a cold knot of fear scrambled into her belly. She whirled around and sighed in relief when she realized it was just a fluke.

A stray moonbeam had lit up Steve's side

3

of their wedding portrait that hung on the wall.

Emily placed the brush on the vanity and chuckled to herself.

For crying out loud. It was now officially October thirty-one and spooky things were supposed to happen. Everyone deserved a good scare on Halloween. It wouldn't be the same if it was treated as just another normal day.

Emily headed to her open bedroom window. Trails of white mist swirled amongst the rocky cliffs below and hovered over the glass-like ocean. The only indication of an approaching storm was the wrinkled black clouds stalking ever closer to the full moon.

When a cool breeze drifted in and whispered a warning against her ear, Emily reached up to close the window. At the same time an odd noise erupted from somewhere inside her tiny lighthouse. The hairs on the back of her neck prickled.

Slowly Emily reached for the can of Mace her fiancé had brought from the States and insisted she keep beside her bed. Trembling, she tiptoed to her open door and peered out. Delicate moonbeams dusted her furniture with an eerie blue glaze.

For what seemed an eternity she stood in the doorway feeling as helpless as a mole, her

4

ears pricked for any sign of something amiss. She noted the pale light erupting through the kitchen doorway and recognized it immediately. Someone had opened the refrigerator door!

Resisting the urge to retreat like a scaredy-cat and escape out the back door, Emily shakily pointed the Mace in front of her and on wobbly legs inched toward the kitchen.

The minute she reached the doorway, she halted and blinked in disbelief. For an endless moment she could only stare at the dark outline of a man's form hunched forward, leaning into her open refrigerator.

He seemed so engrossed in devouring her fried chicken he didn't even notice he'd been caught red-handed. To her horror, he stuck his head deeper into her fridge and reached for another one of the drumsticks she'd slaved over in special preparation for tomorrow's fall fair.

'Touch it and I'll cut off your fingers!' Emily warned.

Startled by her threat, the intruder's head crashed against the inside top of the fridge. A whispery curse quickly followed.

'No sudden moves,' Emily hissed.

The air in her lungs, as well as her nerve, was quickly vanishing. 'I have a gun and I'll blow a hole the size of Shipwreck Island right through your gut.'

Oh God, she sounded like a Texas Ranger in a spaghetti western, but her threat was working, the intruder hadn't flinched a muscle. Hopefully she could usher him out of her home before he noticed her weapon of choice wasn't a gun like she'd said.

'Don't shoot. I'm unarmed.' He called out in an odd whispery voice that made him sound as if he had mild laryngitis.

'That's your first mistake!' She said, trying hard to keep her own voice tough. 'My husband is in the next room. All I have to do is scream, so you better get out!'

'Okay. Okay. Take it easy. I think I'd better explain.'

'Don't bother. Hit the door, buddy.'

'But — '

'Get out! Now!'

When he edged past her, Emily tensed with fright. His dangerous scent swarmed out of the darkness and she couldn't help but inhale. He smelled of the fresh ocean breeze, wave crashed beaches and a deep loneliness that tugged at her heart.

When he reached the door he hesitated. 'I'm sorry, I didn't mean to frighten you.'

'Too late. Leave!'

She tensed when his hand snaked through

the gloominess to flick on the light switch. The harsh light burned into her eyes making her blink wildly. Was he trying to blind her? So he could grab her? Instinctively her finger tightened on the Mace trigger, ready to shoot.

Thankfully he remained by the door, but slowly turned around to face her.

Scarcely breathing, Emily couldn't help taking inventory.

At least one foot taller than her, he was handsome in a rugged outdoorsy familiar kind of way. Sprinkles of gray dusted his collar-length, golden-brown hair.

He had a strong, straight nose. A tiny cleft in his chin. No lines around his mouth. A mouth that suddenly dropped open in surprise at the sight of the Mace.

But it was his eyes that captured her full attention. Sparkling ocean blue, they were filled with layers of emotions. The most prominent, a haunted sadness that ripped at her insides.

His intense gaze unsettled her. It was an oddly familiar gaze. An intimate look that said they'd shared many secrets, yet she swore she'd never laid eyes on this man before in her life.

He seemed to expect her to say something and when she didn't, he smiled a somewhat crooked grin that zapped a powerful jolt of déjà vu straight through her. The spooky feeling urged her not to let this man simply walk out of her life.

Emily inhaled sharply at a glittering gold medallion that hung from his neck. She could barely make out the image, but instinctively knew it would be a portrait of a man carrying a child on his shoulders.

A St. Christopher's necklace! A medal signifying safety to travelers. She'd given her husband, Steve, one like it many years ago.

She watched helplessly as the stranger's large hand twisted on the doorknob.

Let him go! A voice inside her shouted. *He's dangerous.*

A loud, hungry growl escaped his stomach and a pang of guilt slithered through Emily. He turned and stepped across the threshold.

Don't let him leave, her heart begged. Anyone who wore a St. Christopher's medallion couldn't be all bad.

'Wait!'

Her curt shout stopped him cold and his shoulders tensed. Raising his hands over his head, he clamped his fingers behind his neck and waited anxiously. Obviously he figured she was going to call the police and press charges against him for trespassing.

'The least I can do is feed you. You can put your arms down, but stay right there.' She noticed some of the tenseness seep out of his limbs.

He did as she instructed.

Keeping her Mace ready and her eyes glued to the tall stranger standing in her doorway, Emily stumbled toward the open refrigerator. She tried to keep calm, but it didn't work.

Her hands shook as she tugged out the goods she'd made for the fair. To make matters worse she could barely scoop the food onto a plate, all the while her jumbled mind chastised her for not getting rid of the stranger.

She topped the heaping plate of food with more fried chicken. It was a mistake encouraging him to linger. The sooner she fed him the faster she could send him on his way. And yet, there was something oddly familiar about him. What? She couldn't be sure, but something told her she just might be better off not knowing.

With plate in hand she turned to the door and blinked in surprise.

The stranger was gone and her emergency key dangled quietly in the door lock!

★   ★   ★

He stepped onto the wooden deck thoroughly enjoying the crisp autumn wind slice painfully into his face.

He'd seen her!

By golly it was better than he'd ever imagined. The mere sight of her made him feel so alive. So free.

On impulse he'd flicked on the light switch, hoping she would recognize him, wrap her soft arms around his neck and welcome him home with a mind blowing kiss. Deep down he knew it wouldn't happen. The extensive plastic surgery had totally changed his appearance and the damage done to his voice box made sure she would never recognize his voice.

But she sure looked fantastic. Her once long hair was now fashioned into a new shoulder-length curly do and her bangs gone in favor of the no bang hippie look. He'd heard that style was making a comeback. It suited her better, he had to admit, and she looked so healthy, so fresh, so innocent.

Dammit!

He should have stuck to his plan of simply breaking into the lighthouse, grabbing what he needed and leaving. Yet, when he smelled the delicious aromas floating through the air, his stomach had automatically clenched painfully. A gentle reminder he hadn't eaten a proper meal in days.

He'd made a big mistake breaking into the

house while she was home. It still wasn't too late to make it right again. He could simply slip away and break in another time.

Indecision screamed at him as he lifted his head to look at the wrinkled black clouds threatening to blanket the moon directly overhead. In order to keep her safe he needed to leave this instant before bad weather hit, but now that he'd seen her, how could he leave?

A soft noise behind him made him jump and he whirled around to find her nervously sliding a plate of food onto the deck's railing a few feet away from him. His mouth watered and his stomach growled again. Without hesitation he reached out and took the plate.

The tantalizing aromas did the food justice. Like a starving wolf, he downed the crispy fried chicken, the onion-drenched potato salad and the delicious arrangement of other goodies she'd stacked on the large plate.

It wasn't until his plate was nearly empty that he noticed her watching him intently, her face pale and her eyes wide with shock.

He knew fear. Lived with it for years. Smelled it. Saw it in other people's eyes and he saw it in hers now. He hated himself for bringing terror back into her life. But there was something else brewing in those hazel depths. Curiosity.

When she held up the rusty key he'd used to gain access to her home, he stopped chewing. The last bite of food suddenly tasted like sawdust and it took a great deal of effort to swallow it.

'Lucky guess?' she asked coldly.

'Doesn't everyone keep an extra key behind a loose brick in their outside wall near their back door?'

'Sorry, I'm not buying that one.'

'Okay you got me. Your in-laws told me about you.'

'Which in-laws?'

'Your husband's brother, Daniel and his wife, Jo.'

A sparkle of relief shone in her hazel eyes, but he could tell by the way she held her Mace she wasn't sure she should believe him.

'I knew your husband, Steve, too.'

'My husband is dead,' she said quietly.

'I know.' He replied just as quietly, noting the raw pain etching her voice.

Her gaze drifted to his St. Christopher's medallion and a shiver of unease screamed through him. Did she recognize it? Would she ask to take a closer look? He couldn't allow that to happen.

'Why would they tell you about my spare key?' she asked.

'They said you're out on the ocean quite

often harvesting seaweed and I should let myself in if you weren't around.'

'It's midnight, mister. Obviously my boat is docked. I'm here. Why didn't you knock?'

'Didn't want to wake you up.'

'And so you thought you'd make yourself cozy until I woke up and found a complete stranger in my house?' Hot anger tinged her words and a bright pink flushed her cheeks pushing away the sickly paleness. 'You didn't think you'd scare me?'

He shrugged. 'I figured I was harmless.'

'I'm glad one of us thinks so. Why didn't any one tell me you were coming?'

'You'd have to ask them.'

'Don't think I won't.'

'Perhaps I should come back another time?'

'It might be best.'

'I really am sorry for being so rude, Mrs. McCullen. I should have come during the day. It's just that your in-laws spoke so much about you. I feel as if I already know you.'

'Since you know so much about me, how about telling me your name?'

The question floored him and he hesitated. Here was his chance to spill the whole truth, but he couldn't quite bring himself to do it. It would only tear her world apart. He wasn't ready to do that.

He probably never would be ready.

'Chance. Chance Donovan.' He gave her the fake name he'd been forced to use over the past few years.

She nodded slightly and he waited for recognition to flare in her eyes. But nothing happened.

'I don't think my husband ever mentioned you.'

That's because I am your husband, he wanted to yell.

'We go way back,' he said. 'Childhood friends in Montana.'

Emily nodded as a spattering of cold raindrops began to trickle down on them. He noticed she was shivering.

'I'd better let you get back inside. You're getting all wet.'

'It'll be too dangerous to go back out on the ocean. Looks like a storm is brewing. You may as well come in, Mr. Donovan.'

Inside? He hadn't expected her to ask him into the lighthouse. A great deal of mistrust flooded her eyes and she looked very uncomfortable, and that's the last thing he wanted.

'I really should go.'

'No, please come inside. I'll put on some hot tea. I can't very well let a friend of my husband's stay out in the chilly rain and get sick.'

14

He noted the flash of tenderness sparkling in her eyes, a direct contrast to the Mace she still pointed at him. The sight of the can made him uneasy and he wished he could wrench it away from her on the odd chance she decided to use it, but he suspected she'd give him a good shot of the fiery stuff before he even made a move. Over the past years he'd experienced the harsh fact of being pepper sprayed and he wasn't anxious to relive those memories.

He kept a safe distance from her and the Mace and reluctantly stepped back into the lighthouse. She closed the door and headed for the kitchen sink while he stood by the doorway, suddenly feeling awkward.

Earlier, when he'd broken in, he hadn't noticed the changes. First, it had been dark and then when he'd switched on the lights, he'd focused his attention primarily on Emily. Now he realized she'd totally redecorated the kitchen.

The ancient, creaking gray floorboards were now a varnished oak. The plain brown cedar cabinets had been painted a crisp vanilla and the upper doors contained glass panels that proudly showed off an array of fancy dinnerware. Smart brass and ceramic pulls complimented the look.

A thoughtfully designed, elegant island

counter included shelves containing more dishes, drawers, an empty wine rack and a black, marble countertop laden with a giant glass bowl filled with a variety of fresh fruit. A new stove had replaced the old one. The only things she'd kept the same were the 1960's refrigerator and the intimate oak table for two.

She'd always had good taste in decor. Not to mention great taste in nightgowns.

Her feminine peach-colored nightgown was painfully thin and the raindrops made parts of it virtually invisible. Try as he might he couldn't pull his attention away from the wonderful sight. Through the sheer fabric he had no trouble making out her lush shape. She'd changed and definitely for the better.

No longer a rail thin young lady, she'd bloomed into a woman with generous curves. Long legs. Shapely hips. An exquisite waist he ached to touch and perky looking breasts. He closed his eyes as a strong, hot wave of desire washed through his body, leaving him totally tense.

She still had the same overpowering effect on him! Hell, it's even more powerful than he remembered. Being without a woman for so many years probably had something to do with it. He needed to leave before his body and his heart caved in on him.

'You can have a seat in the living room, Mr. Donovan.' Her sweet voice made him open his eyes.

Thankfully she hadn't noticed his intense reaction to her. Her face was turned away from him while she searched for something in an upper cabinet. She dragged down a carton, which he assumed was the tea. She filled a kettle with water and plugged it into the socket.

She turned around and nodded to the doorway she'd been standing in earlier when she'd caught him with his hands on her fried chicken drumsticks. 'Living room is right over there. I'll bring the tea to you.'

He got the feeling she wanted him out of the room and he had a pretty good idea why. He threw a knowing glance at the telephone before he walked into the adjoining room and stepped straight into his past.

He allowed his greedy gaze to suck in the wonderful sight of white painted wood walls, the electric baseboard heaters he'd installed under the giant gable windows, the green overstuffed leather sofa strewn with the same buttery yellow pillows they'd fought with on several occasions, and the braided oval rug that covered most of the living room floor.

The cheerful colors of the carpet gave the room a bright, informal atmosphere that welcomed Chance and he found himself relaxing for the first time in years.

2

The moment he slipped into the next room Emily headed straight for her kitchen phone. Dialing quickly, she inhaled a breath of thanks when her sister-in-law's friendly voice answered after the first ring.

'Hi, Jo! It's me,' she whispered, trying to keep her tone low so the stranger wouldn't hear her talking.

'What's wrong, Emily?'

'Can't pull one over on you, can I?'

'Not at this hour. What's up?'

'Chance Donovan is here.'

'Chance is there? Oh, thank God.' Surprise and relief etched her voice.

'I gather you know him?'

'Yes. We do. He's actually right there? With you?'

'Bold as life. In the living room.'

'Oh my goodness. That's great news. We were wondering where he'd gotten off to. Hold on. Daniel wants to talk to you.'

'Emily, it's me.' Emily frowned into the receiver at her brother-in-law's rushed and frantic voice. 'You said Chance is there? How's he doing?'

'He seems fine to me. A bit hungry.'

Daniel laughed. 'Well, I'll be damned. That's a good sign.'

'He said you told him about me and he decided to drop in for a visit.'

'You sound kind of rattled. Why don't you tell me what happened, Emily?'

Quickly she explained how Chance had used the emergency key to access her home and how she'd discovered him stealing her food.

'He's harmless,' Daniel said warmly. 'Just down on his luck and looking for a place to stay.'

'He says he knew Steve.'

'Oh yes, he knows Steve. I mean, he knew Steve, and the rest of the McCullens. He knows us very well. He's been staying with us for awhile. I mentioned you were living all alone in that big empty lighthouse and suggested he go on over and you'd put him up.'

'You what?'

'I invited him to stay with you for awhile.'

Emily blinked wildly not believing what she was hearing.

'It'll be great,' Daniel continued quickly. 'Maybe he can help you fix up the lighthouse before you put it on the market.'

'Daniel! I don't even know him!'

'He is a very shy fellow. Like I said, down on his luck. I'm sure your home cooking will cheer him right up. He's nothing to worry about, Emily. You won't even know he's there. Listen, I have to go. Sweet dreams,' Daniel said cheerfully and hung up.

Emily frowned into the receiver. What in the world was going on with Daniel? She told her usually overprotective brother-in-law that a total stranger let himself into her home and all Daniel said was 'sweet dreams'? Ever since he'd gotten married, Daniel had been in seventh heaven, maybe all his new found happiness had clouded his judgment.

She remembered all too well that euphoric feeling of being in love.

Twenty years old and innocent, she'd been swept off her feet by the handsome investigative journalist, Steve McCullen. He'd moved into her New York apartment days after they met and were married a few weeks later, coming to her uncle's Shipwreck Island lighthouse for their honeymoon.

At first, Steve hadn't liked it here. He complained about the smell of rotting seaweed and the chapped lips the ocean breeze constantly created. He said the island was far too isolated, being a half an hour boat ride from Prince Edward Island. On top of that his mind was tormented over the recent death of his mother, a woman Emily knew for only a few short weeks and the closest she'd had to a mother since her own had died when Emily was young.

When the honeymoon was over, they'd returned to New York and Steve had immersed himself in his work. She'd been too lenient with her new husband, allowing him to leave on those overseas assignments. He was gone for weeks on end and when he came back home, their time together was intense, romantic and too short.

Finally she'd put her foot down, demanding he stay home more often. To her surprise he agreed. They'd only recently decided to move into the tiny lighthouse when tragedy struck.

She should never have married Steve McCullen. She'd been too deeply in love. A love that had clouded her thinking. Love was painful and she had vowed never to fall in love again.

'Do I pass the test?' The stranger's hoarse voice made Emily's breath catch in her throat.

She whirled around to find him standing in the doorway, his arms casually folded across his chest. He'd removed his green jacket and was wearing a somewhat wrinkled blue turtleneck that fit over his broad shoulders like a second skin.

The blueness of his clothing enhanced the ocean blue in his sparkling eyes and Emily found herself mesmerized by his gaze. His cute mouth, which was inching upwards into that heart-wrenching crooked grin, made her insides quiver with delight.

No man had made her feel this feminine, at least not since her husband, and darned if she would let this stranger make her feel so good.

'Do you make it a habit of listening in on other people's conversations?' she snapped.

His eyebrows lifted slightly in surprise. 'Just wanted to let you know your kettle is whistling Dixie.'

'My kettle?'

'For the tea.' He nodded toward the kettle she'd plugged in earlier.

She grimaced at the shrill whistle piercing the air. 'Oh for heaven's sake. I didn't even hear it.'

Angrily she reached out to pull the plug and inadvertently her arm breezed right over the steam shooting out of the kettle's spout. It blasted a scorching heat against the bottom of her wrist. She screamed from the searing pain.

Before she knew what was happening, the stranger's large hand splayed across the small of her back and he led her toward the kitchen sink. He remained silent as he delicately maneuvered her burned wrist underneath the tap. Cold water splashed against the red welt, but did nothing to douse the fiery tingles his large fingers evoked. Gosh, she hadn't felt such an intimate attraction to a man in years.

Her breath backed up into her lungs when she spotted the soft tenderness brewing in his powerful blue eyes. Emily shifted uneasily at his concern.

If he noticed her uneasiness, he didn't let on. Instead his attention appeared to be focused on the tiny water blisters quickly forming on the burned area. 'Doesn't look too bad. I'll get a bowl so you can soak it while you sit, it'll be more comfortable for you.'

So, he had noticed her move away from him. Did he think she was still scared of him or did he know she was suddenly totally aware of him as a man? Oddly enough since the telephone conversation with her in-laws her fear of him had mysteriously vanished leaving her with this sudden . . . attraction.

A moment later he had her situated snugly on the living room couch, her wrist soaking in the cold water, her mind and body sparring over him while he moved around in the next room. Making tea. For her!

She'd always had a weakness for tall, lean

men and Chance Donovan was all of those and much more. His perfectly shaped lips were so kissable looking, not to mention what she'd like to do to that deep cleft in his chin. His long fingers set every inch of where he'd touched her on fire. The man excited her. Pure and simple.

A noise from the kitchen forced Emily to steady her erratic heartbeat by taking some deep breaths. Heaven knew she didn't want Chance to find her all flustered because he'd know why. A man always knew when a woman was thinking about him. At least it had been that way with Steve.

When she heard Chance's heavy footsteps approaching, she straightened to attention. He placed a tray laden with two steaming mugs of chamomile tea on the coffee table. Her heart sank when she spotted the chocolate-potato brownies she'd made for the Halloween fair's bake sale. All cut up and ready to eat.

'I hope you don't mind. I found the brownies stashed at the back of the fridge. I thought it would go perfectly with the tea,' he said.

'That's fine,' Emily replied tightly. Thank God he hadn't found the pie.

When he sat down on the couch beside her, she shifted uneasily. In a split second his dangerous scent swarmed all around her and she discovered her insides were trembling with excitement like a young teenage girl who suddenly realized why guys existed.

'How's your wrist?'

Before she could answer, he reached out and gently lifted her hand out of the cold water. A wonderful sizzle of pure heat shot through her arm again as his large fingers carefully turned her wrist around so he could get a better look at her injury.

His cute lips turned down into a concerned frown, 'Looks worse than before.'

'Doesn't feel bad. Just stings a little.'

'You have something to put on it?'

'I've got some ointment I can put on later.' The last thing she needed was for him to start applying slippery ointment on her with those lethal fingers.

'Burns need moisture to heal. Don't let the air get at it. Keep it in the water for a while longer, it'll help ease the burning. Then lather lots of ointment on it. Do you have gauze?'

'Yes.'

'Tape the gauze over the ointment. It'll prevent the burn from getting dried out or dirty.'

His genuine concern touched Emily, making her feel guilty at the way she'd yelled at him earlier. 'I'm sorry I snapped at you before when I was on the phone. It's just . . . '

What could she say? His crooked grin and fantastic scent made her swoon? Not to mention angry because she shouldn't be feeling this way about this man, especially since she was getting married to another man in a couple of weeks.

'No need for apologies, Mrs. McCullen. Like I said earlier, I'm the one who is rude for barging in on you. If I might ask, who vouched for me on the phone?'

'Jo and Daniel.'

'Ah yes. The newlyweds.' His luscious lips turned upward into a warm smile. 'Daniel actually said something nice on my behalf?' His voice sounded amused.

'Daniel speaks very highly of you and you seem to have made quite an impression on Jo.'

'Jo is a very nice woman. A perfect match for my . . . friend.'

'I don't recall seeing you at their wedding this past summer.'

'I couldn't make it. Other commitments.'

He took a giant sip of tea and Emily noticed how his large hands dwarfed her delicate teacup. She needed to rummage around and produce one of those big mugs Steve loved.

Chance picked up a giant brownie and

27

shoved the entire thing into his mouth. He grinned and said between bites, 'This, is fantastic!'

'Glad you like it. Um, Daniel mentioned you were looking for some work?'

'He did?'

'You sound surprised.'

An angry burst of wind shook the glass panes in the south windows and Emily noticed him tense at the harsh sound. He sure was a jumpy fellow. He reacted the same way earlier when she'd brought the food to him outside.

Her curiosity about this stranger notched up a few degrees. 'I do have some work that needs to be done. If you are interested?'

Indecision flashed in his eyes.

'I need someone to repair my dock. Help me with the seaweeding. Might take a few days.'

'I don't want to intrude.'

'You already have,' she teased. 'You can use the room upstairs. Sheets are clean and there's a bunch of quilts and blankets up there in case you get cold. Breakfast is usually at six a.m. sharp. Are you interested?'

He bit his lower lip and when she got the impression he might say no, her heart sank. Then he nodded yes and she was surprised at the tingle of happiness shooting through her body.

He drained the rest of his tea then stood.

'I think I'd better let you get some sleep, Mrs. McCullen. Don't forget about the ointment and the gauze to keep the burn moist.'

'Thanks for the advice, Doctor Donovan.'

He smiled and reached for a couple more large brownies. 'Two more for the road.'

Emily laughed. 'I'm glad you like my cooking. Goodnight, Mr. Donovan.'

'Goodnight.'

She listened to his heavy footsteps as he walked up the steep staircase to the spare bedroom. A moment later she heard the quiet click of the door closing. In a flash her thoughts returned to the very interesting telephone conversation she'd had with Jo and Daniel.

Daniel had been thrilled to hear Chance was hungry. The newcomer was a bit on the thin side, but he certainly didn't have a problem with his appetite. Daniel had also mentioned Chance was down on his luck. Had he been in some sort of accident? Lost his job? Or maybe he'd lost someone he loved? Maybe that explained why she sensed his overwhelming loneliness.

And why were Jo and Daniel so concerned about him? Obviously they cared deeply for him. But if he was so close to the McCullen family, then why hadn't anyone ever mentioned him?

They'd been very relieved to discover he was here with her. Had they sent him over as some sort of matchmaking ploy? Daniel made it no secret that he believed Skip wasn't right for her.

But lately she'd grown closer to him. A few weeks ago he'd stated they weren't getting any younger. He wanted kids just like she did, so why not get hitched?

It wasn't a romantic proposal. More like a business deal. But she'd said yes. Oddly enough the thought that she was getting married didn't hold too much appeal. Skip Cole didn't whirl up the intense feelings of wild desire or even the love she'd experienced with her late husband.

On the other hand, Chance oozed masculinity. He'd definitely gotten her motor running again.

'Who are you, Chance Donovan?' she whispered quietly beneath her breath. 'And why does your crooked smile and your touch make my insides jump like a live wire?'

★   ★   ★

Chance sucked in a surprised gasp as he stepped into the cozy upstairs room. Mainly decorated in a bower of blue shades, the tiny area was anchored by a beige iron double bed. An old ladder leaned against a nearby wall with an assortment of colorful quilts layering its rungs. Covering the entire length of another wall hung a rope fishing net decorated sporadically with hand-sized pieces of odd-shaped driftwood ornaments and crusty seashells. He immediately fell in love with the room's casual nature and the delicious aroma of pine.

Crossing the pine-planked floor, he headed straight for the night blackened window and looked out. Aside from the silvery rain dropping like sheets, all he could see was his reflection staring back at him.

A stranger's face. A stranger's eyes. He didn't think he'd ever get used to the shocking blueness of those eyes.

Eyes that had once belonged to someone else. To whom? He didn't want to know. They had belonged to someone who'd died a tragic death in order for him to be able to see again. But now they were a part of him, just as his new face was a part of him.

Chance frowned and felt the muscles tighten around his mouth. Something else he'd have to get used to was the way his muscles did funny things when he smiled, frowned or even laughed, but the doctors said he'd get used to it. It just took time. Time wasn't what he had with Emily's marriage swooping down on him.

He moved away from the window and stretched out on the soft mattress. The truth about his real identity would remain a secret to spare Emily a whole lot of hurt. It was better this way, but why did he feel as if his heart was being crushed to smithereens?

★   ★   ★

Grey slabs of daylight crept into Emily's bedroom prompting her to think about getting up. She'd been semi-awake for hours, her senses never venturing far from the mysterious Chance Donovan. Numerous times she'd wanted to pick up the phone, call her in-laws and get answers to all those nagging questions she had about him.

Knowing Daniel and Jo they'd tease her endlessly, telling her to give up on getting married if the first stranger interested her so much.

Of course they would be right. She should be concentrating on her fiancé and their upcoming nuptials. At the thought of Skip, apprehension shot through her and she forced herself to whip aside the snug blankets and get out of bed.

To her surprise, she felt more alive this morning than she had in years. She applied more ointment to the burn and taped it with gauze, then dressed in a pink wool sweater and a pair of gray wool slacks and headed into the living room.

No sound came from the upstairs room where Chance slept and since they hadn't gone to bed until well after midnight, she opted to let him sleep in awhile longer.

While the coffee brewed, Emily searched the back of some of the cupboards until her hands fell upon the smooth ceramic of the giant mugs she wanted. She couldn't help but smile at the pleasant memories of the days her husband and she had sat at their cozy intimate table for two, giant mugs clasped in their hands as they planned on how many children they'd have together. They'd joked about who would change the diapers and get up for the midnight feedings. Unfortunately their dreams had never been realized because Steve died.

Emily frowned as she poured the hot coffee and headed outdoors.

The crisp, salty ocean air almost took her breath away as she stepped onto the deck overlooking the cliffs. The rain from last night had given way to a beautiful breezy morning. The sky was turning a cool blue and bright sunshine shot sparkles of diamonds off the ocean's white-capped waves.

Two more weeks and she'd leave here, forever. Anxious tears welled up in her eyes, blurring the surrounding beauty. She'd loved it here from the first time she'd seen the lonely little lighthouse when at the age of thirteen her parents had died in a car crash and her uncle Jeb, her only close living relative, told her she was coming home to stay with him.

She'd been furious at her parents for dying and mad as hell at her uncle for forcing her to leave all her friends in Toronto. Thankfully her uncle had been a patient and gentle man. He'd given her only one simple rule. She was in charge of the meals. Before long she'd begged him to give her more chores, and he taught her how to clean the lamps in the lighthouse tower and the surrounding windows so the light would shine brightly through the foggy nights. He showed her how to maneuver his fishing boat, *Sweet Lies*, around the dangerous craggy reefs.

By her fourteenth birthday, Emily knew everything there was to know about running the lighthouse. Then when she turned seventeen a bomb dropped on them.

Uncle Jeb's tiny little lighthouse was no longer needed. A better location had been found a mile down the coast and the new lighthouse would be fully automated and run by the Canadian Coast Guard.

Emily and her uncle were officially out of a job. But Uncle Jeb wasn't one for being down in the dumps for too long. He stepped right into his fishing boat and began raking seaweed and catching lobsters for a living while Emily got a seasonal job on nearby Prince Edward Island. In the town of Cavendish she helped run a souvenir shop for the many tourists who swept onto the island to savor its beauty and who came to seek out the birthplace of Lucy Maud Montgomery, the famous author of the book *Anne of Green Gables*.

While working there, Emily took the opportunity to read Lucy Maud Montgomery's books and was soon bitten by the writing bug. She trudged off to the University of Toronto where she took journalism. During holidays she visited her uncle at every opportunity and learned the tricks to seaweeding. Shortly after graduating, she got a job as a reporter with the *New York Times* and shortly after that she caught the eye of Steve McCullen.

Anger burned through her at the thought of her husband. She hadn't been this angry at him since he'd been alive. Why in the world

35

was she mad now? But Emily knew why. Because Chance Donovan made her remember what it felt like to be a woman. Something her fiancé had been unable to do. Abruptly she tossed the remains of her now cold coffee over the deck railing into the ocean and headed back inside.

★ ★ ★

Emily peeked into the bedroom and smiled. Chance still lay in the same position as when she'd checked on him over six hours ago. Fully clothed, his hands were clasped over his stomach as if in prayer and his chest rose and fell in quiet rhythm.

She tiptoed into the room and peered down at him. Sleep softened his features. His lips were parted and tilted slightly as if he were smiling up at her. Luscious black lashes hid his startling blue eyes and he wore a couple days worth of whiskers. They gave his face a sexy bad boy look she found quite appealing.

On the wicker chair beside Chance's bed she placed a pair of hardly used jeans, a cotton undershirt and a thick denim shirt and a few other items. They had been her husband's. Personal items she'd saved. Clothing she'd touched and smelled and clutched to her heart during the first couple of dark years following Steve's death. When she had finally accepted he wasn't coming home, she'd laundered and folded them and stuffed them into a closet. Now they would come in handy for Chance.

She returned her attention to the stranger. This time to her surprise something powerful stirred inside her chest and two words echoed in her mind.

Déjà vu.

She shook her head and tried to get rid of the uneasy feeling, but it just wouldn't go away.

★   ★   ★

'Hello? Open your eyes.'

The sweet voice seemed to come from somewhere far away, and yet Chance knew she was close. Her sweet ocean scent wrapped snugly around him and he inhaled deeply, allowing her wonderful smell to cascade into every pore. He savored it. Memorized it. Something special for him to hold.

'Are you still alive?' Emily whispered.

At those words, a chill slid up his back forcing him to pop open his eyes. His heart smashed painfully against his chest as he discovered her standing over him. Her bright

37

hazel eyes pierced through the lingering mist of his sleep.

'You were dead to the world, Mr. Donovan. I called up a couple of times, but you didn't answer.'

She smiled down at him and those perfect dimples caved in her lovely cheeks making Chance's heart do an unbelievable number of flip-flops.

'I hope you don't mind my coming up?'

'Not at all,' he answered, thoroughly aware of the way her warm body heat scrambled through his jeans and flirted with his skin.

'Are you up for some lunch?'

'Lunch?'

'It's already past one.'

'Oh! Wow! I'm sorry. I haven't slept like this in years.'

Emily laughed a hearty laugh that clutched at Chance's soul.

'It's the ocean air. You'll get used to it in time.'

He stretched his arms lazily and caught her watching him. She'd told him many times she'd loved his sleepy look when he first woke up in the morning. Was he only imagining that hungry look shining in her eyes? That sexy look that told him she wanted him to make love to her? It was only wishful thinking on his part because she didn't know his true identity.

He was someone else now. A Humpty Dumpty who'd been put together again after falling apart. Only this time around he had a few screws missing. He must be insane to accept a job from his wife. 'I've already slept half the working day away. Not a good way to impress the boss.'

'As long as you don't make it a habit on work mornings,' she said warmly. 'Oh! I brought your duffel bag up from your boat.'

Chance blinked.

'Don't look so shocked, Mr. Donovan. I didn't snoop. But I think everything in your duffel might be soaked so I left you some of my husband's clothes. They should fit you. Seems the clothes you're wearing are a bit worse for wear.'

He glanced down at his rumpled appearance.

'I guess I fell asleep in them.' *While I was waiting for you to go to sleep so I could get what I came for and leave*, he added silently.

She turned to leave.

'Um, Mrs. McCullen?'

'Please call me Emily, Mr. Donovan.'

'And you can call me Chance. Thanks, Emily, for putting up with my bad sleeping habits. It won't happen again. I'll get straight to work.'

'That's something I'd like to discuss with

you over lunch. See you in a bit.'

He listened to her light footsteps as she descended the steep wooden stairs. What did she want to talk to him about? He peered at the duffel bag she'd set beneath the east window. If she'd gone through his belongings, she wouldn't be acting so bright and cheerful.

Had she changed her mind about hiring him? Did his sleeping in ruin his chances of sticking around? He shook the questions aside. What the heck was he thinking? He couldn't hang around Emily. It was too dangerous. Especially for him because she was already interfering with his survival instincts. He hadn't even heard her tiptoeing around up here and to make matters worse he'd slept through his best opportunity for searching the lighthouse.

★ ★ ★

Emily was placing the burgers onto the buns when she heard the shower taps shut off. All morning she'd been cooking and baking, replacing the food Chance had eaten last night. All the while she'd been trying to figure out who he really was. Why did he seem familiar and why did he use her emergency key to gain access to her home?

A shy man, as Daniel had described him,

wouldn't show up in the middle of the night unannounced and he would have knocked. Which led her to the conclusion Daniel hadn't told her the truth about this sexy stranger. And she would get to the truth as sure as her name was Emily McCullen.

She closed her eyes and remembered the sleepy look on Chance's face this morning. He'd erupted those *déjà vu* feelings again and when he stretched those long, muscular arms, she found herself imagining their warmth wrapped around her waist as he pulled her against his hard length.

She nearly gasped out loud when a moment later the door to the bathroom burst open and Chance Donovan stepped out, barefoot and clad only in a snug pair of jeans and the thick denim shirt that had once belonged to her husband. It fit him perfectly.

She drank in his wet, tousled hair, and clean-shaven face and felt her throat go dry. The man looked even better after a shower! Realizing he was watching her carefully, she refocused her attention on the burgers. 'How do you like your burgers dressed — I mean done?'

'Tons of relish, loaded with mustard, easy on the ketchup and mayo and a slice of lettuce if you have it.'

When he suddenly moved closer, her body

tingled with excitement. She felt his warm breath dance across the back of her neck.

'Looks fantastic,' he said. 'I'm starved. Want me to set the table?'

'Sure. Plates are — '

'In this cupboard.'

Emily held her breath as he stretched like a tomcat. The muscles in his arms flexed as he dragged out a couple of plates and two glasses. Have mercy! It suddenly seemed awfully warm in here.

'Um,' she began, trying hard to keep her voice as professional as one would speak to an employee. 'I'm short on time today so I couldn't whip up something more fancy than burgers and fries. I have to get over to Prince Edward Island. There's a Halloween fair on the main island near the North Cape. That's what I wanted to talk to you about.'

He didn't say anything as he placed the plates and glasses on the tiny table.

She grabbed the plate of burgers, and utensils and asked him to sit. She swallowed to clear her dry throat and plunged ahead with her question. 'I wanted to know if you could give me a hand and bring the food over to the fair?'

He shifted uncomfortably and said rather quietly, 'I'm not much for dressing up in costumes . . . or for crowds.'

'I have to tell you I'm not much for fairs either,' she lied. 'Costumes are optional. I'm not wearing one. Besides, I promised to help out at a food booth for an hour or so and then there is something else I need to do. I noticed your boat is a rental from town. We can tie your rental onto the back of my fishing boat, drop it off and you can wander around the fairgrounds until ten. I'll give you an advance and you can ride on some of the roller coasters.'

'Roller coasters?' The tips of his mouth curved upward in amusement. 'Is this chore part of the job description?'

She wanted to say no. Unfortunately, if she did, he would stay here while she was gone. The last thing she wanted was a total stranger among her things. 'Yes, actually it is.'

'You're the boss.'

By the tightness around his mouth Emily could tell he wasn't too happy about accompanying her to the fair.

3

The smell of hot dogs and frying onions assaulted Chance's senses as he wandered away from the giant red tent where he'd left the last armload of food he'd trudged in for Emily. They'd been swarmed by a bunch of gray-haired ladies whose eyes sparkled as they examined her entries for the bake sale. When their attention focused on him, he'd quickly excused himself, but not before Emily slipped some money into his palm and secured a promise from him to meet her back here in an hour for something called the Pie Sell Off Contest.

As he walked up the midway the smells grew stronger and the crowds grew denser. He grimaced at the popping sounds of the .22 rifles in the nearby shooting galleries and tried to tune out the steady cry of the barkers as they lured victims into their booths. Shouts and screams from the people dressed as vampires, witches and the walking dead made Chance edgy. The sounds churned up the memories he didn't care to remember. Images of intense heat, chain link fences, grey cinder block walls topped with rolls of sharp, shiny barbed wire, and screeching seagulls that floated freely above him, urging him to join them in their freedom.

Automatically his hands slipped to his neck, to the tiny St. Christopher's medallion. His uneasiness slipped up a notch. It wasn't there!

Then he remembered stuffing it under the bed after Emily had woken him earlier today. There was no way he could allow her to get a close look at the medallion, because if she read the inscription on the back of it, she'd be firing questions at him, right, left and center.

A familiar chopping sound captured his attention and Chance's spirits soared. Maneuvering himself through the thick crowd, he found the Timber Sports Competition in full swing.

Sweat glistened off the bare backs of the burly men as they swung double-edged axes into giant chunks of pinewood. A roar of cheers went up as a giant fellow chopped through his block first. A few seconds later another ear-splitting roar erupted as two more men split through their logs.

'Well done, men!' a familiar voice yelled.

When he recognized the short, plump, white-haired man screeching into his bull-horn, Chance smiled. Buzz, nicknamed for his short army buzz haircut, had been the fair's Timber Sports caller since Emily had

45

first introduced Chance to the fair years ago.

'Next up is the Double Block Cut. We still have one opening for anyone interested in going up against our current champion.' Buzz hesitated, then looked into the crowd. 'Where is my current champion? Where are you, boy? Show yourself. Ah, here he is. Let's hear a round of applause for our current champion. All the way from the Big Apple USA to defend his title, Skip Cole!'

Chance inhaled sharply at the name. The cheering crowd in front of him wavered slightly and his heart thudded in his ears. His fists tightened into knots and he felt his control slipping as he watched the tall, dark-haired man he'd once called best friend step into the opening. What the hell was Skip doing here? The man was more comfortable following up a story in the war-ravaged streets of some foreign country than playing to a fair crowd.

The caller broke into Chance's whirling thoughts. 'Still an opening. Who wants it?'

'I'll take it!' Chance yelled.

The cheers died and he hunched deeper into the crowd as all eyes locked onto him.

'Well c'mon forward, boy. Don't be shy,' the caller coaxed cheerfully, and before Chance could change his mind, gentle hands ushered him toward the competition's opening.

Toward Skip!

Chance's first impulse was to start swinging his fists at Skip's face and ask questions later. His second impulse was to dive into the crowd, leave the island and forget the past few years had ever happened. Running away, however, wouldn't solve anything.

He'd planned on confronting Skip at one point, but finding him here at the fair totally surprised him. Fortunately, all his uneasiness flowed away when Buzz handed him a heavy ax. Pain rippled through his shoulders as its weight caught him by surprise and the ax slipped from his hands narrowly missing his feet. The crowd laughed.

'Looks like you're out of shape, mister. You sure you want to go up against the defender?'

'It'll be a pleasure,' Chance replied.

'Suit yourself,' Buzz said, his white bushy eyebrows knitted together with concern. 'What size boots?'

'Eleven.' Chance avoided Skip's curious look and grabbed a pair of damp, dirty work gloves from a nearby table.

'Here's your boots. Slip 'em on. What's your name, son? Where're you from?' Buzz whispered.

Chance slipped a sideways glance at Skip, who was pulling on his own work gloves.

'Donovan. Chance Donovan. State of Texas. US of A.'

If Skip recognized the name, he gave no hint of it. He was busy waving to his ever-frantic fans.

Chance slid into his safety boots. A perfect fit.

'Our newcomer hails all the way from Texas,' Buzz shouted into his bullhorn. 'Let's give Chance Donovan a hand for being brave enough to go after Skip Cole, our defending champion for the past six years.'

Chance started. Six years! Skip hadn't wasted any time in taking over Chance's old position as champion of the Double Block Cut version of the Lumberjack Competition.

'All right men! Get ready!'

Chance stepped onto the huge chunk of pine he was about to chop into, nestled his feet comfortably at the edges of the blocks of wood, held the heavy ax firmly over his head and concentrated with all his might on the scratch marks where he was to chop. When the announcer shot off the signal gun, Chance began his downward swing. The blade of the ax slammed into the thick block, sending jarring vibrations through his arms and straight into his neck. His concentration deepened and he kept swinging. Soon he couldn't hear anything but his steady breathing and the blood roaring through his veins. Rivers of sweat cooled down his body and the next thing he knew, burly men with cheerful smiles were slapping his back.

'Congratulations to our new champion, Chance Donovan. All the way from Texas. Winner of one thousand dollars.'

Chance gasped at the sum he'd won. The prize had increased in his absence. Cheers flew into the air.

'C'mon, Chance. C'mon get your prize money!' the caller shouted into the bullhorn.

Excited hands pushed him toward Buzz, who slapped ten crisp brand new hundred dollar Canadian bills into his shaking hand.

'Don't worry they aren't counterfeit.' The caller chuckled and Chance found himself answering his smile.

The cheers and claps shot into Chance again and to his surprise he found himself enjoying all this attention. He smiled sheepishly, rolled up the bills and shoved the wad into his front jeans pocket. The crowd quickly forgot about him as the next lumberjack competition got underway.

A hand slapped painfully onto Chance's back and he froze at Skip Cole's warm voice. 'I've been trying to get rid of that title for years.'

'Why's that?' Chance managed to croak.

'It belonged to a good buddy of mine. Tried to hold onto it in his memory but — '

Skip frowned and shrugged his shoulders. 'Things change, y'know. Life's getting too busy to fly here to defend the title. My fiancée's moving back with me at the end of this month. We probably won't have the time to come to next year's fair so I can't defend the title. Might have a kid by then. She's always wanted a whole passel of them.'

A sliver of reality brushed across Chance as he remembered Emily's dreams of having a houseful of kids. Being an only child herself, she'd always craved the company of brothers and sisters.

Why the hell was Skip telling him all this personal stuff anyway? Was this his way of informing Chance he knew his true identity?

Skip's voice cut into Chance's thoughts.

'You don't sound like a Texan. Lost your accent somewhere?' He slapped his knee and burst into uncontrollable laughter.

Chance didn't know how to react so he stood there inspecting his former best friend.

Skip laughed the same way he always did. Free and easy. Straight up from his chest. When they both began working for the same newbie New York newspaper as investigative journalists, both men had bonded instantly. Chance had sensed immediately that Skip shared the same passion for adrenaline rush adventures he enjoyed. They'd saved each other's butts on more than one harried occasion while smuggling out stories from the war-torn countries. At the same time Skip's easy-going nature and flare for humor had livened up the tension that accompanied their dangerous treks.

When Skip finished laughing at his Texas accent joke, his dark brown eyes held no hint of hatred or betrayal, only humor. 'I suppose you must hear that line all the time?'

Amusement tinged Skip's voice. It seeped beneath Chance's hate and began to gnaw away at it. Chance quickly brushed it aside. 'Actually, no.'

Skip appeared to sense his hostility and immediately sobered.

'Well, I can see you must be rather tired after whacking away at the wood with that heavy ax, so . . . ' Abruptly he stopped talking and his eyes brightened as he peered over Chance's shoulder.

Chance jumped as Skip suddenly started waving and shouting to someone in the crowd. 'Hey honey! Over here!'

Chance whirled around and spotted Emily scrambling through the dense crowd toward them. The last thing he wanted was to socialize with the happy couple. He turned to leave, but Skip's hand curled around his elbow stopping him cold. Before he could yank himself free, Emily's surprised voice captured his attention.

'I thought you couldn't make it in this year?'

'What? Miss the fall fair?' Skip chuckled. 'Not see you? Not on your life.'

Chance's teeth slammed painfully together and his jaw clenched tight with anger as he witnessed Skip kiss Emily on the cheek.

'Mr. Donovan!' Emily's cheerful voice shot through his rising anger.

Chance threw Emily a watery smile.

'You two know each other?' Skip asked.

'We've . . . met,' she said slowly.

Her eyes sparkled and to Chance's surprise her intense gaze never left his face. 'I watched you win the title, Mr. Donovan. Congratulations! Skip's been moaning about getting rid of it all this year. I'm glad it was you who won it.'

She glanced at her watch. 'Oh my! Look at the time! I have to get over to the pie contest. It starts in five minutes. Are you two coming?'

Skip linked his arm with Emily's and threw Chance a somewhat pouty scowl. Chance flipped him a smirk. Skip seemed jealous, but then again so was Chance.

★ ★ ★

52

'Our last contestant is Emily McCullen!'

Her cheeks flushed hot from embarrassment as the announcer called her name. She wiped the perspiration from her damp palms, lifted her pie and headed onto the stage.

'Emily is our final contestant. This Pie Sell Off Contest was her idea and all the money will go toward providing shelter for the homeless this winter on Prince Edward Island.'

Loud claps and earsplitting whistles rippled through the warm tent.

'Emily has made her late uncle Jeb's famous seaweed-apple-blueberry pie. Who wants to start the bidding for an evening date with Emily and a chance to taste her delicious pie?'

When Skip's hand shot up, Emily breathed a sigh of relief.

'Twenty dollars,' he called out cheerfully.

'Twenty-two dollars,' Doctor Baker shouted.

Emily winked at the physician to thank him for his bid.

'Twenty-five dollars,' Skip said with a grin and Emily found herself answering his smile.

She hadn't expected him to show. She'd received an e-mail from him only two days ago. He'd been busy with work and hadn't even mentioned he was coming in today. Obviously he had decided to leave his job to crash the fair. She hated when he dropped in unexpectedly. It made her change her plans at the last minute to accommodate him. God help her when they got married.

'Fifty dollars?' the caller shouted. 'How about fifty dollars for a date with Emily and a taste of her delicious seaweed-apple-blueberry pie?'

No one lifted a hand.

'Oh c'mon, folks. It is for a good cause. No one?' He peered anxiously into the crowd. 'Looks like she might go to Skip Cole. Going once! Going twice!'

'One thousand dollars! Cash!' a man shouted.

Emily blinked in disbelief. The announcer looked shocked. A deadly quiet floated across the crowd. All heads turned toward the back of the tent where the voice had erupted.

'I said one thousand dollars.'

Emily's breath locked in her throat as Chance stepped into the aisle. He flashed a pile of bills in the air.

'Sold! To the gentleman with the bills!' the announcer spat in a flurry of excitement.

Emily didn't miss the curious scowl on Skip's face as Chance strolled casually up to the stage. He handed the one thousand dollars to the announcer and then asked Emily politely, 'The pie and a date with you, right?'

She nodded numbly. He shifted the pie off the table into his large hand.

'The date starts now.' He gently placed his hand on the back of her waist and lowered his voice so only she could hear. 'We'll eat the pie when we get home.'

Amidst hushed whispers, he ushered her off the stage, past the startled onlookers, past a shocked Skip and straight into the dusky evening.

★　★　★

'How about the Haunted House?' Emily shouted with excitement and pointed to the two-story spooky building complete with outside displays of realistic white-boned skeletons whose eyes glowed blood red and jaws opened and closed to the beat of the earsplitting screams floating from inside.

A familiar icy shiver scrambled up Chance's spine. He sure as heck didn't want to go in there. The screams sounded too real and reminded him of the screams he'd heard in his past. Some of them his own.

When a chain-driven roller coaster rumbled out of the creepy building, he jumped. It was loaded with wide-eyed, ashen-faced adults and excited children who imitated the screams from the house. Emily touched his arm and he jumped again.

'Whoa there! You're not one for haunted houses, are you?'

Chance's breath caught in his throat at the concern slicing across her face. Was he that obvious? He'd better keep a tighter lid on his emotions or she'd start asking serious questions.

'Let me see. For someone who doesn't like roller coasters, you've insisted we hit almost every roller coaster at least once, the ferris wheel twice, not to mention how you took over the shooting galleries like a man possessed until you won this — ' She held up the giant, furry, red lobster and her pretty smile widened to the point where he could barely control himself from reaching out and brushing aside the stray wisp of velvet blonde curl covering her right sweet dimple.

'I've discovered coasters are fun, but we've just eaten hot dogs, candy apples and cotton candy and look at those people coming off the Haunted House coaster.' He pointed to the stragglers stumbling down the wooden ramp. 'I think I'll sit this ride out.'

'I'm beginning to think you're right,' she said cheerfully. 'I've never been too good at handling roller coasters with a full stomach. I do, however, have another idea.'

Her eyes twinkled mischievously and at the same time Chance heard soft music float out of a nearby tent. He knew instantly what she wanted.

Before he could protest, she grabbed his wrist. Her hand was a soft, sizzling handcuff he didn't want to escape from and he allowed her to pull him toward the giant tent.

★ ★ ★

'I'm a bit out of practice,' Chance apologized.

Another slice of pain ripped through Emily's toes as he stepped on her right foot for the third time in as many dances.

'You're doing fine,' she encouraged as she moved with him to the gentle rhythm of Shania Twain's 'You've Got a Way.' There was something hauntingly familiar about the way his body glided with hers and she tried her darnedest to figure out why she'd think she'd ever danced with him before. Another burst of pain sliced across her toes.

'Sorry.' He frowned. 'I'm going to have to buy you some steel-belted dance shoes.'

'Then I can join in with you at next year's lumberjack contest?'

A delightful smile brightened his blue eyes. 'You think you got the muscles to take me on?'

'I can take you on any time, Chance Donovan. You name the place and the time, I'll be there.'

'You're on.'

His eyes darkened and to her surprise her entire body shivered with delight. Was she misreading the dangerous desire brewing in the depths of those ocean blue eyes?

'May I cut in?' Her fiancé's deep voice intruded into their dance. Chance's body tensed like a coiled spring. The caring look he'd held for her turned into ice as he glared at Skip. It was the same icy stare he'd thrown at him when Skip had kissed her earlier at the Timber Sports Competition.

She found herself wishing Chance would say no to Skip's request. For some strange reason she ached to stay in his arms forever. The thought rocked her, making her step on Chance's foot. He threw her an odd smile that shot sparkles of enjoyment through her body. When he slipped out of her arms and backed away from her, she almost groaned out loud.

'Go ahead,' he said.

Before Emily could stop him, Chance had disappeared.

★   ★   ★

'I see the way he looks at you, Emily,' Skip said as he took her into his arms for this dance.

58

She noted immediately there were no sparks between them, no body chemistry. He seemed to hold her more like a concerned brother than a fiancée. The realization angered her. 'Oh Skip! For heaven's sake. You're overreacting.'

'I'm not.' His sharp reply captured Emily's entire attention. 'There's something about him. I don't know what it is, but I don't trust him. I want you to get rid of him and come back to New York City with me, tonight.'

'Good grief, Skip. I don't think so.'

'Emily, I'm simply warning you.'

'He bought my pie and a date with me. That's all.'

'One thousand dollars? C'mon! I was so floored I couldn't even come up with a counteroffer.'

As he spoke those words a shiver of unease scrambled up her spine. She'd sensed something about Chance Donovan last night and now Skip was telling her he sensed something too. She tried to ignore the worry lurking in his deep brown eyes and gave him a quick peck on his warm cheek. 'You're so sweet to worry.'

He shifted uneasily and she almost laughed at the hint of a blush crossing his cheeks as he quickly glanced at his watch.

'I get the feeling you have somewhere you

need to be,' she said. 'You don't want to miss your plane. I'll see you at the end of the month.'

'In your wedding gown?'

'In my wedding gown,' she said stiffly.

'The dress is almost finished. Did you know? Just needs that final fitting.'

She found it hard to smile at what should have been welcome news. 'I didn't know it had come in.'

'Helena's going to surprise you by taking you into town for that final fitting. Act surprised when she shows up, okay?'

Emily nodded.

'I still can't believe she's paying for the wedding planner and this whole shindig. She's extremely generous, don't you think?'

Again Emily nodded.

His face fell into a concerned frown. 'E-mail me tonight when you get in. I need to know you made it home safe.'

'I will and I'll fill you in all the gory details about what happened tonight on my date.' She thought her little attempt at humor would bring a smile to his lips, but Skip remained serious.

'I hope you know what you're doing,' he said and gave her a quick brotherly peck on the cheek.

So do I, Emily thought.

When the dance finished, Skip made his excuses and left. The minute he vanished, Chance appeared at her side.

'Miss me?' he teased.

Before she could answer, a spear of sadness clutched at her heart as the next song sliced through the air. 'The Power of Love' by Celine Dion. It was *their* song. Steve's and hers.

Tears sparked behind her eyes and she was about to sit this one out when Chance's large hand splayed across the back of her waist. To her surprise he gently pulled her against his hard length.

'This dance is ours,' he whispered soothingly as his other hand nestled along the curve of her hip.

Emily's knees grew weak with the erotic sensations of his body pressing so intimately against hers and she barely noticed the curious glances the other dancers threw their way as Chance held her. The music faded into the distance as she stared into his eyes.

Shadowed, uncertain eyes and an unsmiling mouth. Yet his entire length evoked a searing heat that caressed her body. She wanted to reach up and run her fingers along his strong jaw and trace the dark shadows beneath his haunted eyes. His sweet cotton-candy scented breath flowed softly against her cheeks and, God help her, she ached to curl her arms around his neck and kiss him. As if he knew exactly what she was thinking, his head began to lower, his mouth opened and she felt his warm breath caress her lips.

'Emily!' a familiar man's voice hailed her.

Chance cursed softly, quickly putting distance between their bodies.

Emily turned away from his heated look to find Dr. Baker peering curiously at them.

'What happened to your wrist?' the doctor asked.

'My wrist?'

'I couldn't help but notice you have a nice sized gauze on your wrist. Thought I'd better check if everything is okay.'

'She burned herself. Hot steam from the teakettle,' Chance said.

The doctor's jaded green eyes slid to Chance and then back to Emily. 'Perhaps I should take a look.'

'I'm fine. Chance here told me to keep it moist with ointment and covered.'

'He's quite correct.' He turned to Chance. 'I don't think we've met.'

'Oh, please accept my apologies,' Emily said as she quickly made introductions. Both men shook hands.

'Pleased to meet you, Mr. Donovan. I couldn't help but notice you paid a thousand

62

dollars for a date with Emily and a go at her pie. Do you two know each other well?'

'Actually we've just met,' Chance said quietly.

'You in town for very long?'

'No. Not long.'

A jolt of sadness speared through Emily at Chance's answer.

'Don't let me keep you two from your dance.' The doctor returned his attention to her. 'Emily, if you think your burn needs attention, please drop in anytime. Mr. Donovan, it was a pleasure meeting you. I hope you enjoy your stay and your date with Emily.'

Chance nodded politely and Dr. Baker quickly slipped into the crowd.

'Small town.' Emily shrugged. 'He's been here about a year and already he's just as nosy as the rest. He's not the first who asked about you.'

Chance frowned.

'You were quite a hit with the older ladies over at the Baked Goods Tent,' she teased.

His frown only deepened and he said quietly, 'We should go home. It's getting pretty crowded in here.'

She scanned the smoky interior of the warm tent. Sure enough the dance floor had gained quite a few more dancers. Gosh, she hadn't even noticed. She'd been too busy staring into Chance Donovan's piercing eyes. Hopefully she hadn't made a fool out of herself. By the way the onlookers were watching them, Emily knew she had given people something to talk about for days. If Doc Baker hadn't interrupted when he did, she would have added even more fuel to their gossip. She bit her lower lip. 'You're right. Let's get out of here.'

★ ★ ★

Hugging the cuddly lobster Chance had won for her, Emily stood at the stern of *her* fishing boat, *Sweet Lies*. She pretended to study the flickering colorful harbor lights as they disappeared into the steel blue horizon behind her, but her thoughts were on him.

When he'd purchased a date with her, he'd said they'd eat the pie at 'home' and then after they'd chatted with Doctor Baker, Chance had once again said 'let's go home'. Why would he consider her lighthouse his home?

Unless . . . he planned on buying it. Was that the reason her in-laws had sent Chance over here? The familiar sadness wrapped around her whenever she thought about leaving. She knew she'd have to let go of her place because in a couple of weeks she'd be

64

married and living in New York City having the babies she'd always wanted.

So, why wasn't she thinking happy thoughts about her future husband? Instead she was reliving how Chance's sweet touch ignited her body into a heavenly state and sent her mind into a jumbled mess. Only one other man had made her react with such ecstasy and she'd married him without a second thought. A lot of good that had done her.

She needed to concentrate on Skip, her fiancé. A safe, reliable man who didn't shoot her insides into a tangled blossom of delight. All she had to do was keep Chance at a comfortable distance, and she could do that by supplying him with loads of work. It would keep them both busy and her mind off her attraction to him. That was all it was, a mere attraction.

Just like it had been with her husband, Steve. Then why had his death left her nursing a broken heart? There was no way she'd ever let another man control her emotions like Steve McCullen had. Never in a million years.

* * *

Chance steered the boat through the thin wisps of white mist toward the dark silhouette

65

of Shipwreck Island. Giant frothing waves crashed against the sides of *Sweet Lies* and he braced his feet farther apart as the boat swayed under the onslaught.

His jaw clenched painfully as he thought about Skip kissing Emily back at the fair. Out of all the men in the world why did she have to pick him? She'd never had any romantic feelings for him in the past. Then again Chance had been gone for about eight years. Plenty of time to get something going.

So why wasn't she deliriously happy about the upcoming nuptials like when they'd planned their own wedding? Their apartment had been littered with bridal magazines, florist shop brochures, catering menus, samples of bouquets, anything that had to do with a wedding. He'd seen no evidence of an upcoming wedding back at the lighthouse. He'd seen no evidence of love brewing between the couple. Heck, they didn't even kiss like lovers. Mere pecks on the cheek sure wouldn't make their marriage last or bring on the kids.

Unless . . . Chance inhaled at an exhilarating thought. Unless she wasn't in love with Skip.

When Skip had intruded into their dance, he'd sensed her disappointment and felt her stiffen in his arms. Why? Why would she react with mild repulsion to the man she was about to marry? When Chance recalled their dance at the fair, his excitement grew. After his initial uneasiness of trying to remember how to dance and stepping on her toes, he'd quickly gotten the hang of it. She had melted in his arms. Just like she'd done in the past.

He was so deep in thought he didn't hear her climb the stairs up to the flying bridge where he stood at the helm. Now her deliciously sexy scent wafted through the cool, salty breeze and a wave of heated desire swept through his every nerve and muscle, threatening to set his entire body ablaze.

'Why do you dislike Skip?' she asked softly.

Chance's grip tightened around the steering wheel and he kept his eyes glued to the looming silhouette of the lighthouse. 'What gives you that idea?'

'The way you tense up whenever he's around.'

'I've got nothing against your fiancé,' he lied.

She didn't say anything.

'What does he think about you letting me stay out here at your place?' he asked.

There was a long silence and then she sighed lightly. 'I didn't tell him.'

Chance laughed. 'Why not?'

'He didn't ask and I didn't tell. No harm

done. Besides he's gone.'

'Sore loser.'

'He had business to attend to.'

'He's engaged to the most beautiful woman in the country and he'd rather do business?'

He heard her draw in a sweet breath at his comment. It was a sensual sound he remembered well and suddenly he wanted her. Ached to taste her sweet lips on his mouth. Needed her beneath his body, craved her legs to clasp around his hips. He wanted to feel like a man again and he wanted to hear those sexy little gasps when he made love to her.

Her frightened cry doused him back to reality. 'Someone's in the lighthouse tower!'

A slither of dread shot into Chance's limbs and he scanned the rocky shoreline ahead. He barely made out the dark silhouette of the buildings partially hidden behind the white swirls of fog. Nothing appeared out of the ordinary.

'Look up in the lamp room,' Emily hissed.

No sooner had she said the words than he spotted the tiny flicker of light flash in the glass windows.

'We have to hurry,' she urged.

Chance didn't hesitate. He shoved the throttle forward into a faster speed while his heart painfully cracked against his chest.

Someone was in the lighthouse. That meant only one thing. Skip must have recognized him and that's why he'd left the dance early.

Dammit!

Now Chance had put Emily into danger once again simply because of his twisted need for revenge.

Within minutes he'd maneuvered *Sweet Lies* to the dock and cursed viciously beneath his breath when she hopped out of the boat and disappeared into the misty glow.

4

Emily stood just inside the open doorway of the lighthouse tower and stared into the gloomy interior to the dim light shining way up at the top. After a few nervous seconds she heard Chance's rushed footsteps cross the wood deck behind her.

'Don't ever pull a stupid stunt like that again,' he muttered hoarsely as his solid form brushed angrily past her.

'Chance . . . don't go up there.'

'Stay there!' He disappeared up the curling stairs.

His brisk remark pushed aside her fear and shot a jolt of hot fury into her veins. She wasn't about to let some man fight her battles for her!

Ignoring his order, she followed behind him. Darkness closed in around her and she used the rounded wood walls to keep her balance as she practically ran up the curling stairs to catch up to Chance. When he realized she followed him, he emitted a gentle curse, grabbed her hand and began pulling her along behind him. By the time they reached the top step, Emily was huffing and puffing, her lungs frantic for air.

The instant they stepped into the watch-tower, the dim light flicked off and a shadowy figure crashed into Chance, knocking him off his feet. Emily screamed as the intruder brushed past her and disappeared through the doorway they had just entered. His hurried footsteps clattered wildly as he ran down the narrow staircase.

'Chance?' Emily called out as she gazed into the darkness. She heard his heavy breathing from somewhere nearby and then his voice floated to her thankful ears.

'Here. Just had the wind knocked out of me. Are you okay?'

'I'm fine.'

At her confirmation, Chance rose out of the darkness a few feet away from her, his silhouette tall and menacing against the icy blue night sky behind the glass windows.

From somewhere down below the sound of an engine captured their attention.

'He's docked a boat on the north shore,' Chance said. 'C'mon!' He grabbed her hand and pushed open the nearby door. Crisp, salty air blew against her face as he led her onto the Observation Deck of her lighthouse. 'Down there!'

A lone figure sat hunched low in a speedboat that left mist-streaked waves in its wake as it quickly disappeared around the point.

'You recognize the boat?' Chance asked.

'No,' Emily whispered hoarsely. 'I'd better go downstairs and see if he stole anything.'

She headed toward the stairs and cried out when her foot cracked painfully into something lying on the floor.

'What's wrong?'

'I don't know. Hit something.' She made her way to the nearby wall and switched on the lights.

When she spotted the black lump on the wooden floor, she gasped and blinked with disbelief. 'This is unbelievable! It's my husband's old laptop computer.'

A strange kind of joy sifted through Emily. A bittersweet happiness one feels when one finds a wrapped Christmas present in a closet after someone has died. 'I haven't seen it in years.'

'Is it damaged?' Chance's voice sounded somewhat strangled.

Emily swooped over and picked up the heavy computer. She rapped her knuckles on the lid. 'It's as solid as concrete. They don't make them like this anymore. And it sure is heavy.'

'I'll carry it down for you.'

He made a move to take the laptop, but she

didn't want to let go of it.

'No, I'll take it. Let's go downstairs.'

★ ★ ★

Half an hour later, Chance had retrieved both Emily's furry red lobster he'd won for her at the fair and the seaweed pie from the boat.

She had brewed some coffee and they sat in silence as he dug into his second helping of the deliciously sweet apple-blueberry-seaweed pie. She watched him eat. Her eyes were bright with excitement over finding the laptop, her cheeks were flushed and her hair was all mussed up from the wind they'd encountered on the way home.

He knew instinctively she was studying him, trying to figure out if she could trust him with something that was nibbling away on her mind. In the meantime he couldn't help but cast quick glances at the laptop computer that sat sentry between them on the tiny table for two.

His laptop. Loaded with all his files. His gaze dropped to the disk slot and he breathed a sigh of relief. The disk was still there.

'Did my brother-in-law tell you what happened to my husband?'

Her soft question pleased Chance. She was testing him. He knew it without a doubt. The information she gathered from him would show her exactly how much Daniel trusted him and in turn how much trust she should place in him.

He thought for a moment before answering. 'He said Steve had just quit his job in New York and caught a flight out to Charlottetown. A friend of his picked him up and drove him to where he had *Sweet Lies* docked near the North Cape. After he boarded the boat, he was arrested because a substantial amount of heroine was found on board. Within four hours of his arrest he apparently committed suicide in jail.'

'That's a lie!'

Emily's angry outburst startled Chance. For the first time he caught a glimpse of the hell he'd put her through all these years. Correction, the hell they'd both endured because of Skip.

'I said apparently,' he soothed. Her eyes continued to blaze with unbelievable fierceness.

'Did he tell you we all had doubts?' she asked.

Chance nodded. 'Especially when you demanded to see your husband's body and were given his ashes instead.'

'Convenient wasn't it? A mix up in paperwork they said. He tell you what a

74

stupid thing I did after I got my husband's ashes?'

'You scattered them in the ocean. He also told me you were very distraught at the time. It's understandable, Emily.'

'My mourning screwed everything up. Throwing his remains in the ocean prevented any sophisticated forensic tests to be done.'

'Don't you think it was him?' He held his breath and anxiously waited for her answer.

'It's not that. My main concern is they probably cremated Steve to prevent us from finding out he was murdered.'

'They?'

'If I knew that answer, I'd have put them behind bars a long time ago.' She gazed down at the laptop. 'Why would someone bring Steve's laptop back after all these years?'

A shiver of dread shot through Chance.

'It wasn't brought back.' Emily frowned at his words. 'I saw a wall tile missing near the doorway that led up to the lamp room. I think Steve hid the laptop in the wall.'

'Why would he hide this in the lighthouse tower?'

'Maybe he used to go up there and write his articles? It's a great view for inspiration.'

'He really did love it up there. It still doesn't answer my question of why Steve's laptop was up there?'

'He probably kept it there because it was inconvenient to lug it up and down all those stairs.' Chance forced himself to jab at another piece of the seaweed pie. He hoped Emily was buying it, because it was the truth.

Her frown deepened.

'Is this the first time you've had a break-in since Steve died?'

'I had a couple shortly after he died.'

'Anything stolen?'

She shook her head. 'They ripped everything apart as if they were looking for something. Shortly after the second break-in, Steve's two brothers made me go into hiding until they could figure out who killed Steve. I was in hiding with my brother-in-law, Daniel, down in Mexico for a few years and then I just had to come back home. Despite his protests. He is so overprotective.'

'Better safe than sorry.'

She looked at him and smiled. Chance inhaled sharply as her dimples caved in her cheeks.

'You've got a piece of pie on your lip,' she whispered.

To his surprise she reached over and dabbed her warm finger across the left side of his mouth. Suddenly he wanted to take her hand and kiss her delicate fingers, one by one. That was just for starters.

As if sensing what he must be thinking, her gentle caress slowed and she drew her finger away.

God she was so cute when she got nervous. He ached to lean over and kiss her pretty mouth. Instead, he cleared his throat and looked down at his half-eaten second helping of pie. She followed his gaze.

'I've been meaning to ask you. Why on earth did you pay one thousand dollars for a date with me?'

'Wasn't you I was after,' he replied, trying to keep his voice causal.

A somewhat disappointed look swept across her face.

'It was your pie I wanted.'

A bright smile lit up her delicate red lips and he felt his loins tighten even more, if that was possible.

'Better eat that piece you have there on the plate because you are going to need all your energy tomorrow.'

'What's on the agenda for tomorrow? Or should I ask?'

'Tomorrow you're going on a seaweed harvest.'

'Excellent.' Chance leaned forward. Using his fork, he chopped off another piece of the heavenly smelling desert. 'Then you can bake me more pies.'

'Can you afford the price?' She smirked.

'I'm sure we can come to some sort of suitable arrangement.' He shoved a forkful of the treat into his mouth. He didn't miss the tinge of pink that swept across her cheeks before she hurried away to retrieve another cup of coffee.

★   ★   ★

'Lucas,' Emily whispered. Lucas was the name Steve and she had planned on naming their first-born son.

She quickly typed the name into Steve's laptop computer and hit the enter key.

The amber-on-gray screen produced one word, 'ACCESS DENIED.' She frowned for a moment, then her face lit up with a smile.

'Elizabeth.' She typed in the name they'd picked for their first-born daughter.

The machine whirred and the same two words flashed across the screen. 'ACCESS DENIED.' She added the two names to the piece of paper containing the growing list of names she'd already tried.

'What else could he have used?' She scrunched her eyes together and concentrated for the hundredth time on what had been going on in their lives at the time Steve died.

He'd been actively investigating allegations

about a crooked police chief in New York City and another story about organ transplants. The passwords in those areas were endless. She was positive he would have used a personal password. Something near and dear to his heart. She'd already used everyone she knew and their birthdays.

Absently she twisted her finger through a few strands of hair that fell over her face and remembered the last time Steve had twisted his fingers through her hair.

They'd been standing on their dock, right below the lighthouse, saying goodbye . . .

'You sure you're going to be all right here all alone for one night?' He whispered softly against her ear as his fingers sifted through her hair toward the back of her head.

'It'll be torture tonight, but it'll be twice as sweet when you come tomorrow.'

'MMMMMMM. I like the sound of that.' He smiled, revealing a flash of white teeth.

She didn't smile back at him. The eerie uneasiness dogging her every waking hour since yesterday hadn't faded. If anything, her fear for his safety was growing by the minute. Everything in the past few weeks had been too perfect. She'd finally convinced him to quit his dangerous job as an investigative journalist and move back here to Shipwreck Island.

She was too happy and from past experience when things went along too smoothly, something tragic always happened to ruin her happiness.

Steve's hand loosened from her hair and curled gently around her shoulder. He frowned at her. 'Emmie? You've been too quiet this morning. What's wrong?'

'Nothing. I'm just going to miss you like crazy.'

Steve's lips tilted upward again and those generous lines around his mouth popped up, making Emily catch her breath.

'I'll be back before you can even blink.' His right hand lifted from her shoulder and he brushed his warm thumb against the side of her mouth. 'Smile for me so I can see those cute dimples one more time.'

She forced herself to smile.

'That's better. Now hold that smile because I want to see it there when I get back tomorrow.' His hand dropped away from where he'd been caressing her mouth and he made a move toward *Sweet Lies*.

'Wait!'

At her shout he turned back around. When he spotted the glittering gold medallion she dangled from her fingers, his eyes widened slightly.

'It's for you.'

'Isn't that your uncle's?'

She nodded. 'It's for good luck. A St. Christopher's medallion. Gives safety to travelers and since you're going off again, I want you to wear it for luck.'

'You're all the luck I need, babe.'

'There's an inscription on the back.' She turned the medallion over so he could read it.

'To Steve. Your Endearment Always. Love Emily. Sounds nice.' He leaned close to her, their lips inches from each other. His green eyes sparkled warmly and his outdoorsy scent wrapped around her. All she wanted to do was kiss him, lose herself in the welcome warmth of his strong, hard body.

'I know I shouldn't say anything and I don't know why I'm telling you, but I have a bad feeling about you going off this time. I want you to be careful.'

'I'm only quitting my job.' He chuckled. 'Nothing is going to happen to me.'

A roaring wave crashed against the pier, making them both stumble.

'I guess I'll have to fix the dock when I get back.'

'You can fix other things too,' she said softly.

'We'll start on making a baby when I get back, okay?'

'Promise?'

'Promise,' he vowed and planted a mind-busting kiss on her eager lips. When he finally pulled away, she slipped the necklace around his neck.

'Have supper waiting on me when I get back. I'm going to need all the energy I can get when we get started on our little project.' He winked and she almost cried when he slid from the safety of her arms.

A moment later the boat's engine rumbled to life. She waved to him and kept waving until *Sweet Lies* disappeared around the point.

It was the last time she ever saw him.

Emily sighed with sadness, leaned back against her chair and gazed thoughtfully at the blinking amber cursor.

'Sweet Lies,' she whispered beneath her breath. 'Of course. The password is 'Sweet Lies'. How could I have been so stupid?'

Excitement surged through her veins and she quickly typed in her boat's name then hit the enter key. The computer whirred a few seconds then stopped.

ACCESS DENIED.

Dammit! It was going to be a long night.

★ ★ ★

Chance stared at the dim light escaping from beneath Emily's bedroom door. No one had to tell him what she was still doing up at this ungodly hour of one a.m. She was trying to crack the password.

Unless . . .

A shiver of unease slipped down his back. Unless she'd already guessed it and gained access to the disk. Chance leaned forward and pressed his ear against the door. The distant sound of Emily's fingertips busily pounding away at the keyboard sounded like music to his ears. She was still trying to crack it. He would have been worried if she'd been quiet. That meant she was reading.

He ran a hand over his bristly chin as he remembered tonight's intrusion up in the lighthouse tower. When he'd seen his laptop computer lying on the floor of the observation room, he'd just about passed out from the shock. All the horrible years had faded away and he remembered when he'd slid aside the wall tile, slipped his heavy laptop up onto the thick log support beam and slid the tile back into place.

He hadn't meant for the wall to be a hiding place. He'd placed the computer up there so he wouldn't have to lug it down the long flight of stairs back into the house. He'd only be gone twenty-four hours and then back up here tapping away on his articles.

Freelancing was going to be tough, but he

had accumulated loads of contacts over the years. He'd call in a bunch of favors and have his articles selling like hotcakes in no time flat. In the meantime, they would eke out a living with the seaweed business Emily planned to start.

Things had gone totally awry when he'd quit his job and been thrown in jail on drug charges. He'd had years to try and figure out what in the world these people who held him prisoner wanted and it always led back to the mysterious disk he'd found that morning on the front doorstep of the lighthouse. The disk had piqued his interest the way it had shown up the same day he quit his investigative journalist job.

He'd backed up the disk onto his computer hard drive and made another backup disk. He pocketed that, left the original in the drive and stashed the laptop in the secret wall compartment.

His gaze dropped to the light still seeping out from beneath Emily's bedroom door. Damn it. It looked like he was in for a long wait.

★ ★ ★

It wasn't until a strange knocking sound nibbled through her many layers of sleep that

Emily groggily realized she'd overslept. Due to the excitement of last night's break-in and staying up late trying to crack the password into the computer, she'd forgotten to set the alarm clock.

When her eyes finally fluttered open, she fully expected the knocking sound to be Chance tapping on her bedroom door, in an effort to wake her. Then she realized the noise sifted in from somewhere outside. She strained her ears to distinguish the sound. Someone was hammering.

Within minutes she donned her long johns, jeans, turtleneck and a cozy sweater coat, then headed outdoors.

A blast of cold wind almost blew her right back into the lighthouse and she realized today would be too dangerous to go seaweeding. Obviously, Chance had realized the same thing and decided to start working without her.

As she picked her way down the steep, rickety rock steps that meandered along the red cliffs, Emily inhaled the bracing wind. The air was drenched with the smell of rotting fish and sea salt. She could even taste the grittiness of the sand blowing against her face.

She glanced around. Chance was nowhere in sight. A touch of nostalgia seeped into her.

On the sandy beach below she spotted neatly piled lumber. He must have found it in the shed. Beams that Steve had purchased days before he died.

A noise from immediately beneath her feet captured her attention and she scrambled down the grassy slope to the beach where she found Chance.

Eight feet up, he sat proudly on a brace between the pilings. Several long nails protruded from his cute mouth and he was positioning a two-by-four with his large hand. In the other, a hammer was poised ready to strike a nail. He hadn't seen her and she couldn't resist watching him work.

He wore tattered dungarees and an old moss green sweater. Steve's clothes fit Chance, although a bit loosely.

Through the clouds a ray of sunshine washed over him, enhancing the contours of his broad shoulders, the powerful muscles in his legs. Even his hands looked larger in the light. Strong fingers clasped the hammer, and yet the gentle way he held the wood made Emily remember how his hot hands had rested along the curve of her hips during last night's dance.

A memory from the past floated up from the depths of her brain. Her husband perched beneath this same dock years earlier, sitting almost exactly the same way as Chance was sitting right now. Steve had already begun nailing up some of the braces the day before he left. She'd come down to call him in for supper. When he climbed off the pilings, he'd taken her into his arms and kissed her.

Steve had always been a spur of the moment kind of guy. Impulsive. Without warning he'd reach out and take her into his arms. Hug her. Kiss her. Tell her how much he loved her.

She missed those strong hugs and passionate kisses. Missed them with all her heart.

They'd stripped off their clothes and made love in the tall grass beside the beach. She could still feel how the cool grass had cradled her body, could still smell the faint scent of Steve's salt-tinged skin as he pressed against her. The sounds of their lovemaking had intermingled with the cries of the seagulls circling overhead. Late evening sunshine had brought out the golden highlights in Steve's sandy brown hair too. Just like the morning sun was doing to Chance's hair.

She froze at the thought. The sun slipped behind the gray clouds and the golden highlights vanished. An icy shiver of *déjà vu* rammed through her veins.

Trick of the light? Yes that's all. Besides,

lots of men had golden highlights in their sandy brown hair.

'Emily?'

When she heard Chance's gravely voice, her breath backed up in her throat.

'Good morning!' She forced a cheery note into her voice and headed under the wharf to stand beneath him. 'Looks like it was my turn to sleep in.'

'Happens to the best of us,' he said between the nails still hanging from his lips. 'I heard on the radio there was a high wind warning in effect. Supposed to calm down later this morning. Figured you wouldn't go out in this. So I thought I'd start bracing up the dock before she sets out to sea.' He cast her a curious look. 'That is if it's okay with the boss?'

'Of course it is. Did you need a hand? Or are you hungry?'

A luscious smile curled up the corners of his delicious-looking mouth and his piercing blue eyes held hers for a long moment. Her heart began to pound wildly in her ears.

'Sure. I could use a hand for a few minutes. Unless you think your muscles aren't up to the task?'

He was teasing her just like he'd done during their dance last night. Her mouth suddenly went dry at the thought of what had almost transpired between them while dancing. If the doctor hadn't interrupted them during last night's dance . . . Emily tried to stifle the warm flush heating up her face.

'C'mon, I'll give you a lift up.' Chance held out his large hand.

Without even thinking, she placed her hand in his and started at the shocking heat that sliced up her arm. In an instant her brain was sending messages of alarm down to her parts south. The temperature only seemed to increase as he hoisted her up to sit next to him on the beam.

And then he was looking at her rather oddly and she instinctively sensed he'd felt something too. Reluctantly he let go of her hand.

She inhaled a few breaths in an effort to calm herself. It didn't work. Especially since she could feel the burn of his thigh pressed intimately against her hip. His ocean blue eyes were mere inches from hers and they seemed almost . . . sexual looking.

When he broke the heated gaze and repositioned himself on the beam, he broke the spell and the searing touch between them. Maybe she'd just imagined the look glowing in his eyes. Maybe she was reacting this way because she'd been too long without a man.

Yes that was it. She'd been too long

without and in a couple of weeks that problem would be solved when she got married. To another man. She needed to keep that one thought squarely in her mind and she'd have no problems with Chance.

'Can you hold the two-by-four up, like this?' he said between the nails as he held up the eight-foot-long piece of wood.

His gorgeous blue gaze locked onto her eyes again, regarding her with that sexual look again. She noticed his Adam's apple bob nervously as he swallowed and then cleared his throat. 'I'll start hammering at the other end.'

She reached up and taking great care not to touch his hot fingers, placed her hands on the board.

'Got it?'

She nodded and he maneuvered along the awkward brace like a sure-footed panther.

He stopped at the other end of the piling, then lifted the wood up over his head. He removed a nail from his mouth, set it against the piling and with a concentrated twist to his lips began to hammer.

Emily stared as his sweater hiked up to reveal a flat belly and thin crisp-looking hair that ventured beneath the waist of his jeans to the well-endowed bulge. Her pulse quickened and her face grew hot as she fantasized what it might be like for Chance to make love to her. Would he be gentle? Savage? Or a wild combination of both, like Steve had been?

The sound of hammering ripped through her fantasy and she sucked in a hot breath. Her eyes drifted up to his sleek arm muscles straining against the sweater. The hammering stopped. He reached for another nail and in a moment he began to hammer again.

Strange how a few minutes earlier she'd thought she'd spied those McCullen golden highlights shimmering in his hair. Last night while they'd danced, she'd experienced the eerie *déjà vu* of having danced with him before.

When Chance's fingers settled onto the piece of wood beside her hand, Emily jumped.

'Sorry didn't mean to spook you. You can let go now. I've got it.'

Reluctantly, she withdrew her hand and watched him pry another nail from his mouth.

'Daniel mentioned you were getting married in a couple of months.'

His casual question almost knocked Emily off the beam where she perched.

'I haven't noticed any wedding stuff lying around. Ordinarily,' Chance said as he positioned the nail against the wood, 'when a couple is getting married, they have wedding things lying around the house.'

'We have a wedding planner.'

'I see.' He began hammering again.

When he finished, he removed the last nail from his mouth.

'Isn't a wedding planner a little . . . formal? I mean, shouldn't planning your own wedding be more . . . intimate? With the couple and their wedding party involved?'

'We don't have the time to do it ourselves,' Emily said, suddenly feeling defensive.

'A couple should make the time for each other.'

She noted the disapproval in his gravely voice and wondered why his opinion suddenly mattered to her.

'If a couple doesn't make the time to plan their own wedding, they sure won't make the time for each other during their marriage.' He pounded another nail into the brace.

She had to admit he had a point. 'And what about you, Mr. Donovan? Are you married?' The shout slipped out of her mouth before she even knew what she was saying. The hammering stopped and she looked up to find his warm blue eyes studying her face.

'I was married. A long time ago.'

She noted the excruciating sadness in his voice, a vast array of emotions tinged his eyes.

Love. Pain. Sadness and guilt. 'What happened?'

'Unforeseen circumstances ripped us apart.'

Emily expected him to expand on these 'unforeseen circumstances,' but he didn't.

'Before we got married, my wife had all kinds of wedding things strewn around our apartment and she encouraged me to participate in helping her to plan.'

Emily found herself smiling as she remembered all the wedding items littering the apartment before her wedding. 'I had to encourage Steve to help me too.'

'I expect he enjoyed it in the end, like I did.'

'As a matter of fact, yes he did. Especially the food aspects. He hit all the catering businesses and brought home dozens of brochures outlining the menus. Steve always had a ravenous appetite.' For more than food, Emily silently added.

'Speaking of ravenous appetite . . . '

'I get the hint, Mr. Donovan. I'll get breakfast going. That is unless you still need me?'

Chance didn't reply. Instead his lips curled upward into a seductive smile. Emily's attention drifted to his mouth, which hovered dangerously close to hers.

'Mushroom omelet,' he said. There was

unmistakable passion in his rough voice and it didn't have anything to do with a passion for food.

'Is that a request?'

He drew in a ragged breath and nodded.

'I'll call you when it's ready.' She made a move to get up and her throat went unbelievably dry as his hot hands spanned possessively around her waist.

'Let me help you down.' His warm whisper was mere inches from her ear.

She caught a whiff of his seductive masculine scent.

Feeling flushed, hot and tipsy from his touch, she allowed him to hoist her to her feet. Without thinking, she grabbed his shoulders in an effort to steady herself.

Warm muscles flexed beneath her fingers and his breath caressed her lips. In a split second visions of his hot moist mouth upon hers, his long fingers touching her in the most intimate of ways. Moving beneath him as he entered her . . .

Her dead husband's face flashed before Emily. Her wonderful, sweet Steve. She'd always been achingly aware of him. He'd evoked these same passionate emotions inside her, made her mind and body whirl with excruciating need. A fiery need only he could quench.

Now she was reacting the same way to Chance. Not good. Too dangerous. It would be too easy to kiss him, to fall into bed with him. He wanted her. She could see it in his smoldering gaze, the way his fingers possessed her waist and the way his head was lowering toward her mouth.

Despite all those tumultuous warnings, she couldn't move. Couldn't break the magnificent pull between them. Apparently he could. His hands released her waist and he stepped away from her. There was a touch of humor in his ocean blue eyes, and also a shadow of regret.

Regret at wanting to kiss her? Or stopping himself from kissing her? Perhaps he'd remembered her fiancé. A fact she'd forgotten.

Reluctantly she slid her hands from his shoulders. 'I'll get the omelet going.'

'I'll be up in a few minutes.'

She nodded and on trembling legs picked her way back down to solid ground.

She felt his heated gaze upon her as she climbed the grassy knoll. It took all her strength not to look back. If she did, she wouldn't be able to stop herself from inviting him to make love to her right there on the beach.

5

Chance fought his agonizing hunger for Emily as he watched her head up the incline. It had been a mistake accepting her invitation to stay at the lighthouse and another mistake to allow her to get so close to him up here on the beams under the boardwalk.

His senses had stirred violently the instant he grabbed her hand and helped her to her feet. His body blazed to life when his thigh brushed against her hip and she watched him pounding those nails, her eyes wide with need, her kissable mouth downturned into a desirous pout.

When he hauled her to her feet, her hot hands had curled around his shoulders like they'd done in the past. He'd just about given in to the hot desire racing like wildfire through his veins. He wanted to kiss her so fiercely, it hurt. The way he throbbed so savagely against his prison-tight jeans, he would have taken her right then and there on the beach. She would have let him too.

The sizzling look in her eyes was unmistakable. Desire. Raw hunger. Lust?

His guts tightened up in frustration and

anger. Yes, he could take her. Just like he'd taken her years earlier, when she came down to the beach to call him for supper the night before his life ended and Chance Donovan's began.

Her cheeks had been flushed from the salty air, her long blonde hair tousled by the summer wind and the look of desire she always held for him prompted him to kiss her and make love to her. Their coupling had always been intense. Sometimes he'd been scared he'd hurt her and yet every time he made love to her, she always matched his savage thrusts. That particular summer afternoon on the beach years ago he'd felt an overwhelming need to possess her entire body, to brand her his own, to make sure she never forgot him. It was as if he'd somehow known deep down, he'd only have a short time with her.

This morning the look of need on her face was unmistakable. Giving in would ease the crackling tension between them, but if he did make love to her, he knew he'd never be able to leave her, and she'd want to know everything that had happened to him. Everything. Every sick detail.

Chance cursed beneath his breath, jumped onto the beach and yanked up another board. He picked up where he'd left off reinforcing the braces so the dock wouldn't collapse, but doubted his marriage would hold up under the strain of Emily knowing the truth. She'd never forgive him for breaking up her engagement with Skip, especially if there were no clues on that disk in his old laptop.

His comments about hiring a wedding planner had produced the desired effect. It had brought up memories of their own engagement. He'd seen the love sparkling in her hazel eyes as she remembered. She was better off with warm memories of their past and a hell of a lot better off hating him for doing her a favor by getting rid of Skip Cole, the man who had so violently ripped them apart.

★ ★ ★

Emily hoped she hadn't made a complete and utter fool of herself. She wouldn't blame Chance if he thought she was a loose woman because of the indiscreet way she'd practically thrown herself at him even though he responded. How else would a red-blooded male react when a woman couldn't seem to keep her hands off him?

Shaking her head in disgust, she whipped the ingredients of the omelet with renewed frenzy. The man hadn't been here forty-eight hours and she'd almost been kissed twice. More times than Skip had ever tried.

No wonder she wanted Chance's kisses! Why did her body have to betray her with such hot, delicious yearnings she couldn't seem to control?

Just thinking about him made her body heat up with want. He was a stranger. A handsome, stranger who should be forbidden fruit to her.

Their brief chat under the boardwalk spilled into her thoughts. *A couple should make the time for each other.* His exact words. Boy, he certainly had zeroed in on Skip and her relationship quickly, hadn't he? Skip and she hadn't even talked about the wedding arrangements, leaving everything to his boss. Helena was a dear friend, who'd even hired private investigators to search into Steve's death. The inquiries had come up empty.

Pointing out his charming gentleman qualities, she'd pushed Emily to accept Skip's proposal. He had a sweet sense of humor, a handsome salary, good looks and he wanted to settle down with a good woman and have babies.

Whenever he stayed over, which was quite often in the past few weeks, he never once approached her in a sexual nature, stating he was an old-fashioned guy and wanted to save himself for the honeymoon. She'd almost laughed out loud at that one. Wasn't that usually what a woman said to her intended instead of the other way around?

He was romantic though, wining and dining her at the most exclusive restaurants on Prince Edward Island. On several occasions he even chartered an airplane to New York for them to catch an elegant dinner and Broadway play or a Yankees' baseball game.

Other than brotherly pecks on her cheek and an occasional display of affection by surprising her with a bouquet of fresh flowers, he was a perfect gentleman. The total opposite of her husband.

Steve always placed a protective hand against the small of her back when he led her into a restaurant. Held her hand while they walked down city streets or along red sandy beaches. No pecks on the cheek from Steve! Only fierce, passionate kisses that made her blood boil and her hair curl as if she were being electrified.

Chance seemed to be the same type of man. After he bought a date with her at the fair last night, he'd placed a possessive hand against the small of her back. When they'd toured the fairgrounds, he held her hand.

Only when he shot those rifles with fierce determination had he let go of her hand, and then he won the stuffed lobster that now sat on her bed. At the dance he looked at her with those seductive eyes, dark with desire. Just like he'd looked at her today under the boardwalk. On both occasions her body had reacted with violent need.

Chance reminded her of how it felt like to be a woman. To want a man to caress her breasts. To want his muscular legs intertwined with hers. To want him to fulfill her every sexual desire.

Oh dear! What was she going to do about this fatal attraction? The only way she could think to solve the problem was to ask him to leave. Yet it wouldn't be very nice to kick out an old friend of her late husband and his family.

She reached for the frying pan and shook her head. That's exactly how her life was at this point. In the frying pan. If she wasn't careful, she'd soon be jumping straight into the fire.

★ ★ ★

Chance smelled the mouth-watering scent of mushroom omelet the instant he stepped onto the deck. The aroma shot memories through his system of late nights, working on a deadline and Emily prodding him awake in the mornings by making his favorite mushroom omelet. More times than not, it ended up burning and he'd be late for work because he dragged his sweet Emily right back into bed with him.

He opened the door and stepped into the kitchen. He found Emily at the stove, her back turned toward him. Rolling up his sleeves, he headed for the kitchen sink to wash his hands.

'I'm famished and the omelet smells fantastic,' he said casually as if nothing had happened between them under the boardwalk. She remained silent and when he finished, he wiped his hands on a towel and sidled in next to her to take a peek at breakfast. She stiffened. A sick heaviness wrapped around his guts, and he moved away from her. Obviously, she was upset with him at the way he'd come on to her under the boardwalk.

'Omelet will be done in a minute,' she said softly. 'Why don't you grab yourself a mug of coffee.'

Chance reached for the mug from the dish rack and poured himself a cup. He didn't offer to get hers because he knew she preferred to drink it steaming hot, instead of it sitting on the table cooling while she prepared breakfast.

He grabbed the cream from the fridge, dumped in a hefty dose and shoveled in three spoons of sugar. He loved his coffee extra sweet and creamy, and Emily had always kidded him he should cut down on the sugar and cream before he got fat.

He took a giant sip and savored the roasty flavor. Alarm slithered up his spine when he noticed her watching him, her face pale. 'What's wrong?'

'Nothing.' She turned away and picked up the spatula.

'Don't tell me nothing's wrong. Your hands are shaking. Is it me? The way I behaved under the boardwalk? I'm sorry. I came on too strong. Especially since you're engaged. I should have kept my hands off you.'

'No, it's not that. I didn't mind . . . I mean it just brought back memories of Steve and me . . . down there. And I just realized you take coffee the same way he did.'

Chance swallowed the lump of fear knotting up his throat.

'And mushroom omelets were a favorite of Steve's.'

'The McCullens always made them when I went to visit their ranch,' Chance said quickly. 'I guess being around you reminds me of those days.'

Her face lost some of its paleness and he exhaled a sigh of relief.

'Omelet's finished. Take a seat. I'll bring it over.'

He pulled out a chair and took a seat so he could watch her work.

She'd always been beautiful, but suddenly she seemed even more beautiful. Maybe because he knew he couldn't have her or maybe because of what she'd said of how he reminded her of Steve.

The magical connection was still there. Unbroken after all these years of separation, and stronger than ever. What happened under the dock this morning proved it.

He studied the shape of her body like he'd always loved doing. This morning though, it was more than enjoyment that seared through him as he watched the seductive way her breasts pushed out against the thick turtleneck she wore.

He remembered how soft and warm she'd felt this morning against his body. Raw desire sawed through his insides and he shifted uncomfortably as she leaned over him to place the steaming omelet onto his plate. Straining for control, he shoved himself and his chair farther beneath the table so she wouldn't see his arousal. He forced himself to pick up the knife and fork and proceeded to dig into the heavenly smelling food.

Just then, the phone rang. Emily picked it up. 'Hello.'

'Daniel! Hi!' She smiled into the receiver then listened for a moment. 'He's eating breakfast.'

She turned to Chance and waved him to come over. Reluctantly he left his delicious smelling omelet.

'Hi!' was all he could think to say when he pressed the receiver to his ear.

'You dirty dog!' Daniel chuckled in a teasing tone. 'Obviously you've worked up quite an appetite. Hope you aren't doing anything you shouldn't be doing.'

'Wouldn't you like to know?' Chance grinned.

'The wife was worried about you so she told me to phone and see how it's going.'

'Quit hiding behind your wife. It was your idea to call or she would have done it herself. You're too nosy for your own good.'

'Speaking of wives, I get the feeling you haven't told Emily yet?'

Chance's grip on the telephone tightened and he snuck a peek at Emily who was watching him curiously.

'That won't come up,' he warned.

'I thought I'd better remind you about your check up appointment next week.'

'I hear you.'

'It's important, kiddo. Keep an eye on your health. Watch yourself.'

'Yes, Mother.'

'I'm serious.'

'Okay.'

'Now there's another reason I called.'

'Besides checking up on me?'

Daniel chuckled softly. 'Put Emily on the phone with you.'

Chance waved to Emily, then held the phone so they could both listen. Her body heat swarmed all around him.

'She's here,' Chance said.

'Jo's pregnant,' Daniel replied.

Chance held his breath as a nice fluttery kind of feeling scampered around in the pit of his stomach at the news. A soft gasp from Emily made him put his arm around her waist.

'Daniel! This is so wonderful.' Emily laughed. 'It is the best news.'

'That's not all. Brother Mathew and his wife, Sara, are expecting too. I just talked to them on the phone and they told me.'

'You boys sure have been busy.' Chance chuckled into the receiver.

'How far along are they?' Emily asked.

'Jo's three months and Sara's two,' Daniel replied. 'I'm not even supposed to be telling you this over the phone. Jo wanted to come visit and tell you in person, but I couldn't wait. The minute she was out of sight I had to call.' His voice suddenly softened with disbelief. 'Oh God! I'm going to be a dad! Hold on. I have to sit down.'

'Easy there, man.' Chance laughed. 'Got smelling salts handy?'

There was silence on the other end.

'Danny?'

'I'm here. I think reality just hit me. I've got to open up a college fund for the kid. Find out where he or . . . God! What if he's a girl? How am I going to keep the guys away from her?'

'Daniel,' Emily broke in, 'first you need to get the baby a room to sleep in. A nursery. With a crib. A mobile with some relaxing music so the baby can fall asleep. And the baby's going to need some clothes . . . '

'Right. You're right. A bed, clothes, mobile.'

'Are you by any chance writing this down?' Chance smiled at Emily. Her hazel eyes were beginning to fill up with huge watery tears.

'Write it down? Good idea. Oh darnit! I hear Jo coming. Don't tell her I called you. Gotta go. Bye!'

The instant they were disconnected Chance became very aware of the tears trickling down Emily's cheeks. He knew why she was crying and experienced the same agonizing pain of loss. Of what could have been. Of what would never be.

'Don't cry, Emily,' he said softly.

'I'm sorry. I can't help it,' she sobbed. More tears spurted from her beautiful eyes and she quickly brushed them away.

His body ached to hold her close. To comfort her, reassure her, but he knew this time if he held her, he'd lose control.

Instead he reached out and touched his trembling fingertips to the corners of her eyes in a desperate effort to wipe away the continuous stream of hot tears. Damn she smelled good. A tinge of fresh air, delicate baby shampoo and mushrooms. Very appetizing indeed.

'I'm so happy for Jo and her sister, Sara. And for the McCullen brothers,' Emily whispered as she stared up at him. 'It's just . . . Steve and I never had the chance.'

She gasped down a gulp of air then continued. 'We were married only a few short weeks before we decided to move in here. I'd already quit my job and wanted to get into a seaweeding business. Steve wanted to freelance, and went to quit his job. When he came back, we were going to start a family . . . but . . . he never came back.'

I am back! Chance wanted to yell. Instead he said, 'Now Steve's brothers' wives are having babies and you're not.'

'Neither is Steve. He should be here experiencing the same joys of fatherhood.'

'Daniel didn't sound too joyful once reality hit,' he teased.

She looked up at him and her face broke into a breathtaking smile. He'd never wanted to kiss her like he yearned to kiss her right now.

'All his insecurities will fade into the background,' she said. 'He'll be a wonderful father. All the McCullen men make wonderful fathers.'

A surge of pride flowed through him at her confident words.

'Anyway I don't know why I'm telling you all this. Your omelet needs to be reheated and I've got to pick up some baby wool the next time I'm in town so I can get started on some clothes.'

Chance inhaled a big gulp of relief as Emily's smile grew stronger.

'They'll both be spring babies. One month apart.'

He watched in awe as she headed back to the microwave with his omelet.

'Sara and Mathew's son is a year old now. He's going to have a new brother or sister.' Emily laughed and pressed the required buttons to nuke his breakfast. 'Sara's going to have her hands full when the new one arrives. She might need a baby sitter and so will Jo.'

Chance found himself smiling as she continued to chatter cheerfully about the new arrivals. Typical Emily. Wore her emotions on her sleeve. She cried, then always managed to pull herself together and look on the bright side of things.

He'd always admired her strength. She never leaned on anyone. When life threw her a punch, she ducked right under it and came up smiling twice as hard. He had no doubt she'd be baby-sitting her heart out within a few months time. She'd go on like a trooper once he removed her fiancé from her life.

★ ★ ★

For the remainder of the morning Chance worked himself half to death nailing the braces into place beneath the wharf. His emotions about his brothers' news were seesawing all over the place.

He remembered the last time he saw his only nephew on the Fourth of July when his oldest brother, Mathew, and his wife, Sara,

110

dropped in unexpectedly for the fireworks festivities. J.D., short for Joseph Daniel, had just turned eight months old. When the little tike had spotted him, Chance had been scared.

Emerald green eyes, wide with wonder, stared at him. J.D. had examined the bandages covering Chance's nose and chin from his most recent reconstructive surgery. A distant smile hovered on the baby's pursed rosebud lips and then recognition flared across his chubby face. The robust baby had then held out his pudgy arms to Chance.

'He remembers you from our last visit,' Sara had laughed.

Overwhelming love burst inside his heart as he'd accepted the warm, soft bundle who promptly kissed his cheek and began poking curious chubby fingers at his white bandages. Chance chuckled at the warm memory. Now two more snugly bundles were on the way. He'd have to put his uncle skills to work.

Suddenly he heard the smooth sound of an approaching motor out on the ocean. Chance's heart picked up the beat and uneasiness slammed through him. What if it was Skip? Or his henchmen? Lifting his head, he spied a somewhat large motor boat heading directly toward the wharf. *Toward him!*

He was vulnerable out here. Maybe he hadn't been spotted yet. Maybe he could get up into the lighthouse without being seen. He could get his weapon from his duffel bag.

A split second before he jumped from his perch beneath the rustic wharf he froze, and gasped softly when he spotted a familiar face. His ex-boss, Helena Whitney, stood at the bow of the boat. She was staring straight at him!

In the past he'd always been glad to see Helena. Her charming, easy-going smile never failed to make him feel welcome and at ease. She wasn't smiling now and he sure wasn't feeling welcome. Her tightly pursed lips and narrowed icy eyes bored right into him and he shivered involuntarily. His fingers automatically tightened around the hammer in his hand.

Helena was definitely not happy to see him. Then again why would she be? To her he was a complete stranger dangling beneath Emily's dock.

On suddenly trembling legs Chance jumped into the soft sand and headed up to meet the woman he hadn't seen in eight years. When his feet hit the creaking planks on the wharf, Helena was already being helped out of the boat by a man Chance recognized as the fellow who'd rented him a boat days earlier.

The man nodded politely and Chance nodded back.

'Good afternoon,' Helena called out cheerfully as Chance approached her.

The frown on her face had been replaced by the familiar warm smile he remembered so well. Unfortunately her smile didn't quite reach her gray eyes. Intense eyes examined his face to the point of making him feel uncomfortable.

'I'm Helena Whitney,' she finally said and extended her hand.

'Chance Donovan.' He hoped the shakiness he felt didn't appear too evident in his voice. He accepted her hand. It was small and bony, but still held a strong grip. Chance felt the eight years of not seeing her begin to dissolve.

'The man who paid one thousand dollars for Emily's pie?'

'That's me.' He studied her face. She hadn't changed much. Not a gray hair flew out of place in the decreasing wind. Every strand coiffured neatly into the same 1960's baby doll style she always wore. She had a few more wrinkles on her otherwise immaculately cosmetic-plastered face and the same overwhelming scent of magnolia perfume sifted through the air.

She glanced down at the hammer he still held clasped firmly in his other hand. 'And I

113

see you are doing some handiwork for Emily, too.'

He noted the thinly disguised disapproval in her otherwise courteous voice. He didn't know why he suddenly felt so defensive.

'Where is Emily?' she asked.

'By now she's probably browsing through some patterns for knitting baby clothes.'

The utter look of shock on Helena's face almost made him laugh out loud.

'Skip and Emily must have decided not to wait for the honeymoon. My goodness I hope this doesn't mean the wedding gown won't fit.'

A spear of anger shot through him at her comment. 'Emily's not pregnant.'

'But you just said — '

'Her two sisters-in-law are expecting. We just heard the news this morning.'

'This is marvelous news, Mr. Donovan. I'm sure it will give Emily and Skip incentive to get working on a family of their own. They do make such an adorable couple, don't they?'

Chance fought down intense anger as she studied his face, obviously awaiting an answer. She sure as hell wasn't going to get one.

'You do know she's engaged to be married?'

'I've heard.'

114

'How long do you plan on staying?

'Until Emily asks me to leave.'

'I'm sure it won't be too long. She is getting married in a couple of weeks and she's putting her lighthouse on the market. Perhaps you'd be interested in purchasing it?'

Her gray eyes swept across his face again and he shifted uneasily under her obvious stare. What the heck was her problem anyway? Staring at him as if he were some two-headed creature not to mention constantly throwing Emily's upcoming nuptials in his face.

He shouldn't be blaming her for being so curious. She didn't have a clue to his true identity and she was most likely concerned about Emily being out here alone with a stranger. It hurt nonetheless at being reminded his wife was going to give up her dream of living here on Shipwreck Island so she could have kids with a man whose idea of a kiss was a peck on the cheek. Emily was a passionate woman. She deserved to be kissed properly.

'Mr. Donovan?'

'What?'

'I asked you if you had any plans of where you'll be working when you leave here?'

'Plans?'

'I could use a handyman at my newspaper

branch in Toronto. It's a bustling city in Ontario, Canada. Emily went to journalism school there.'

'I know.'

Her eyes widened. 'You know?'

'She mentioned it,' Chance said quickly realizing his mistake.

'As I was saying, I noticed your marvelous handiwork beneath the shabby wharf as we were sailing in. Are you interested?'

'No, thanks.'

'Then you must already have plans?'

'I don't have plans, Miss Whitney. I'm just drifting.'

'I see. How about experience in journalism? I'm always looking for excellent journalists to send overseas to cover wars. Emily's late husband was my best investigative journalist, but obviously he had emotional problems I wasn't aware of. He hanged himself in jail after being caught with drugs.' Helena shook her head in apparent disgust.

Chance found it difficult to remain calm. She obviously believed the lies the authorities had spawned.

'Miss Whitney, why don't you go on up and visit with Emily. I've got work to do.' Chance turned away from her, but Helena's hand snaked around his elbow stopping him cold.

'Mr. Donovan. You haven't given me an answer.'

'To which question?'

'Do you have any experience in journalism?' she asked softly, her gray eyes assessing his face again.

'I appreciate the job offers, Helena. I'll think about it.' The thought of getting back into journalism certainly did give him a certain degree of excitement.

'Splendid! I'll look forward to hearing from you.' Suddenly her head snapped up and a huge smile slipped across her face. 'Emily! Darling!'

Chance swung around to find Emily waving to them as she skipped down the rickety rock steps onto the dock. In a flash the two women were hugging each other.

'Helena! I'm so happy to see you.' Emily chuckled as she withdrew from Helena's embrace.

'You look absolutely lovely, Emily. Your engagement must agree with you.'

Chance noticed Emily's smile drop a degree at Helena's comment.

'Doesn't she look lovely, Mr. Donovan?'

'She's beautiful,' Chance whispered and his insides brightened as Emily's smile widened at his comment.

'I've come to get you for your final fitting,

darling,' Helena said.

Chance gritted his teeth and his fingers tightened around the hammer as Emily said rather meekly, 'Of course. It sounds wonderful.'

She definitely did not sound like an excited bride.

A surge of protectiveness ripped through him. 'Maybe you should pick up that baby wool while you're in town. Didn't you say you needed some?'

'What a good idea, Chance,' Helena said. 'It'll give Emily some incentive.'

He wished he could deck Helena. Instead, he smiled and continued speaking in as casual voice as he could muster.

'I could use more wood to replace some planks on the dock,' he lied. He had more than enough, but the thought of Emily being out there all alone without him to protect her made him uncomfortable. She seemed almost relieved that he was inviting himself to join them. Helena, on the other hand, looked far from happy.

'I'll go and lock up,' Chance said. Without waiting for any objections Chance headed toward the towering lighthouse.

6

'The wedding dress looks absolutely magnificent on you, Emily. A perfect fit. Twirl around so I can see the back.'

Emily did as Helena instructed and tried to keep the smile plastered on her face as the sales lady also nodded approval.

'The scalloped v-neck certainly does suit you, Mrs. McCullen,' the sales lady said. 'Now step up on the footstool and I'll pin the length for the hem.'

Emily stepped up on the stool and brushed a stray strand of her wind-whipped hair out of her face. If she blurted out she wasn't so sure about marrying Skip, what would Helena say? Emily knew the answer to that. After these last few weeks of planning and even paying for the wedding, Helena would be horrified and most likely faint right here in the bridal boutique.

'The bare back is absolutely gorgeous, Emily,' Helena said. 'It will pique the male onlookers' interest. They will be so jealous Skip caught you first. Oh, and I've already ordered the flowers for the church and the reception. Yellow roses and miniature red roses with baby's breath. Such a beautiful combination. Darling, why are you frowning so?'

Emily looked up to find Helena scrutinizing her in the mirror.

'Oh, Helena! I don't know what to do,' Emily burst out, unable to keep her thoughts a secret any more.

'But those are the flowers you wanted. Have you changed your mind?'

The look of horror on Helena's face made Emily feel even worse.

Yes! She wanted to scream. *I've changed my mind about the wedding. I don't want to get married.*

Instead she bit her lip and steadied herself against blurting out more. She wouldn't disappoint Helena . . . or Skip.

'My matron of honor is three months pregnant. My bridesmaid is pregnant too.'

'Your Mr. Donovan already informed me. I will get in touch with our mothers-to-be and see about getting their dresses refitted. Is that what has you so concerned?'

'Yes,' Emily lied. 'And . . . do you think I could get lupins added to the flower arrangements?'

'I'll call the florist right away.' Helena flipped open her cell phone and began to dial.

Lupins were Steve's favorite flowers. When

Emily walked down the aisle, she'd look at the flowers and think of him. She could do anything if his spirit was with her. But if that were true, why did she feel, with each passing day, that another nail was being driven into her coffin?

* * *

Chance couldn't shake the feeling he was being followed. The tiny hairs on the back of his neck had sizzled a warning the instant the hardware store employee and he had finished stacking the pile of lumber he'd ordered onto the deck of *Sweet Lies*. Since then, he'd wandered up the main street and cast quick glances into the store windows in an effort to catch a glimpse of the culprit. He didn't spot anyone suspicious.

He checked his watch and realized he still had a few more minutes left before meeting Emily and Helena back at the boutique directly across the street.

Helena had tried to persuade him to join them inside earlier, but he noticed Emily squirm at the invitation. It sure wasn't high on his hit list of things to do. Last thing he needed was to see her decked out in a fancy, silky white wedding dress. Especially since he wasn't the groom.

What he needed at the moment was a stiff drink to shake off these spooky feelings of being followed. Since Jake's Bar and Grill hovered right in front of him, he might as well take advantage of the situation.

Inside the narrow hallway, he allowed his eyes to adjust to the dimly lit interior. Things sure hadn't changed much since he'd been here last. A thick cloud of blue cigarette smoke hovered amidst the thin spattering of rough spoken fishermen hunched on bar stools. A fifties tune reverberated from the same ancient jukebox situated in the middle of the dining area off to the left of the bar. The red Coca-Cola refrigerator still held its prestigious place beside the jukebox.

Chance wandered into the room and noticed all eyes turn on him. The small town was a tight-knit community, and he remembered all too well how he'd received curious stares the first few times he walked into Jake's establishment a little over eight years ago.

'If it ain't the pie lover.' The ribbing remark came from the young bartender who stood behind the bar casually wiping a beer glass with a dirty white cloth.

Chance plopped himself onto one of the available bar stools immediately in front of him. At first sight Chance didn't recognize him, but as his gaze roved over the scruffy blond hair tied back into a ponytail, the little scar on his chin and the trademark chocolate brown eyes, recognition dawned. Garrett Rustico.

An eerie sadness embraced Chance at the loss of missing Jake's youngest son grow up from the gangly pimple-faced teenage boy Chance had sometimes helped with his English homework over a bowl of his dad's homemade chocolate-covered pretzels. Not to mention helping Garrett work through his immense crush on Emily.

'Was the pie worth the grand?' One side of Garrett's mouth tilted upward in the all too familiar amused smirk.

'You should know, Garrett. You've had your share of her pies.'

The young man's smile disintegrated at Chance's comment. Puzzlement shot across his face. 'Do I know you?'

'I don't know, do you?'

Garrett's Adam's apple bobbed as he swallowed. His chocolate brown eyes studied Chance's face but no recognition showed.

'I'll have a bottle of Jake's home brew,' Chance said. 'With lots of ice. And a bowl of chocolate-covered pretzels if you still make them.'

'Ice in your beer?'

'And chocolate-covered pretzels.'

For a split second recognition flared in Garrett's eyes and then it was quickly extinguished as he grabbed a beer bottle from under the counter and snapped off the lid. Thick white foam bubbled from the mouth of the bottle. He kept his eyes on Chance as he filled the mug with ice. After gently placing the mug and beer bottle onto the counter in front of Chance, Garrett disappeared through a doorway.

Chance chuckled to himself. He knew he shouldn't be fooling around with the sensitive kid this way, but it was one way to keep the kid from asking him more questions about Emily and her pie.

He poured the beer over the thick ice cubes. Then he lifted his mug to the curious onlookers, said a quick cheers and proceeded to drink. The ice-cold beer hit the spot. Smooth, sweet with a tinge of salt fish. Just the way he remembered it.

Garrett set a heaping bowl full of chocolate-covered twisted pretzels in front of Chance. 'Anything else?'

'This'll do for now.'

Garrett nodded, the puzzled expression now firmly in place as he grabbed the dirty towel and a somewhat cloudy-looking beer mug from a half-full dish tray. He resettled himself against the sparkling mirror that lined the whole back wall.

Chance knew from previous experience the kid was now working hard to figure out something. It sure wasn't his homework. 'So, where's your old man?'

'Retired. Moved to Florida.' He nodded his head as if he finally figured it all out. 'You know my dad.'

'I met him a few times. Long time ago. How's he doing?'

'He's happy as a clam dropping out of a net. Found himself a woman. They're living together in a retirement village in some trailer park south of Homestead.'

A warm feeling slithered through Chance hearing Jake had finally settled down again. Jake Rustico's wife had died tragically when a vicious storm capsized the fishing boat they owned. He hadn't been able to save her. In an instant he'd turned into a widower with four kids to feed. The oldest was fifteen, Garrett, the youngest, had been seven. Jake took out a loan, started up Jake's Bar & Grill and raised his kids making each one promise they would never work the sea. From the looks of Garrett acting as barkeep, at least the youngest had kept his word.

'How do you know my dad?'

'Lived around here for a short time. Way back.' Chance helped himself to a handful of the tiny pretzels. It wasn't a lie. Emily and he had flown from New York for many weekends until they moved here permanently.

Garrett nodded, then his eyes casually glanced over Chance's shoulder. He knew instinctively Garrett had spotted something awry.

'You've got yourself a tail,' Garrett said matter-of-factly.

'How do you know he's tailing me?'

'Hey man, I'm a barkeep during the day. At night I'm a cop. I know a tail when I see one.' Garrett casually placed the mug he'd been cleaning onto a nearby shelf and threw the dirty towel over his shoulder. 'Besides, came in right after you. He's just inside the hallway. Hasn't taken his eyes off you since you arrived. Want me to get rid of him?'

'I'll handle it. How much do I owe you?'

'On the house. For old times sake.'

Chance nodded his thanks. 'Mind if I use your bathroom?'

'All yours. While you're at it the exit is that way too.'

'Thanks, Captain.'

The puzzled expression sauntered back onto Garrett's face. Chance had always called the kid 'Captain' because of his dream of captaining his own fishing boat one day. Obviously he'd listened to his old man

126

instead of following his heart.

Chance eased himself off the barstool. Without looking at the door or the shadowy silhouette, he ignored the old cronies' curious glances as he sauntered toward the back hallway.

The instant he slipped out of sight, Chance eased himself into another hallway that he knew led to the outside. He resisted the urge to head for the exit. Resisted the urge to run. Instead, he stopped.

Cautiously he slid out the gun he'd brought along. He'd secured it into the waistband of his jeans when he'd gone back to the lighthouse to lock up. In quick unison he slid off the safety catch, checked to make sure the clip was full and then held the gun firmly in his right hand while he got ready to reach out to grab the culprit with his left.

He didn't have long to wait. The old floorboards creaked a warning as one set of fast paced footsteps headed down the hallway.

His fingers tightened on the trigger and the instant he sensed the intruder within reach, his reflexes, honed from many years of fighting to survive, went into action. Jerking the person right into the hallway with him, he shoved the intruder smack up against the wall. Before he could even blink, Chance had the gun pressed against a soft temple. Wide hazel eyes blinked wildly up at him.

'Emily! What the hell are you doing here?'

She didn't answer. As a matter of fact her face had turned as pale as a ghost, and her entire body trembled with fear against him.

He dropped the gun from her head and closed his eyes as a massive wall of fear threatened to knock him over. 'I almost blew your head off.'

'What's with the gun?' she whispered shakily.

'I thought you were somebody else.'

'I'm glad I'm not.'

'I'm so sorry. I thought I was being followed.'

'What do you mean followed?'

Alertness crept into her voice and Chance ignored her question. 'Did you see someone lurking in the doorway when you came in?'

'No.'

'He must have slipped out.'

'Who?'

'What are you doing here? I thought we were meeting at the boutique?'

Now that the danger was over, he felt the warmth of her body begin to seep through his clothes, making him fully aware he was pressing Emily into the wall.

'I saw you come in here. I just had to say

goodbye to Helena. That's why I took so long.'

'She's gone?'

'Yes, she had an appointment.'

Chance sighed with relief. Helena and her nosy questions were gone.

'For heavens sake put that gun away. Canadians don't own fancy handguns like that. I hope you have a permit for carrying it in this country.'

Chance grinned despite himself. Emily had always hated guns. Another reason she'd left the States and come back to her homeland of Canada. He slid the safety catch into place and shoved the gun back into the waistband of his jeans.

'Well? Do you?' she asked.

'What?'

'Have a permit to carry it here?'

'No.' Her eyes widened at his admission. 'I do have it registered in the States. I snuck it through customs while I hitchhiked over.'

'My God, Chance. You live too dangerously. Hitchhiking and smuggling illegal weapons are not good habits to have.'

'Maybe you can try and break me of these bad habits.' He chuckled. 'Although . . . us being so close is a habit I'd like to keep. Thank you very much.'

Her heart pounded frantically against his

chest and he knew instinctively the fear had slid from her body, replaced by something else. Awareness. Of him.

He sure as hell was becoming blatantly aware of her, too. Wide, sparkling eyes stared back at him. A man could drown in those bottomless eyes and never find his way back out. If he were smart, he'd stop staring into them before she pulled him under her magnetic spell and he lost all common sense.

Then again, he figured it was already too late to regain common sense. Especially since Emily's luscious, warm curves snuggled seductively against his muscles. He found himself growing hard.

She must have felt his blossoming arousal because a shiver trembled through her body. Past experience told him she was responding to his desire. Her sweet, feminine scent swarmed all around him. Captured him. Prevented him from releasing his grip on her.

Examining her silky looking mouth, he wondered if she still tasted as heavenly as he remembered. 'I think I'm going to kiss you.'

To his surprise she smiled and Chance's heart filled with love. Her eyes closed and her beautiful rosebud lips parted as he lowered his head.

'Should take that to the hotel next door.'

Chance groaned at the familiar voice and

looked up to see Garrett Rustico watching them.

'That fellow that was following you just slipped out the front door,' Garrett said.

Chance stepped away from Emily and turned to leave. Her firm grip on his elbow stopped him cold.

'Don't go,' she said. Alarm sliced across her ashen face.

'She's right,' Garrett replied. 'He's long gone. I do have a description if you're interested?'

'Shoot,' Chance said.

'Six foot two. Black hair. Crew cut. Well-trimmed black moustache. Thin slit of a mouth. Wearing a black suit. Smells like a cop, but more likely a government lawyer of some kind.'

An icy shiver shifted aside all the heated desire Emily's body had created and Chance found himself cursing quietly beneath his breath.

'You know him?' Emily asked.

'No,' Chance lied.

'I can get a sketch artist to draw up the face,' Garrett said.

'I'm sure it's nothing. Case of mistaken identity.'

'Seems to be a lot of that going around today,' Garrett said quietly.

131

'What do you mean?' Emily asked.

'Inside joke, Emily.' Garrett said. 'Listen, I have to get back to the bar. The dinner hour group is starting to come in.'

'Thanks, Garrett.' Chance extended his hand and they shook.

'Anytime, Captain.' Garrett winked.

Chance inhaled sharply at the remark. Had Garrett figured out Chance's true identity? Or was he merely repeating what Chance had called him earlier? He warily watched Garrett who waved goodbye to Emily and disappeared.

'What is going on?' The alarm in her voice made Chance frown.

'It's nothing. I've just been spooked since the break-in at the lighthouse tower. That's all.' He slid his hand in hers and ushered her toward the back door. 'Let's go home.'

* * *

'So? What was with the jumpy routine back at Jake's?' Emily waited until they were halfway back to Shipwreck Island before asking the question so he wouldn't be able to run away and not answer her.

'Case of mistaken identity. I already told you.' He kept his eyes glued to the salt encrusted front window of *Sweet Lies* as he

132

expertly guided the boat along the generous ocean swells.

'It's not every day someone sticks a gun at my head, Chance. I deserve an explanation.'

'I just told you.'

'I know, mistaken identity. Sorry, but I'm not buying it.'

'I'm not selling.'

She didn't miss the sudden trembling of his hands as he turned the wheel.

'I saw how you reacted when Garrett told you the man's description. You were afraid, Chance. Just like you are now.'

'The guy was tailing me. I was curious as to why. That's it.'

'Bull!'

He glanced at her and a shiver of unease sliced through her.

'Leave it alone, Emily.'

Her heart scrambled into her chest. 'So, there is a story. Someone is following you. What about the break-in? It had to do with you, didn't it?'

'The subject is off-limits.'

'When you're living under my roof, the subject is open for discussion.'

'The living arrangements can be changed,' he said.

'You mean you'd move out before telling me what's going on?'

He didn't answer, but the firm set to his jaw and his tense stance told her he would.

'Typical man.'

'What's that supposed to mean?'

'It means you'd rather keep all your emotions bottled up inside instead of telling me what's going on.' She tried to reign in her anger by inhaling a deep breath. It didn't work. 'I have a right to know if you're in danger.'

'Since when? We're not a couple.'

'Could have fooled me,' Emily muttered beneath her breath.

'Listen, I'm sorry about what happened back at Jake's. It was the adrenaline rushing through my system. I was saying things I shouldn't have. Especially to an engaged woman. I was wrong. It won't happen again. Another bad habit I need to break.'

His confession made an eerie sadness clutch at her heart. 'Fine. You're still not off the hook, Chance. Are you in danger?'

'Everything is under control. You don't need to worry.'

'I won't worry if you don't.'

He threw her a disgruntled glance then focused his attention back to the ocean ahead.

Emily bit her lower lip. Someone was after Chance. He was scared. She could smell the raw fear lurking all around them. Keeping quiet never solved problems. She'd always tried to knock that phrase into Steve's thick skull, too. He never listened to her either.

She hugged herself as another icy chill bit through her insides. No one was going to harm Chance Donovan. Not if she had anything to say about it.

★ ★ ★

Emily shook her head in puzzlement as she tried to think up yet another password to enter into the laptop. The hammering she heard drifting up from the beach made her thoughts return to the mysterious Chance Donovan and their conversation as they'd returned from town.

The subject was off limits, he'd said. Like hell. He had thrown her against the wall and poked a gun against her temple for a reason. Someone was following him. Who? Why?

Garrett had mentioned the man looked like a cop or some kind of lawyer. What kind of trouble was following Chance?

Why hadn't he denied the lighthouse break-in had to do with him? The person who'd broken into her tower had been looking for something, but what?

Emily closed her eyes and rubbed the tense

muscles cramping painfully throughout her neck. Another question nagged at her. Why had Chance once again said 'Let's go home' before leaving Jake's Bar and Grill?

He said those words as if he already owned her place. Why didn't he just come right out and tell her he wanted to buy her home?

How could he afford it? The man had admitted he'd hitchhiked up here for heaven's sake. If he had money, then surely he would have found a safer form of transportation.

What was with the gun? She'd always disliked guns. Probably because she'd grown up in a country where guns just weren't readily used except for hunting. Maybe if she'd grown up south of the border, she wouldn't be so frightened of them.

Nothing to fear but fear itself, her uncle Jeb had always told her when he'd captured her disapproving glances while he'd cleaned his hunting rifle. With grave patience he'd explain to her how people feared guns only because they weren't familiar with them. When people knew how to handle them and how to store them safely, the fear subsided into a sensible respect for the weapon.

In her reporter days she'd seen the damage a bullet did to a body. Gangland shootings where the back of a teenager's head had been blown away or a child who'd accidentally shot himself or someone else because a parent hadn't stored the gun properly.

Now Chance, the man who evoked such intense yearnings inside her body, a man who looked at her with such tenderness in his eyes, a man who admitted and then denied he wanted to kiss her, also carried a deadly weapon.

The sound of hammering stopped the route her thoughts were going and she found herself smiling despite her anger at him. He certainly did have a way with his hands. He'd worked straight through dinner. Then he'd switched on the floodlights claiming he wanted to get the job done tonight so they could go seaweeding tomorrow without worrying about the dock heading out to sea.

She suspected there was another reason he stayed outdoors and away from her. Perhaps he didn't want to pick up where they'd left off when Garrett Rustico had interrupted them at Jake's Bar and Grill. She couldn't blame Chance for staying away especially since she'd already allowed another man to lay claim to her by agreeing to marry him.

★   ★   ★

When he finally laid the hammer to rest inside the toolbox, Chance's muscles ached like the dickens. Night had dropped a few hours ago and a cold chill claimed the misty air. From his perch inside the leaning shelter he peered through the open door up at the towering white painted lighthouse and the white clapboard keeper's house nestled snugly beneath the tower's shadow. To his disappointment Emily's bedroom light still shone a buttery glow from her windows.

No doubt she'd be pecking away at the keyboard valiantly trying out some new passwords. Too bad they'd forgotten to pick up some knit wool. He'd been hoping knitting baby clothes for the upcoming arrivals would keep her off the computer.

It wouldn't have kept her anger at bay during their return trip from town. She had every right to be red-hot mad at him. He'd pulled a gun on her. He'd pressed himself against her. Almost kissed her.

Then on the boat on the way back here he lied like hell when he'd told her she was merely a bad habit to him. A bad habit he had to break.

She'd tried to conceal her hurt by keeping a stiff, calm voice, but he'd always been able to see her true emotions. It was now quite obvious to him she didn't love Skip. For God's sake she had just finished trying on the wedding dress she'd be wearing down the aisle for another man, when he'd told her he was going to kiss her. She'd merely accepted her fate with a lovely smile on her lips.

If Emily was in love with another man, she would not behave in this way. Instead, she would be kicking and scratching out Chance's eyes. Speaking of eyes, he needed to get something to eat and take his medication.

He stepped through the open shed doorway and shivered as the cold ocean air sliced through him. The clang of a buoy out in the water made him peer across the calm sapphire blue ocean for anything suspicious.

The feeling of being watched had disintegrated upon leaving town, but it didn't mean they weren't out there. Watching. Waiting.

An icy sensation crept up his spine as he remembered Garrett's description of the man he'd spotted following Chance into Jake's Bar and Grill. The man could have been anyone. If Chance had paid attention to his finely tuned survival instincts, instincts that had kept him alive through the brutal horrors he'd experienced over the past few years, he might have caught the culprit following him. Instead, he'd been thinking about Emily, the darn wedding dress and reminiscing about the past.

Clearly being around her wasn't in either of their best interests and obviously Skip had recognized Chance's name when he'd bla-tantly announced it at the fair. He needed to figure out a way to persuade Emily to go and stay with Daniel and Jo before these people made their next move. He could trust his brothers to protect her and it was up to him to get rid of the danger lurking after them.

Chance leaned over and picked up the gun from the picnic table where he'd left it for easy access. Checking to make sure the safety was on, he shoved it into the waistband of his jeans. Jeans that had once belonged to him. He'd been surprised to discover Emily had kept them. Another indication she hadn't totally forgotten him.

A white twinkle far out to sea captured Chance's attention and he automatically stiffened.

A boat?

He narrowed his eyes and squinted through the thin trails of mist forming over the water. He couldn't take any chances. Settling himself on the picnic table he watched and waited, all the while thinking about Garrett's description of the man he'd seen. If the identification was correct, then the break-in was just the tip of a fast approaching tidal wave with more bad things on the way.

7

'You sure you're up to this?' Emily laughed as she watched Chance pull the long handled seaweed rake through the shallow ocean waters from his perch at the stern of *Sweet Lies*. The frown of concentration he toted vanished and he lifted his head. To her surprise his eyes shone with excitement.

'This is great!' Immediately he returned to his job of raking the seaweed, the cute frown of concentration back on his face. Within a few seconds he slapped his first haul onto the deck.

'Hey, not bad for the first time.' Emily chuckled as she leaned over and ran her fingers through the slippery brown sea plants. 'Still good quality for this late in the season. Probably because of the excess of sunny days and the unusually warm ocean temperatures this time of the year.'

'Now what do we do with it?' Chance asked.

'Haul it into the middle of the net I've laid out here on the deck and then when there's a huge heap at the end of the day, I use the winch and hoist it up. Then we bring it into town.'

'Sounds like a simple enough way to earn a living.'

Emily grinned. 'You won't be saying that after ten hours of work.'

'Ten hours?' He gaped in disbelief.

'That's not including an hour lunch break and two fifteen minute breaks or the ride back to town.'

'I think I catch your drift.'

'Not to worry, Chance. Since it's your first day out, I'll only work you eight hours. How's that?'

'You're a slave driver,' he grumbled beneath the teasing look he threw her way.

She inhaled sharply when his muscles strained against his turtleneck as he hoisted the seaweed laden rake into the air and maneuvered the seaweed into the middle of the net where he dumped it.

'I hear seaweed is pretty good fertilizer for farmers. Is that where these are going?'

'Some of it goes to farmers so they can replenish the trace minerals they lose due to the conventional overfertilization with chemicals. The rest depends on what orders are waiting in town at my seaweed factory.'

'Your seaweed factory?'

'Actually I own half of it.'

'The McCullens didn't tell me you owned a factory.'

'They don't know. I haven't told them yet. I wasn't sure it was going to fly.'

'But it is, isn't it?'

'This summer has been fabulous, we've got tons of orders. That's why we're out here so late in the season. I'm trying to make profits look good so my partner, Jen, and I can get a bank loan and purchase a second fishing boat. We're going to hire someone to look after the factory and Jen wants to captain *Sweet Lies*. Garrett Rustico, you met him at Jake's yesterday, has expressed interest in captaining the new boat if we get one.

'You're kidding? I thought he was a cop?' Chance sounded very surprised.

'He is. I might add you two appeared quite chummy yesterday. Hit it off quickly, didn't you?'

'He's a likable fellow.' Chance eyed the seaweed in the net. 'What else can they use this stuff for?'

'Oh, Mr. Donovan, haven't you heard?'

Chance shook his head.

'Times have changed. Seaweed is not only good for the farmers, it's good for your body. Now we harvest seaweed as sea vegetables.'

'Sea vegetables?' He twisted his face into a sour grimace and Emily had to laugh.

'Sea vegetables are an excellent source of iron, Vitamin A, and Vitamin B12, all of which are found in our fruits and vegetables. It's also high in fiber and is a good source of protein.'

Chance looked doubtfully at the clump of seaweed at his boots. 'This ugly stuff? Hardly looks appetizing.'

'I didn't get any complaints from you the other night or at breakfast this morning when you devoured the seaweed pie.'

He smiled sheepishly. 'I hope you brought some of it along?'

'I did.'

He rubbed his hands together with appreciation. 'Yum. Let's break into it now.'

'News flash.' Emily grinned. 'The vitamins you ingested at breakfast will get you through to lunch.'

'A guy can try, can't he? What else is it good for?'

'Are you asking for a lesson in the uses of seaweed?'

'Might give me an incentive to work harder.' He grinned.

'It's used as a thickener in soaps, shampoos, ice cream and other foods. It's a million dollar plus industry on Prince Edward Island and other coastal provinces and states. And it's also used in cosmetics and skin care products. Did you know that recently a Japanese conglomerate invented a way of extracting algin molecules that bind tightly to water and they'll be used in longer lasting lipstick?'

'I don't know what you said about the Japanese scientific jargon, although I do know you don't need any lipstick.'

She glanced up at his gentle voice. His eyes seemed a richer blue and she felt his warm breath sear her lips. Only a cool ocean breeze fought the sizzling sparks blazing between them.

'You look pretty damn good the natural way.' Without saying another word he broke the intense gaze and returned to the stern where he sliced the rake back into the shallow water where she'd anchored the boat.

Emily sighed heavily at the interaction that had just taken place between them. He obviously was attracted to her too. What in the world was she going to do?

She lifted her own rake over the port side and found it difficult to concentrate on scanning the rocky bottom of the ocean with him around. Whenever he moved, she couldn't help but watch his muscular arms or long legs or his cute frown of concentration. She wished it was summer and hotter than blazes. Then he'd remove his shirt and she could enjoy the scenery.

Warmth blushed across her face and it sure

wasn't from the autumn sun. Her fingers tightened on her rake. She had better keep her mind and eyes on her job and her thoughts on her wedding, which was less than two weeks away.

★ ★ ★

Cold wind snapped against Chance as he took a momentary break from rearranging the morning's catch of seaweed in an effort to allow it to bake on the deck in the hot glow of the early afternoon sun.

Today the sky was a wild, sharp blue with dots of black clouds hovering in the northeastern horizon. Bright sunshine shot silver sparks off the whitecaps that danced on top of the ocean waves making him blink in awe at the beauty of Shipwreck Island.

Over the years he'd dreamed of this secluded island many times. His desperate mind spit out memories of this sun-drenched coastline like a drowning man frantically grabbing onto a life preserver. His mind's eye had scanned every craggy crevice of the red rocky cliffs that stretched down to the equally rusty red sandy beach. In all those dreams, Emily had been with him, just like she was with him now.

A momentary tinge of panic nudged away

the shaky calm that had enveloped him since he'd arrived on the island. Was he dreaming? Was he still being held prisoner? Had his mind snapped and crossed over into forever ever land? Or was he really here?

One look over his shoulder confirmed he was sane. Emily stood at the helm, her eyes squinting into the sunshine, her blonde hair tucked into a black woolen fishing cap. She looked so cute as she tapped her fingers on the steering wheel to the catchy melody of the Canadian singer Shania Twain's song 'Will You Remember Me?'

He reached for the rake, trying hard not to wince as his sore muscles pulled and tightened with these new movements. A low chuckle erupted from behind and he lifted his head. Emily stood smiling at him.

'Sore?'

'Nothing I can't handle.'

'Good. What do you say we forget about lunch and get straight into this afternoon's catch?'

His mouth dropped open in shock and Emily burst out laughing. 'You should see your face! Thought you could handle it.'

'I lied.'

'There's a great spot for lunch just over there.'

He knew where she pointed even before he

spotted the tiny peninsula jutting into the cove. It had always been one of her favorite spots to picnic. He nodded his approval. Throwing the rake aside, he got ready to cast out the anchor. At that moment his back prickled a warning and he immediately heard the low purr of a motorboat mingling with the cries of seagulls.

A small speedboat idled about a half mile out near the mouth of the cove. He stiffened. He'd seen the boat a couple of times during the morning and it was always far enough away so he couldn't make out any identifying features. It left him to wonder if the intruder might be the same person had been inside Emily's lighthouse the other night and who followed him in town yesterday.

★   ★   ★

Emily sat down heavily on the warm piece of driftwood. Her body was tired, but it was a healthy tired. She could only imagine how Chance must feel on his first day out.

She remembered the uncomfortable achy feelings very well. Every spring, after a winter's long break, her muscles ached in places she'd forgotten she'd even had muscles. The aches only lasted the first few days until the body became reaccustomed to the new movements. And by the way Chance winced every now and then when he picked up a piece of driftwood for the fire, she knew he experienced those same aches.

She was surprised he'd even volunteered to build a fire after all the work he'd put in this morning. To keep the chill out, he'd said.

When he had an armload of wood gathered, he tramped over to where she sat dishing out the food filled Tupperware. The black remnants of an old fire were barely visible and that was the exact spot he picked to set up the campfire.

She hid a smile when he grimaced once again as he squatted down, struck a match and lit the newspaper under the kindling house he'd erected. The edges of the paper curled into black. Gray plumes of smoke billowed momentarily then the paper burst into flame that eagerly licked the dry pieces of twigs and driftwood. When the fire crackled to life, he heaved a huge sigh of relief and promptly crashed butt first upon the rusty sand close to the fire.

'Be warned.' Chance chuckled heartily as he rubbed his red hands over the warmth of the flames. 'I've worked up a serious appetite.'

Taking that as her cue, she unscrewed the thermos lid and poured him a healthy dose.

'Hot coffee with plenty of sugar and cream.'

'And caffeine,' he added cheerfully. 'To keep me revved up so I can work all afternoon.'

Emily had to laugh. 'I knew your tough guy attitude was just an act, so I came prepared.'

He grunted, took a swallow of his coffee, nodded his approval and lay back against the log on which she sat. She handed him a lobster sandwich, a tuna sandwich, potato salad, an orange, and a banana.

He cocked a curious eyebrow at her. 'You feeding an army?'

'If you eat it all, then I'll treat you to some chocolate potato brownies and a slice of seaweed-apple-blueberry pie.'

In answer he took a huge bite of the lobster sandwich and once again nodded his approval. They ate in a comfortable silence, but she didn't miss his wary gaze thread across to the opening of the cove.

'Wind's picking up,' he mumbled fifteen minutes later as he greedily worked away at his slice of pie. 'Might be a storm brewing.'

'It'll probably come ashore in a couple of days.'

He threw her a curious grin.

'I heard it on the radio this morning.'

'Ah, yes. I forgot about the modern conveniences in this rustic setting.' Once again he glanced out across the ocean.

'The storm got you worried, Chance?'

'Huh?'

'You've been looking around all morning. You don't have to worry. The lighthouse has survived many hurricanes and wild storms. I'm sure it'll survive more even after I've gone.'

'Daniel told me you were selling.'

'Are you interested in buying the lighthouse?' Emily blurted out. 'Is that why you're here?'

'Actually . . . I do love it here.'

'You want to buy it?'

'Unfortunately I can't afford to.'

'So? Why are you here?'

Yesterday he'd clammed up when she'd asked him, but hopefully today with a full belly and being tired he might give her a clue as to why he was here.

He placed his empty plate down on the sandy beach beside him and rubbed his hands over the crackling fire.

'I want the truth, Chance. Are you hiding from the law? Is that why Daniel sent you here? Was that a lawman following you yesterday?'

'Daniel didn't send me here, Emily,' he said softly. 'I came here of my own free will. Just to say hi to an old buddy's wife.'

'Then why haven't you mentioned Steve anymore?'

'Figured you'd bring him up when you wanted to talk about him. Since you've brought him up, why are you selling the lighthouse? Are the memories you two had together here bad ones?'

Emily sighed. 'When I marry Skip, I'd rather not be reminded of what this place meant.'

'You aren't selling because he wants you to, are you?'

She shrugged and took a delicate sip of her coffee. 'He's never asked me to sell.'

'But he's never talked you out of it either.'

'No. It's my idea. It's taken me a long time to decide to sell. Now I just want to go on with life. Put the memories behind me and start living again.'

'So, the memories are bad?'

His soft question made her look at him. Sweet tenderness glowed in those wild blue depths, a tenderness she ached to experience.

The breeze ruffled his sandy brown hair and the crisp sun played with the faint lines of silver white and shimmering golden highlights. Her husband had golden high-lights and if she stared hard enough at this stranger in front of her, she could almost see Steve's face staring back at her. Her heart responded violently to the thought and she inhaled sharply. She felt uncomfortable with the way her thoughts and this conversation were going.

'Are the memories bad?' he asked again, his voice still soft but now etched with a tinge of desperation.

'They are wonderful memories,' she found herself whispering, unable to unlock her gaze from his eyes.

He seemed to approve of her answer with a gentle nod of his head, yet his voice turned hard. 'Then it means you are selling out to break your connection with your husband. Hardly a reason for getting rid of a place you obviously love.'

An icy chill swept through Emily at the truth in his words. Chance was right. The only reason she was selling her lighthouse was because of good memories and to finally break with her past. Could Chance blame her for wanting to break the connection?

Every ounce of Shipwreck Island and the lighthouse contained some memory of Steve and their dreams. This tiny peninsula had been a favorite picnic spot of theirs. A place she'd avoided coming to because of those painful memories, and yet for some odd reason today she'd just naturally steered

Sweet Lies into this cove without even a second thought.

Chance remained silent for an endless minute, his intense gaze piercing her heart, searching her soul. 'You're just settling for this Cole fellow.' It was a statement not a question. 'You probably figure you aren't getting any younger and it's time to start that family you've always wanted.'

'I don't see how that is any of your business,' she snapped.

'Did I strike a nerve?' He casually placed another piece of driftwood on the fire.

'Why are you being so nosy?'

'I guess I did touch a nerve.' His soft whisper unraveled her.

'Okay! I'm not in love with him. I do care for him, though. That's good enough for me.'

Chance looked up from the fire with obvious disapproval flashing in his eyes. A shiver of guilt speared her body.

'Cold?' he asked.

'I guess so.'

Without warning he stood and lifted the knit wool blanket she'd brought along from the boat. He unfolded it, slipped it over her shoulders and then to her horror slid onto the log beside her and wrapped the other end of the blanket over his shoulders. Immense body heat sizzled against her and she found herself enjoying his closeness. He remained silent now, his attention once again focused on the ocean.

The flames from the fire danced wildly in the wind, offering little heat. Then again she didn't need any heat, did she? Especially with him sitting so close she could smell a trace of the soap he'd used in this morning's shower. The combination of the soap, his sweat, and his unique male scent urged her to snuggle a little closer to his strong, lean body and to put her head on his shoulder and know she was not alone anymore. She sighed with contentment. It had been so long since a man's scent had aroused her.

'Emily?' At his soft whisper she snapped up her head. Totally disbelieving what she'd just done she began to apologize, but his heated look stopped her from saying anything.

His eyes were no longer dark and dangerous, but tender, caring and full of desire. She felt herself melt under his gaze and allowed her lips to part.

His mouth devoured her lips. A wild fire exploded inside her abdomen. His tongue tasted, questioned and teased her lips with such urgency it frightened her.

It excited her!

Her hands slipped beneath his shirt and scampered over his taut belly up over his chest and over raised welts . . . scars?

He pulled away and cursed heavily.

'Chance?' she whispered, wanting him to keep going.

'Don't say a word,' he whispered coolly as he peered over her shoulder.

She didn't miss the alarm in his voice. 'What's wrong?'

'Shhhh!' He placed his finger on her passion-swelled lips.

Before she knew what was happening, he sprinted from the log and rushed toward the nearby cluster of scraggly spruce trees. When Chance dragged a tall, skinny teenager out of the thicket, Emily blinked in surprise.

'Let me go!' The boy screeched as he tried to wriggle free from Chance's iron grip on his elbow.

'Chad Sullivan! You Peeping Tom!' Emily shouted.

The teenager's face blushed a crimson red.

'You know this kid?' Chance asked.

'The baker's son.'

Chance's eyes narrowed into dangerous slits. 'Who hired you to spy on us?'

Emily couldn't believe his accusation. 'Chance! Stop it! He's just a curious boy!'

Chance shook his head. 'This curious boy has been tailing us all morning.' He gave the kid a vicious shake. 'He's the one who was in the lighthouse last night.'

'How can you be so sure it's him?'

'His after shave is the same smell.'

He turned to Chad and threw him a scowl that made the boy shiver with fright. 'The truth, kid. Or I'll stick your hand in the fire until you talk.'

'It was her fiancé,' Chad gasped.

'Skip?' Emily couldn't believe it.

'He wanted me to keep an eye on you. To tell him what you two were doing today.'

'Cole wanted you to search the lighthouse, right?'

'Aw c'mon. No one hired me to steal anything or search Mrs. McCullen's place. Just to check if she made it safely home.'

'How'd you find the laptop?' Chance asked.

The boy's face flushed a deeper shade of red. 'Aw man, I found the ancient thing when I was trying to pry the wall slat away so I could jimmy the door open easier and get inside the lamp room to see if you were coming.'

'The door to that platform was locked,' Chance said. 'That should have been your first clue to stay out.'

'Chad Sullivan!' Emily admonished. 'I thought your parents taught you better than breaking and entering!'

The teenager shifted uncomfortably under her intense stare. 'I didn't break in. The main level door to the lighthouse was unlocked. Just the one up to the next level was locked. I wanted to see if you were coming, like Skip asked me to do at the fair.'

'Do you know you could have broken your neck going up there without proper supervision?' Chance said sternly. 'And you can go to prison for what you did last night. Trespassing, stealing and assault when you crashed into me. You're setting yourself and your parents up for some heavy duty grief.'

Chance's voice turned soft and gentle. 'Do you know what happens to a young man like yourself in prison?'

The teen's eyes widened into worrisome saucers and his Adam's apple bounced uncontrollably.

'You don't want to ever find out, kid. Believe me. If I ever hear you're in trouble again, Emily and I will come forward and report what happened at her lighthouse the other night. They'll slap ten to fifteen years onto your sentence. Hell that's conservative, twenty years, and with any luck you'll get out when you're an old man like me. Is that clear?'

Chad nodded his head slowly, his face showing all the fear a sixteen-year-old's imagination could conjure.

'Now I want you to apologize to Emily,' Chance commanded.

'I'm sorry, Mrs. McCullen. I truly am.'

'I wish I could say it's all right, Chad.' Emily sighed.

'Yes, ma'am.' The boy's face turned pale as a ghost. Obviously it had sunk in how extremely lucky he was to be let off so easily.

'I will have to speak to your parents about this matter the next time I'm in town,' Emily said.

The boy shook his head, his wide gray eyes pleading with her not to do that.

'That won't be necessary, Emily,' Chance said. 'He understands. Don't you kid?'

'Yes.'

'Next summer you'll work at seaweeding here with Emily. It'll keep you out of trouble.'

'She's selling her place, sir.'

'No, she's not.'

Emily started at Chance's words. How dare he say she wasn't selling the lighthouse.

'She'll be in touch next summer,' Chance said.

'Yes, sir. Thank you, sir.'

'Now, tell Cole I want to speak with him at his earliest convenience.'

'I can't,' the boy cried.

'Why the hell not?'

'I don't know how to contact him, sir. He said he'd contact me tonight.'

'Tell him when you hear from him then.'

'Yes, sir.'

Chance released the boy and Chad sped off like a bullet headlong through the nearby bushes.

'You let him off way too easy, Chance. If he were my kid . . . '

'He's almost a man, Emily. Do you know how humiliated he would have been if you'd told his parents?'

'As well he should be. What he did is serious. He could have fallen and been seriously injured or most likely dead.'

'If you treat him like a criminal, then he'll turn into one. Just the threat of his parents ever being told about this should hold him in line.'

'What if it doesn't?'

'Has he ever been in trouble with the law before?'

'No. Maybe he's never been caught. You could be encouraging him by letting him get away with it. He might try something again.'

'I think I'm a pretty good judge of character. He strikes me as the type of kid who's very sensitive to other peoples' opinions about him.'

'Yes, he is. I've known him since he was

about eight, but kids change.'

'It's called growing up, Em. For a young man it's tough enough. It's kind of nice when someone cuts you some slack once in a while. Makes you think twice as hard.'

'You speaking from experience?'

He laughed. 'I was sixteen at one point.'

'And . . . what about your jail speech? Is that from experience too?'

Chance stiffened.

'Something bad happened to you in the past, didn't it?'

'Why don't we keep my past out of the present,' he said curtly. 'Let's get back to work.'

He began piling the Tupperware containers into the empty cooler. Obviously it was her turn to strike a nerve. And by the way his jaw was clenched, it was a very painful and raw nerve.

8

'So this is your factory?' Chance said as he scanned the rundown-looking warehouse dominating most of the nearby shoreline.

Emily smiled to herself. Thankfully he wasn't holding her earlier curiosity against her. As the afternoon wore on his tension had eased and he'd returned to his normal sexy self.

'Used to be the local fish processing plant until it went belly up. We bought it and the weed is dried inside before shipping it out to the separate factories to do with what they will. I know it doesn't look too impressive from the outside, but we're expanding slowly.'

'That's the best way to go. Nice and slow. Don't make as many mistakes that way.' He lifted his hand to wave to someone. 'Who is that lady over there? She seems excited to see us.'

Emily spied the tall, dark haired woman who was waving wildly at them. 'That's Jen, my partner. We went to high school together and then she moved to British Columbia to work in a greenhouse and nursery. She came back last year and we hitched up as if the

162

years hadn't slipped away between us.'

'Hi, Emily!' Jen shouted from the wharf. 'Slip 10 is open. Bring her in.'

Emily waved back acknowledgment and steered *Sweet Lies* toward the end of the wharf. A few minutes later, they climbed out of the fishing boat and she made the introductions. 'Chance Donovan this is Jen Crystal. Jen, this is Chance.'

Chance extended his hand and they shook. 'Pleased to meet you, ma'am.'

'Ma'am?' Jen laughed. 'Please, Chance, leave the ma'am out on the ocean for the boss lady. She'll appreciate it more than I ever will.'

'Will do.' Chance chuckled.

Jen placed her hands on her hips and shook her head as she stared curiously at Chance. 'I heard about you. You're the one who outbid Emily's fiancé for a date with her.' She didn't wait for an answer as she turned to Emily. 'I got your wedding invitation in the mail a few days ago.'

Emily's heart sank at the news.

'That's my cue to cut out,' Chance said. 'I've got a few errands to run unless you need help unloading?'

'The workers unload.' Jen grinned. 'That's what we pay them the big bucks for.'

'Don't you want to come inside and take a

look around? Get some more info about seaweeding?' Emily teased.

'I've seen enough seaweed today.' He winked. 'Thanks, but I'll take a rain check.'

Emily nodded. 'One hour long enough?'

'Should do.'

'Meet back here?'

'Sure thing,' Chance replied. 'Nice meeting you, Jen.'

'Likewise,' Jen said cheerfully.

Emily watched as he sauntered off down the pier.

'Nice buns!' Jen shouted after Chance.

He threw them a sheepish grin over his shoulder.

'My God, Emily. Where did you fish him out from? He's absolutely to die for.'

'He's an old friend of my husband's.'

Jen nodded knowingly. 'An old friend of Steve's, eh? He sure doesn't like the idea of you getting married. He's got the hots for you.'

'I brought a big load of seaweed, Jen,' Emily said quickly, trying to change the subject. It didn't work.

'Girl! By the way you're blushing I'd say you're interested in him, too. What has been going on between you two?'

'Nothing.' Emily avoided Jen's curious stare.

'Nothing, my behind.' Jen grinned. 'More like something. A little la-de-da before the wedding? If you know what I mean?'

She wriggled her eyebrows up and down a few times before throwing her arms around Emily to give her a comforting hug.

'I'm only teasing you, eh? I know you wouldn't do something like that. You have been thinking on it, haven't you?' She let Emily loose. 'It did cross your mind, didn't it?'

Emily laughed. 'Yes.'

'Good. You wouldn't be normal if you didn't think about it.' Jen winked and Emily found herself smiling at her friend's bold teasing.

Jen looked over Emily's shoulder and her eyes twinkled happily as she surveyed *Sweet Lies*.

'Looks like you hauled in a good catch. You two do good together. Now let's get this stuff unloaded. I've got me a passel of nervous employees who are sitting on the edges of their seat waiting for a pink slip. Your haul will keep them employed for an extra day or so. You going to be bringing in more weed?'

'As long as the quality and weather hold.'

Jen nodded her approval.

'The workers will appreciate it. It's not easy going this late in the season, what with the crazy weather around this time of the year. I have to warn you, there's a storm that might be heading up this way in a couple of days. A big one. They're saying it might turn into a hurricane. You might want to keep your ear on the radio.'

'Heard about it.'

'Good.'

Jen headed for the boat and whistled at the fishing net bulging with seaweed as it swayed in the stiff evening breeze. 'Did I say you two work great together?'

'Yes, you did.'

'Did I?' She chuckled. 'Well . . . let's get 'er unloaded, eh?'

★ ★ ★

Chance stared down at the tombstone and tried hard to remain emotionless. The person lying beneath the sparkling gray one had sacrificed his life to help him. He exhaled a shuddering breath and knelt onto the yellowing cold lawn beside the gravestone. Kind of hard not to feel for one of the most important people in his life. With shaky hands he placed a bunch of purple lupins intermixed with pink and blue bachelor buttons into the vase.

'Thanks, buddy. I finally made it out.'

Tears sparked at the back of his eyes and he quickly stood. On wobbly legs he walked away from his past.

★　★　★

Emily waited until Chance left the cemetery before leaving her hiding spot behind the nearby giant pine tree. She stared down at the tombstone that he had visited. The mysterious grave had appeared late last fall. She'd wondered who he'd been and how he'd died. She'd never seen anyone visit or put flowers on the man's grave . . . until today.

She looked at the pretty bouquet of sharp purple lupins and the dainty bachelor buttons. Why would Chance bring this man flowers? There was an inscription etched into the stone too. 'A good friend. Free At Last. May you rest in peace.'

Her gaze wandered to the man's name, Michael . . . Was he a friend of Chance's? He'd been very emotional during the visit.

She removed a daisy from the bouquet she'd brought for her uncle Jeb and placed it into the vase on the stranger's grave. 'I don't know who you are, mister, but whoever you are, you made some sort of impact on Chance's life.'

Emily sighed with relief when she spotted Chance turn the corner of the warehouse and stroll casually toward where she stood at the stern of *Sweet Lies*. There wasn't a hint of the emotional turmoil she'd seen brewing in him back at the cemetery. If anything, he seemed quite cheerful as he shifted a couple of paper grocery bags in his strong arms.

'Glad you could make it back,' she teased as she accepted the two bags from him. 'Thought I'd have to sail without you.'

'Made a couple of pit stops.'

She stretched her neck to peek inside one of the bags. His amused chuckle stopped her cold.

'Don't look in there. It's a surprise. Just put them in one of the coolers and I'll cast off.'

He turned away and began untying the lines while she fought the urge to stick her nose into the bags. His occasional knowing glances tempered her curiosity. She wouldn't give him the satisfaction of catching her snooping. She dumped the bags into the nearest cooler and climbed the steps up into the flying bridge. She waited until he was safely on board before turning the ignition key. The rusty boat roared to life. Pushing the throttle forward, she eased *Sweet Lies* away from the slip.

They moved slowly past many other fishing boats, lobster boats and tugs motoring to town to sell their daily catch. Most were smaller than hers, but just as rusty.

Working in the fishing industry was a tough way to make a living. For most of these people fishing, lobstering and seaweeding were the only work they knew. Their fathers, grandfathers and ancestors before them had worked the ocean. It was in their blood. Just like it was now in hers.

Rain or shine there was always a haul for her to chase. Especially when her workers had bills to pay and food to set on the table. No air-conditioned offices in this neck of the woods. Only the cool breeze off the ocean to keep her company.

Emily recognized many of the men and women in the boats. Most wore the traditional black wool caps to keep their heads warm from the chilly November winds and all waved to her. Even Chance waved cheerfully or shouted a hello from his perch on the bow.

Soon the town was left behind and they were cruising swiftly over the long ocean swells. A stiff breeze had blown up while they were in town and the bow bounced, casting a blinding shower of ocean spray along the sides of the boat. If Emily hadn't spotted Chance sneaking down below earlier, she would have panicked thinking he'd fallen overboard.

The weak pink sun struggled slowly past the horizon and she felt the first throes of the cold night air slam into her. She pulled up the collar on her red and black hunting jacket and nestled in for the half-hour ride home.

'How does a mug of hot chocolate sound?'

Emily whirled and her mouth dropped open in surprise. Chance stood at the edge of the flying bridge, an uncertain look glued to his face. He held a steaming mug in one hand and a giant platter heaped with a variety of crackers, cheeses, thick slices of fruits and vegetables and what appeared to be her favorite, lobster and cream cheese dip.

'Oh my God! You went to Bernie's.' Emily laughed.

'You approve?'

'Of course I approve. Bernie's is absolutely my favorite restaurant. But it's so expensive, Chance. You shouldn't have.'

That look of uncertainty deepened.

'I'm so glad you did. I'm absolutely starving.'

He grinned and slid the platter onto the dash beside her.

'I'll take the helm,' he said. 'You enjoy the hot chocolate before it gets cold.'

They switched places and she eagerly wrapped her hands around the hot mug he held. She inhaled the misty chocolate aroma, then gasped when she spied the miniature marshmallows dancing amidst the thick foam. 'Mr. Donovan, you are spoiling me.'

'You deserve to be spoiled. Especially after the hard day you put in today.'

'I did have lots of help. You deserve it just as much as I do.' Impulsively she grabbed a baby Gouda cheese and held it up to his sexy lips. 'Open.'

He did and she slipped it between his teeth and watched him chew. His mouth looked so appetizing and she found herself anxiously awaiting another kiss like she'd experienced this afternoon.

When he turned from studying the ocean, Emily quickly avoided his sharp blue eyes and focused her attention back on the giant platter. She didn't want him to know what she'd been thinking, because if he did and they picked up where they'd left off at lunch time, there sure wouldn't be any interruptions way out here. She picked up a cracker and dipped it into the lobster cream cheese and shoved it into her mouth. 'I think I've died and gone to heaven,' she said between the delicious bites of the expensive delicacy. He threw her an amused grin. A sexy grin that made her insides quiver with excitement. With suddenly shaky hands she lifted the mug up to her lips and took a quick gulp of the sweet liquid. 'You make hot chocolate exactly the way my husband's mother used to make it. Smooth, sweet, a dash of whipping cream in the milk, tiny white marshmallows and a generous helping of wine. Absolutely fabulous.'

He didn't say anything, but by the way his eyes crinkled slightly at the sides, she knew he loved her compliment. She slid another cracker into her mouth and turned to look at the increasingly dark sky. Suddenly a flash of light streaked across the sky.

'Quick! Falling star! Make a wish!' Emily shouted. She scrunched her eyes tightly and made a wish. When she opened her eyes, she found Chance's dark blue gaze upon her face.

'What did you wish for?' he whispered.

'I can't tell you. It won't come true.'

He smiled. 'Give me a hint?'

'True love.'

'True love?'

'Yes. True love.'

He shrugged his shoulders and looked out across the dark sky and the rolling white-crested waves. 'I thought you'd wish for something different.'

'Like?'

'I don't know. Something more practical, I guess.'

'What would be more practical than true love? Don't you believe in it?' She held her breath as she waited for his answer.

'I do. What's your interpretation of it?'

She shrugged, quite surprised he'd ask a question like that. She took a delicate sip of her hot chocolate and savored the tart sweetness for a moment. 'I don't know. What do you think it should mean?'

'I never thought about it. I kind of figured if you fall in love everything just kind of fits right. Your turn.'

'Well . . . I think a relationship should be based on honesty. Trust. No secrets. No sweet lies.'

Chance nodded. 'Sweet lies. Like the boat.'

'That's right. My uncle Jeb named her *Sweet Lies* to remind him not to trust another woman. You want to hear the story?'

'Sure.'

'He fell deeply in love once. The woman was the sweetest most innocent creature he'd ever laid eyes on. She was perfect in every way. Too perfect it turned out. She told him she loved him and wanted to marry him. Apparently there was a problem.'

'She was already married.' Chance grinned.

'Hey, I'm telling the story.'

'Okay.'

'She was already married.'

'Told you.'

'My uncle found out through a friend that the woman's husband worked on some oil rig in Alaska. He confronted her and she admitted it. She admitted she didn't have the heart to tell him the truth. Uncle Jeb cut off any further chance of relationship right then and there because he figured if she lied to him once, she'd do it again.'

'Sometimes people tell lies to protect other people.'

'And themselves,' Emily replied. 'There's never any good in keeping secrets and telling lies because they eventually come into the open and hurt twice as much.'

Chance remained silent for a long time before saying quietly, 'The island is coming up.'

He eased back the throttle to slow down *Sweet Lies*. A moment later he slid the boat expertly alongside the wharf and she quickly jumped out and secured the lines.

A few minutes later they'd gathered the food and were heading up the stairs when he pointed out to sea. 'I don't want to scare you, but it looks like we've got company.'

Emily immediately saw the dark silhouette of a boat anchored about one half mile offshore. An uneasiness slithered along the entire length of her spine. 'It might simply be a fisherman.'

'Or it could be someone else Skip hired to spy on us. Let's get inside.'

She followed Chance as he cautiously strode through the semi-darkness toward her lighthouse while throwing curious glances at the mysterious boat. She had half a mind to send Skip a scorching e-mail chastising him for not trusting her.

Emily frowned at the thought. She shouldn't be mad at him. She had to tell him she'd kissed Chance. Although by now Chad might already have relayed that message. Even if he hadn't, she'd have to tell Skip because she didn't want any sweet lies between them before they got married.

Skip had every right to know what had transpired between Chance and herself on the beach today. Her betrayal would break Skip's heart. He'd probably call off the wedding. Or tell her to get rid of Chance.

Any normal, sane, engaged woman would be turning the boat around and dropping him off in town. So why wasn't she doing it? Probably because she wasn't like many other engaged women. She was an oddball and had proven it by giving up a lucrative career in journalism to come back home to eke out a meager existence slinging seaweed, all alone, on a rusty old fishing boat in the middle of a dangerous ocean. She wouldn't give it up for the world.

That thought smashed into her brain like a bullet. Wasn't that exactly what she was doing? Giving up the way of life she loved to move to the city, get married and have babies with a man she did not love?

Chance had been right this afternoon. She wasn't pursuing a dream. She was settling. There was a heck of a big difference between the two. God, why had she been so stupid that she hadn't seen it herself?

Goodness. She had gotten herself into one heck of a pickle, hadn't she? Teenagers breaking into her home, spying on her and a sexy stranger who made her forget her fiancé. What in the world was going to happen next?

★　★　★

From his bedroom window Chance stared out at the mysterious boat anchored in the ocean waves as it drifted in and out of the white mist. The muscles around his mouth tightened from the frown he'd toted since the conversation about sweet lies.

He had told Emily his share of lies and up until tonight he'd thought they had been to protect her. Now he wondered if maybe he'd been protecting himself too. He didn't want her to know the hell he'd been through these past few years. He didn't want to see the guilt push aside the happiness gleaming in her eyes. Guilt because she hadn't been able to help him and the overwhelming anger she'd feel at the culprits who had ruined their life together. Telling her the truth would only shatter the tranquility she'd created for herself here on Shipwreck Island, and if he didn't get what he came for and soon, then all his lies just might bubble up to the surface like she had suggested.

He listened to the light clicks of Emily locking the doors and then allowed his thoughts to wander back to the boat. It was still there. Wearily he pressed his fingers to massage away the throbbing pain in his temples.

The kid he'd caught today during their lunch hour had appeared sincere. He'd told them Skip had asked him to make sure Emily got home safely the other night and to keep an eye on them today. Why had Skip hired a kid? Why not a professional? Someone who wouldn't be easily detected. Luckily the kid had shown up when he did because if he hadn't . . .

Chance inhaled softly at the memory of holding Emily in his arms. It had been years since he'd been with her. The softness of her body pressed against him had totally thrown him off balance. Flattened snugly against his chest, the softness of her breasts made him bold. For a few seconds he'd held heaven in his arms and then that gangly teenager had appeared.

Just like the other night. If the kid hadn't found the laptop, then Chance would have it by now and have disappeared before giving Emily a memory of a stranger who'd kissed her at the picnic spot on Shipwreck Island.

Instead he sat on his bed waiting. Waiting for her to go to bed so he could search her room and wondering how he could keep himself from kissing Emily tomorrow. Once again he peered out the window at the boat that bobbed against the dark horizon. Who was out there? If it was the man who'd been following him around town the other day, then Emily and he were in extreme danger.

★   ★   ★

Emily awoke to the feeling of someone moving about her room. A horrific slice of fear forced her to hunch deeper into her blankets as a dark shadow moved in front of her window. In a split second she recognized the silent profile of Chance. Instead of being terrified at finding him in her bedroom she felt oddly thrilled.

'What are you doing in here?'

The sound of her whisper brought him instantly to attention. He drew away from the window, strode to the foot of her bed and grinned down at her. 'Caught again.'

Her heart suddenly picked up its beat and she found herself staring at his broad chest and shoulders and his lean hips. He still wore the same clothes he'd worn yesterday.

'Haven't you gone to bed yet?'

'No,' he said softly. 'Thought I heard a noise so I decided to look for the Mace.'

'Do you think someone's here?' Alarm slithered through her and she made an attempt to get out of bed. Chance's gruff voice stopped her.

'Don't get up! I'm sure it's nothing. Just the wind.'

'The Mace is over here.' She pointed to the night table beside her bed.

Chance didn't approach. Instead he headed for the portrait on the wall. 'So, this is your wedding picture. Steve wasn't a bad-looking character when he wore a tuxedo, was he?'

'He was quite a dashing groom.'

Chance nodded. 'The bride on the other hand is absolutely breathtaking. I wonder who she could be?'

When he turned in the semi-darkness and his smile widened into that irresistible crooked grin, her breath backed up in her lungs. The realization hit her like a thunder-bolt. Chance, who stood directly beside the portrait of her also smiling late husband, had an almost identical smile to Steve's.

Could this be why she was so drawn to Chance? Because he vaguely reminded her of Steve? Not a very good reason to start a relationship with him.

Good heavens! She didn't mean she would start one!

Temporary insanity. That's what it was. Or maybe pre-wedding jitters? Yes, that's it — pre-wedding jitters. She was reaching for an excuse not to get married and Chance just happened to be that excuse. Why did he have to be such an attractive one?

'Emily?'

His soft voice prodded into her thoughts and she blinked to discover he had moved away from the portrait and slouched deeper into the shadows. His smile was gone, but he watched her with curious eyes. Deeply dangerous and delicious eyes. The intensity of his stare once again sent chills of thrills shooting through her body.

'Goodnight, Emily.' There was such a sadness in his voice it sliced straight into her heart.

'Goodnight, Chance,' she whispered back.

Without saying another word he picked up the Mace can and left the room. Although gone from sight he still hovered in her mind. Forty-eight hours ago she hadn't known Chance Donovan existed. But since he'd come into her life, everything had turned upside down. He'd destroyed any semblance of peace she'd managed to scrape together over the last few years.

Something deep inside her screamed she should know Chance Donovan and yet all she had to go on were these déjà vu feelings that crept over her every once in a while and the overwhelming feelings of attraction that sizzled between them.

She wanted to question him about his past, but he obviously didn't want to talk about it. She'd picked up that hint when she asked him during lunch on the peninsula.

What she wanted to know was why she got the distinct feeling he cared very deeply for her, a woman he barely knew.

Chance slid the can of Mace onto the loft's windowsill. He didn't need it. He'd lied to Emily. There hadn't been any noise. He'd used it as an excuse because he'd been caught snooping around her bedroom looking for the laptop.

He'd banked on her still being a sound sleeper. Obviously she wasn't anymore. Unless he'd been noisier than necessary, subconsciously hoping she'd stop him before he could grab the disk and the computer. Then he'd have no choice but to disappear. His plan was growing harder and harder to stick to with every passing hour. He sensed it wouldn't be long before he finally caved in and blew her world apart.

When he'd turned away from the wedding portrait to look at her, he'd been shaken to the core. She'd been looking at him with that familiar warm sparkle of love shining in her eyes. The same way she'd looked at him in the past, when he was Steve.

His heart had leapt with joy, and he'd wanted to tell her everything then denial flashed in her eyes. It had stopped him cold. Yes, she'd been thinking of Steve. Unfortunately he was dead and Chance was the leftovers.

Despite not being good enough for her he ached to touch her sleep-tousled hair, to feel her delicate lips brush against his mouth like they'd done during the picnic on the peninsula.

She'd always possessed absolute power over him. From the moment he'd spotted her at the White House press conference years earlier. When she was a newly-hired cub reporter with the *New York Times*, she'd asked the president a question. She'd smiled at his satisfactory answer. The breath-taking hint of dimples in her cheeks had totally captured Chance's attention.

He'd made it a point to get into the same elevator with her. He must have been staring too hard because she turned around and smiled at him. Instantly he realized he was in love with Emily Montgomery. He still was in love.

Chance shook his head in disgust. Maybe it was lust. After all he hadn't been with Emily in years and tonight, when she wanted to get out of her bed, he'd stopped her cold. He knew if he saw her in that thin peach nightgown again, he wouldn't be able to keep his hands to himself. Worst of all he'd have to spill all his secrets because there was no way he could ever keep his true identity from her if he decided to stay. Which he wasn't going to do, not under any circumstances.

9

The next day a northeast breeze promised a cold day. In the morning the mist dangled all around them. The water was choppy and the seaweed difficult to spot, but Emily and Chance worked the beaches, gathering the weed by hand and dragging it onto the boat with baskets. It was a technique used in the pioneer days before the use of horses and modern machinery. However the piles of seaweed that had washed ashore from last night's wind was too tempting to ignore.

They picnicked on board *Sweet Lies* during lunch. As much as she craved to take the break in the same cozy cove as yesterday, it was too far away from where they worked today.

Besides, she was terrified of what would happen if Chance kissed her again.

It didn't look like she'd be lucky enough for a kiss today anyway. He'd kept a cool, respectable distance from her.

Finally it was quitting time and Emily heaved a sigh of relief. Her muscles ached and all she wanted to do was deliver today's catch of seaweed to town, take a hot shower, grab a hot meal and climb under her snug covers. Unfortunately *Sweet Lies* had other plans.

She had just turned the ignition key, eased the throttle forward, and inhaled a nauseating lungful of diesel fumes when the engine sputtered and promptly died. She groaned, turned the ignition key again, but the boat merely coughed.

'Uh, oh,' Chance shouted from where he stood beside the net of seaweed he'd just winched into the air. 'Sounds like we're out of diesel.'

'We can't be out of fuel,' Emily said.

'I'll go down and check.'

Her heart pounded as she waited impatiently for him to return. What if it was something serious? The engine was so old anything could go wrong at this point in its life. What if they became stranded? What if they had to spend the night on board *Sweet Lies*? Together. In the tiny bed. The idea was both frightening and exciting.

'You're out of diesel,' Chance called as he climbed out of the hull. He stood at the base of the flying bridge, hands on his hips, looking up at her. His mouth twisted into a somewhat half-hearted smile. 'If I didn't know better, I'd say you staged this whole thing so you can be alone with me.'

'Chance, this is not funny. Just use the backup diesel drum.'

His smile dropped into a serious frown that sent shivers up her spine.

'What's the problem?'

'The extra diesel drum is empty.'

'It can't be. It's full. I just had it filled a few days ago.'

'I'm serious, Emily. It is empty.'

She studied his stern face and realized he wasn't kidding around. 'I can't believe it! Someone siphoned my fuel!'

'Can you blame them? With the way prices are going up these days?'

Now he was teasing, but she also sensed an underlying tenseness in his voice.

'You think it might have been someone from that mysterious boat last night?' she asked.

'Thought crossed my mind.' His frown deepened. 'Where'd you put the laptop?'

'They won't find it.'

'You sound mighty confident.'

'You're sounding too spooky, Chance. You make it sound as if someone has deliberately stranded us.'

'You said it, I didn't.'

'You're thinking it.'

He nodded then scanned the fog-enshrouded sea. For what was he looking?

In this thick soup he'd be lucky to see anyone to flag down for help. His jaws clenched so tightly a muscle twitched in his cheek. Déjà vu spilled over her at the sight. When Steve had been worried, the muscles in his cheeks had jumped in a similar fashion. She shook the weird feeling aside and reached for the CB.

'Do you know how embarrassing this is? For an old pro like me to get caught without extra diesel on board? I'll never live it down.'

'What do you care?' Chance said. 'You won't be living here any more. You're selling out, remember?'

His rude jab made Emily mad and she violently clicked her thumb on the talk button. 'May Day. May Day. May Day. This is *Sweet Lies* looking for some assistance at Shipwreck Cove. Anyone in the vicinity? Over?'

'Emily! Stop!'

His angry shout startled her and she removed her thumb from the button. 'What is wrong?'

'Don't call for help!'

'Why not?'

'Just don't,' he said tightly.

His anger frightened her and she turned around to replace the CB on the hook. With full intentions of confronting him as to why they shouldn't be calling for help, she whirled around and cursed. Chance was nowhere in sight. Why did he do that? Here one minute. Gone the next. Just like a darn ghost.

'Chance?'

'Down here,' he shouted from below.

She found him in the cabin, searching the tiny kitchenette's cabinets.

'What are you looking for?'

He didn't say anything, but continued to search behind her canned goods.

'Are you hungry again?'

'No.'

'Extra clothes are in the bunk below the bed.'

'Guys don't get cold.'

This time his face was slanted in a way she could read his features. The frantic look on his face sent a sliver of fear shooting up her spine. 'What are you looking for? Or do I want to know?'

He didn't reply, but his search intensified and then suddenly his arms stopped moving and he inhaled sharply. 'It's happening again.'

'What's happening again?'

To her horror he withdrew a litre-sized clear plastic bag stuffed with a white powdery substance.

'Please tell me that's sugar,' she begged.

'It's sugar.'

His wobbly smirk told her he was only trying to humor her. 'How'd you know you'd find something?'

'Just a hunch. I was hoping I was wrong. If someone removed the diesel, they wanted us stranded for a reason.'

'What the hell do they want us stranded for? And who are they?'

He didn't answer. Instead he grabbed a knife from a drawer, sliced a small hole in the top of the bag, licked his finger and then touched the white powder. The powder stuck to his finger and he brought it to his tongue. His reaction was violently quick.

He spit it out, cursed and raced toward the tiny porthole above the bed. He opened the window and carefully stuffed the bag out into the cool night air. With his other hand he used the knife to slice it completely open, then dumped the contents into the ocean. He dropped the bag out the porthole too. When he turned to her, she shivered at the raw fear shining in his eyes.

'Better go topside. Check everything. Cans. Drums. Pails. Freezers. Engine room. Anything that can hide a litre bag.'

She nodded numbly.

'Take this knife.' He handed her the knife he'd just used. 'If you find something, get rid of it. Do it the same way I did. Pour it

189

overboard. Don't get any of it on the side of the boat. Don't get anything on you. Wipe the knife clean of your fingerprints and throw it over too. Go!'

She whirled around and headed for the stairs.

'Emily!' His sharp voice made her halt half way up. 'Move fast. We may have company.'

She nodded again and her limbs trembled as she frantically scrambled topside.

Damp air greeted her and she quickly scanned the dark mist hovering around the boat. She saw nothing. Heard nothing but the howling wind and the waves crashing against the sides. That didn't mean someone wasn't lurking nearby.

Move fast. Chance's words echoed through her brain, prompting her into action. She searched everywhere. Cans, pails, drums, coils of rope, ice chests. Everywhere she could think of where someone might hide illegal drugs. When she finished with the obvious places around the deck, she climbed up the ladder to the flying bridge and checked any cubbyholes. Thankfully she found nothing.

Climbing back down from the flying bridge, she knelt, raised the hatch cover over the engine room and descended the ladder into the dark and oily-smelling hole. Flipping on the light, she did a thorough inspection. Just when she thought she'd covered the whole area, she spied something white and out of place peeking from behind the electric pump. Blood curdled in her veins and with shaky hands she picked up the evidence and headed topside. Leaning over the port side, she sliced open the bag and dumped the contents into the ocean. The plastic bag quickly followed.

She scanned *Sweet Lies* trying to figure out if she'd missed anything and suddenly realized she hadn't searched the bow area. Before she could make a move toward the area she heard the low hum of a finely tuned engine.

'Chance!' She yelled.

'I hear them,' he said from behind her.

Whirling around she spotted Chance holding another litre plastic bag filled with heroine. 'Dear God! Get rid of it!'

He moved quickly. He took the knife from her and threw it and the entire bag overboard. To her surprise he pulled her against his body. Without warning he crushed his lips over her mouth. Unfortunately she was so terrified she could only hang onto his hard muscular arms until he decided to come up for air.

A spotlight suddenly flashed upon them,

blinding her. She clamped down on the overwhelming urge to dive into the ocean.

'This is the Coast Guard!' A mechanical voice erupted from a large boat that gently nudged the starboard side of *Sweet Lies*.

Chance drew away from her and lifted his arm to shield his eyes against the light.

'We are boarding your vessel,' the mechanical voice blared.

Chance smiled and threw a friendly wave.

'Did you cover everything?' he asked from the corner of his mouth.

'Missed the bow.'

He cursed under his breath, then said, 'Stick close to me.'

She nodded and followed him as he strolled toward the starboard side where two uniformed officers were climbing down a rope ladder onto her boat.

Hi!' Chance greeted the first officer as he stepped onto the deck. 'What can we do for you?'

'More like what can we do for you? We heard your call for help over the radio, but couldn't get a response.'

'That was me, sir,' Emily said. 'The radio is old and it's on the blitz half the time.'

'What's the problem?'

'It's all my fault, officer,' Chance said. He acted as if they hadn't just found a bunch of drugs on her boat. 'The little lady told me to put an extra drum of diesel on board this morning, but I forgot. Too many other things going on. It never ends, I tell you. It never ends.' Chance shook his head slowly and heaved a sigh.

'Do you mind if I get a drink of water?' The second officer came forward.

Emily felt Chance stiffen and automatically sensed his hostility.

'Sure. I can get you a glass,' he replied in a somewhat strangled voice.

'Oh no. I can get it myself.' The officer began walking past them. 'It's this way, right? Down those stairs?'

Emily nodded not believing the audacity of this fellow to invite himself into her cabin.

'I'll show you,' Chance said coldly.

'Oh, no need.'

'I insist.'

An icy sliver of fear crawled across Emily's back at Chance's cold command. His jaw was tense, his eyes dangerous slits as he passed her and followed the officer down the stairs into the cabin.

'Ma'am, how much diesel do you need?' the remaining officer asked.

'About five miles worth. It'll be enough to get us home.'

'I'll get it for you. Back in a minute.'

193

When the officer turned and hopped onto the rope ladder that led up to his much higher craft, Emily sighed with relief. After he was out of sight, she held her breath and listened for any sounds from *Sweet Lies'* cabin. All she heard was a couple of creaks of a cabinet door opening and closing. Had the second officer used the excuse he was thirsty so he could execute a search? Oh God, please don't let him find anything.

When a shadow appeared in the stairwell, she jumped. A split second later she recognized the officer. Thankfully his hands were empty, but the scowl he threw her way as he stepped onto the deck made her cringe. When Chance, toting an equally fierce look on his face, joined them on deck, Emily breathed a sigh of relief.

A clatter of footsteps behind them captured Emily's attention and she turned to find the other officer jumping off the transom onto the deck, a ten-litre drum of diesel fuel hoisted on his shoulder.

'Ma'am, here's the diesel. Where can I put it?'

'I'll take it,' the officer who'd gone down into the cabin with Chance said quickly. He made a move forward, but Chance was quicker as he accepted the drum and shoved it onto his shoulder.

'I'll take care of it,' Chance said.

The officer who'd given the drum to Chance frowned at his companion's behavior. 'You can go back to the ship, Northam. You're not needed here any longer.'

'Yes, sir.' As Northam departed, he threw another dark scowl over his shoulder at Chance and Emily.

'How much do we owe you?' Chance asked.

'Since this is your first time, it's on the Canadian Coast Guard. Next time there will be a hefty price for the diesel. Best be careful and keep extra fuel on board.'

'We will. Thank you for coming to our rescue,' Chance said. 'We sure do appreciate your help.'

'Glad to be of assistance. I'll leave you to your business. Have a good evening.'

Emily held her breath as the officer headed back to the rope ladder. A few minutes later the Coast Guard's cruiser roared to life and disappeared into the curls of mist. Emily slumped onto a nearby cooler. 'My God, that was so close.'

'You stay here,' Chance ordered. 'Keep watch. I'm going to get the diesel into the system and then we're getting out of here.'

He hoisted the drum a little higher on his shoulder and disappeared. Emily looked up to the dark mist-covered sky and thanked their lucky stars tonight hadn't turned into a horrible catastrophe.

*   *   *

Five miles later Emily shook from both frustration and anger as Chance helped her climb out of *Sweet Lies*. He didn't let go of her hand as he quickly led her through the darkness up the rickety rock stairs toward her home. All the years she'd lived here she'd never been afraid of the lighthouse. Tonight, however, the towering silhouette appeared ghostly, foreign and menacing. It looked down on her as if it might crash right on top of her. She shook her head at the silly thought.

She was tired from a hard day's work and frustrated because she didn't understand why someone would plant drugs on her boat. She was also angry at Chance for not trying to soothe her ruffled feathers. He'd been totally silent on the ride back. After he'd taken charge of her boat and maneuvered around the rocky outcrops she made sure nobody was following as she'd checked the bow area. She'd come up with nothing, but that didn't mean someone hadn't stashed drugs inside the walls of her boat.

God! Was she being too paranoid? Or could someone have put drugs inside the walls? A drug sniffing dog sure would find them and then they'd be in trouble.

Anyone could be lurking around here in the foggy shadows. Any second a garrison of lawmen could surround them and haul them off to jail.

She should have kept an extra container of diesel in the shed. She usually did. However since she was going to sell the lighthouse, she'd used it all except for the extra one she kept on board *Sweet Lies*.

She should have asked for more diesel, enough to get to town and get some help. Even if they could get to town, to whom could they tell their story? The cops? They'd want to know what happened to the drugs. That is if they believed their story. With her luck they'd execute a search of *Sweet Lies* and conveniently find more drugs.

Chance's unexpected whisper almost unraveled her, making her jump in fright. 'When we get inside, I'm going to hit the showers and crash.'

Emily pulled away from his grasp. 'How can you even think about sleeping?' she said to his broad back. 'Any second the cops could storm this place and search for planted drugs. And with our luck they'd find them this time.

Who knows who was in here today.'

'Emily, just go take a shower and relax. I'll check around.'

'No way. I'm sticking to you like glue.' Ignoring his concerned grin, she grabbed the back of his jacket. As Chance unlocked the door she braced herself, anticipating that someone would jump out at them.

Nothing happened as they stepped inside. When he flicked on the lights, she scanned the kitchen. Everything seemed to be in place. Then again everything had seemed fine on *Sweet Lies* until Chance had discovered the drugs.

To her relief he reached around and took her by the hand. She followed him like a second skin while he checked the doors. Everything was locked up tight.

'You'll feel better once you take a shower,' Chance said again as they entered the living room.

'Why do I get the feeling you want to get rid of me?'

'Go. Take a shower. Take as long as you need. I'll be right here when you get out.' He plopped down on the couch and threw her a somewhat reassuring smile that did nothing to ease her increasing anxiety.

'Okay, but I don't think I'll ever feel relaxed again.'

Chance waited until he heard Emily turn on the shower taps before moving to check the windows. He breathed a sigh of relief to find she had replaced all the older style windows on the first floor with new storm windows, but that didn't mean someone hadn't jimmied one open.

She was right. How the hell could he even think about sleeping tonight? Especially with someone obviously after them.

If that were the case why had the Coast Guard let them go so easily? Unless whoever was behind this was playing with him. Letting him know they knew he was back. Or warning him this time they were going to involve Emily and not just threaten to do it like they'd done over the years.

He inhaled deeply at the thought of Emily. She was exhausted. Strained to the max. He was surprised she'd even agreed to take a shower, but he'd figured it was the safest place for her to be while he checked around.

Visions of the movie *Psycho* suddenly danced around in his head. Wasn't there a creepy shower scene in that movie? A woman in the shower and a knife slashing through the shower curtains, stabbing her?

He gritted his teeth against the goose

bumps racing up his spine and forced himself to shake those silly thoughts away. He needed to talk to someone who could calm him down. Someone who would believe him and get Emily off this island before something else happened. He'd call Daniel and tell him what had happened tonight. He'd know what to do.

Chance picked up the phone and a horrible slice of dread ripped into him. There was no dial tone.

★   ★   ★

'What a day!' Emily sighed as she allowed the hot penetrating spray to ram into her tense shoulder muscles. Now she knew how Steve must have felt when the Coast Guard boarded *Sweet Lies* all those years ago. He must have been absolutely horrified at having drugs on board and then stunned. She hadn't been able to do a darned thing to help him because she'd been safe and sound at home building a nest for them.

She closed her eyes and felt the hot sting of tears crash against her eyelids. Poor Steve. He sure could have used Chance's help.

Thank God Chance had been around for her today. If she'd been alone, the Coast Guard would have found the drugs and she'd be in jail right now. Awaiting the same fate as Steve.

What a nightmare! Thankfully Chance had known what to look for and what to do.

It's happening again. Chance's exact words and her exact thoughts while she helplessly watched him pull the white bag full of drugs from behind her *Sweet Lies'* kitchenette cabinet. He must have been thinking about Steve and how he'd been framed this same way. Obviously whoever had been behind Steve's frame-up had resurfaced. Why now? Why after all these years?

Questions with no answers. It was enough to throw her hands up in the air and scream in frustration.

★　★　★

'Before you hit the shower I need to ask you some questions.'

Emily's strong tone made the uneasiness he'd been experiencing since finding those drugs swirl into the pit of Chance's stomach. His head snapped up and he saw the raw angry sparks shooting from her hazel eyes.

When she noticed he was placing a couple of blankets on the couch, she frowned. 'What are you doing?'

'Thought I'd sleep down here tonight.'

She seemed to tense at the idea and a split second later she relaxed.

Chance fluffed up the pillows and asked. 'What is it you want to know?'

'How did you know it was the Coast Guard coming?'

'Saw the emblem on it's side as it pulled up.'

'What if they weren't the authorities? What would you have done?'

'Grabbed you, dove overboard and then kissed you.'

'Chance, be serious. How did you know these people weren't simply imitating the Coast Guard?'

He relaxed. He'd expected curious questions from her. Thankfully she hadn't figured out his true identity. 'Emily, people don't go around imitating the Canadian Coast Guard. They infiltrate it. I was looking for a suspicious character. When the man asked for water, I suspected him and that's why I stuck to him like glue.'

It wasn't the truth. Another sweet lie to protect them. The minute Chance had spotted the fellow he'd recognized him as the same man who'd found the drugs on *Sweet Lies* years earlier. Whoever was behind this nightmare was using the same techniques and same people they'd used in the past.

Obviously they knew he was back.

'Someone tipped him off?' she said in disbelief.

He nodded.

'The Canadian Coast Guard is crooked?'

'No. Just one man. I think the next time we're in town I'll hit the library's Internet and send the McCullen brothers an e-mail. Tell them what happened and to check into this guy's background. I'm sure they'll find something.'

'You can use my Internet, or you can call them.'

'Someone is probably monitoring your e-mails. It's better if I use a neutral computer.' He opted not to tell her about the phone not working.

She nodded. 'What do we do now?'

'They'll try again. I think it's safer if you go and stay with Daniel and Jo.'

'You've got to be kidding.'

'Don't be stubborn about this, Emily. This is serious. We'll take the laptop to their place and see if we can crack the code.'

'No, I'm going to try to crack it myself.'

'I'm telling you they will try again. Next time it won't be pleasant.'

'They?'

'If I knew that, Emily . . . '

'Give me twenty-four hours. Then we get

the McCullens involved.'

'I can live with that,' Chance lied. Anything could happen in twenty-four hours.

She didn't say anything, but he noticed her shoulders relax slightly. It sure felt good to know she trusted him and he felt better being closer to her tonight. Even if it was only on the couch.

'I'm going to try and break the code to the disk,' she said. 'Unless . . . you need something?'

'Go ahead. If you get sleepy, just turn in. I'm keeping watch. I'll wake you up if I need you to spell me. If you need something, come and get me.'

'Thanks, Chance,' she said softly.

'For what?'

'For being there tonight. For knowing where to look for the drugs and getting rid of them before the Coast Guard showed up . . . and for being here tonight. I feel much better knowing you're here.'

Her words made him feel so good. 'You're welcome.'

She nodded and, to his disappointment, disappeared into the bedroom.

10

Chance peered up at the living room's knotty pine ceiling. For years he'd dreamed of being back here in this cozy little lighthouse, peering up at this ceiling or lying beside his wife. For years he'd awakened and found himself staring at the round, black metal bars holding him prisoner, totally alone.

Surprisingly, thinking about his hellish past didn't spark the usual raw anger. Something had changed inside of him over the past few days. Maybe it was the salty smell of the fresh ocean air, the physically challenging work of lugging in the seaweed or even the scenic rock-cradled beaches that had helped heal some of his inner turmoil.

If he were a betting man, he'd put all his money on Emily being the one responsible for making him feel like a normal man. Just to be near her, talk with her and tease her gave him the confidence he needed to start living again.

Throwing back his covers he tiptoed to her open bedroom door. She lay fast asleep, her head nestled snugly on a fluffy pillow. His heart swelled with love. She was so perfect, in every way. Physically, spiritually, emotionally. She allowed him to feel so peaceful.

The realization washed over him in a pleasant wave and he chuckled. Peace. Blessed Peace. He'd found it. Right here on the tiny, lonely gem of a godforsaken rocky island he'd once hated and had learned to love.

He reached out and touched a silky strand of her soft honey blonde hair, traced his finger feather light down her right cheekbone to her rose petal-shaped lips. Lips, both sweet and demanding at the same time. Quite a lethal combination.

Slowly he lifted his finger from her face and held his breath as she nestled more snugly beneath her blankets. She remained asleep.

He knew how Emily felt. He wanted to stay cuddled up pretending that everything was all right. The truth of the matter was if he didn't get her out of here, away from the danger that followed him like a plague, there would be no chance at a future between them. For some strange reason, this morning he actually thought there just might be a chance for them.

First he needed to think up a way to get her safely off the island.

★   ★   ★

Tantalizing aromas of fresh brewed coffee sifted through the thick layers of Emily's sleep and unleashed a memory of Steve and how he'd start the coffee machine every morning. The peaceful vision made her wake up and reality crashed in around her once again.

Yesterday Chance and she had almost ended up in jail. Now she had less than twenty-four hours to find out what Steve had hidden on his computer, if anything.

Funny after everything that had happened yesterday, she'd been totally convinced she wouldn't sleep and had done the opposite, sleeping through the entire night without even waking.

When she entered the kitchen, all she found was a steaming coffee pot set on the coffee machine heater and a note sitting on the counter. Quickly she picked up the piece of paper and breathed a huge sigh of relief. *Up in the lamp room.* Now, what in the world was he doing up there?

★   ★   ★

Chance stood at the railing just outside the lamp room and peered out across the green-blue ocean. Even though the day looked fresh and clean, he distinctly smelled a

207

disturbance in the air. Gray-tinged white clouds drifted low over the moody ocean and the crisp air seemed heavy with different scents. The pungent seaweed and the foul odor of rotting fish intermingled with other more pleasant aromas of ocean salt and the sweet pine that drifted from the nearby stunted trees cradling the shoreline. A sound behind him made him whirl around. To his delight he found Emily standing in the doorway. She wore a dark blue knitted sweater, a white turtleneck and form hugging jeans and she was holding a breakfast tray.

'I would have said breakfast in bed or more appropriately breakfast on the couch, but you were already gone.' She smiled and he found himself grinning at her. Under the circumstances he wouldn't have been surprised if she were still uneasy and snappy after everything she'd been through.

'So, it's breakfast in the lighthouse tower instead.' She placed the tray on the wide windowsill and peered curiously at him. 'Phones are out. I get the feeling you already knew that. I'm sorry I forgot to mention to you that yesterday was the day the phones were to be disconnected anyway.'

Immense relief swept over him, followed quickly by a ravenous appetite.

'I believe you are up here for a reason?' she asked.

'Trying to flag down some help. See if we can get off the island.'

'You said I had twenty-four hours to get the password.'

'We're sitting ducks here, Emily. If you're so determined to get into the laptop, then we'll shack up at some hotel on the mainland. Staying here isn't an option.'

'Of course. You're right. I guess I wasn't thinking straight last night.'

'Not to worry. You're thinking straight today.' He eyed the breakfast tray and rubbed his cold hands together in appreciation as the taste bud arousing aroma of crisp bacon and fluffy eggs drifted from the two aluminum-covered plates on the tray.

'Dig in.' She lifted a cover and handed him one of the plates.

The dish felt warm against his cold hands and he wasted no time in digging into the food.

'How did you plan on signaling the boats for help?'

'I know enough about SOS signaling,' he said between bites. 'Been practicing with the lamp for the past two hours.'

'I do hope you know you'll be in for a long wait. We're not in the middle of the shipping lanes. They're on the south side of Shipwreck Island. The Coast Guard put up a modern lighthouse over there. This one is considered obsolete.'

'Then we'll go to the other lighthouse.'

She shook her head. 'No way you can get in. Everything is bolted up tight as a drum.'

He nodded as he continued to eat her delicious cooking.

'I do have another idea,' she said.

He stopped chewing and cocked his head sideways in question.

Suddenly she peered at him strangely and for a split second he got the feeling she knew who he was, but that wasn't possible.

'What? Have I got egg on my face?' he said nervously. The odd look in her eyes vanished and he relaxed.

'It's nothing.'

'So? What's the idea?'

'It's a long shot. I'll tell you after you finish your breakfast.'

Suddenly he got the distinct feeling he wasn't going to like what she had brewing on her mind.

★ ★ ★

With sadness in her heart Emily watched Chance untie the ropes holding her boat securely against her dock.

'Are you sure you want to do this?' he asked as he held the lines in his hand.

'There's no other choice.'

Reluctantly he threw the lines into the boat and gave *Sweet Lies* a swift push. Her boat and the full cargo of seaweed drifted away.

One foot. Three feet. Six feet. Nine feet.

'Do you think it'll work?' Chance asked.

'I don't know. The wind's almost right. Hopefully she'll get blown into the shipping lanes and someone will recognize her.'

'What if she falls into the wrong hands? Are you sure you're prepared for that?'

She swallowed the thick lump of emotion lodged in her throat. For all she knew this would be the last time she'd ever see *Sweet Lies*. Anyone could find her and decide to lay claim to her. They would refit her, repaint her, take her for their own. Even worse, whoever had planted the drugs on her could find her and come straight back here. That's why they'd opted not to leave a note of help inside.

As if sensing her sadness, Chance placed his strong hands on her shoulders and squeezed reassuringly. 'Even if no one recognizes her out there and the bad guys don't see her berthed here, they might think we aren't here and not show.'

She nodded and watched the boat drift toward the point. 'Or she might simply get dragged out to sea, or capsize against the rocks and be lost forever.'

He didn't say anything. She knew he was thinking the same thing.

★ ★ ★

Two hours later the sadness at the loss of her boat still clutched painfully at Emily's heart. Even concentrating on trying to crack the password was useless. She tried everything she could think of and nothing worked.

Her eyes smarted from staring at the computer screen, yet her mind and hands ached to keep herself busy. She peeked out the window and saw Chance's stiff form up in the Lamp House. He was still peering out across the ocean.

Earlier when she'd told him she had another way to help get them off the island, he'd cocked his head slightly to one side. Déjà vu had staggered her. When curious or puzzled Steve had also cocked his head in exactly the same way. It was an endearing habit she'd always loved. Today it had been anything but endearing. Creepy how many similarities the two men possessed — similar crooked grins, golden highlights, cocking of

212

the head, her insane attraction to them. Yet Chance was different in many ways. Not as relaxed or confident as Steve had been. Somewhat uneasy at times and uncertain.

It seemed an eternity since he'd shown up. A lifetime. As if he'd always lived here with her. As if . . . Steve had never left. She stopped herself. Her thoughts were going haywire. Chance Donovan and Steve McCullen were two totally different men with similar personalities. In this world it was quite possible two men could have the same type of personality, wasn't it?

She flicked off Steve's laptop in sudden frustration. She needed to do something else to keep her mind occupied and she knew just what to do.

★   ★   ★

Emily was probably waiting lunch on him, but Chance needed to get a quick peek around the bend up ahead. He'd wanted to let her know he'd seen the motorboat off the northwest point, but the sound of the vacuum cleaner whirring in the loft made him change his mind. By the time he got upstairs, told her what he'd seen and then headed out to the beach, the boat might be gone.

He'd spied the laptop sitting open on the

kitchen table and stiffened at the sight. It would take him only a minute to get inside. Then he could see what information the disk contained. But Emily came first. If he could flag down that boat he'd seen, they could be off the island within minutes. The disk would have to wait.

A wicked flash of lightning forked out of the black billowing clouds flowing up from the south. The storm was almost upon them. By his estimate it would strike Shipwreck Island within the hour.

Up ahead he spotted the boat pulled up on the beach and his heart picked up the beat. Perhaps the owner had also seen the storm heading their way and decided to take shelter. Maybe he could persuade the owner of the boat to brave the storm and get Emily and himself to Prince Edward Island. At that thought he broke into a trot.

He squinted as the cool wind blasted sprinkles of rain into his eyes and the roaring crash of the white-capped waves drowned out the sound of his pounding heart and any other warnings he might have heard. When he saw the familiar dark haired man with a moustache step out from behind a clump of gnarled pine trees, Chance came to a screeching halt. In a split second he realized it was too late to make his escape.

Emily had set about cleaning the tiny lighthouse with a vengeance. She'd vacuumed the first floor and looked up to the tower to see Chance still silhouetted up there. A quick glance at the kitchen clock showed it was almost lunchtime. He would be hungry, but first she'd quickly clean the loft.

She'd lugged the heavy vacuum cleaner up the narrow stairs to the loft and started vacuuming the rugs and then under the bed. She was about to turn and leave when she spotted his green duffel bag still propped against the wall where she'd placed it the morning after he'd arrived. Apparently he was one of those men who didn't like to unpack.

Looking down at it, she shook her head. Didn't he realize all his damp clothes needed to get dried? With all the excitement she'd forgotten to tell him to bring down the clothes that needed washing or drying.

Opening the drawstring, she lifted out two wrinkled shirts and a pair of heavy track pants then heard a strange rattle at the bottom of the bag. Digging past some underwear, she gasped when she spied three pill bottles.

A shiver of unease curled through her belly as she withdrew one. She read the label.

Prednisone. The name sounded awfully familiar. Reaching inside, she retrieved another bottle. Cyclosporine.

A shiver of alarm ripped through her as she remembered why people took these types of medications. Both were anti-rejection drugs.

Chance was an organ transplant recipient!

★   ★   ★

Chance drew in a shaky breath as he stared straight into the face of the man who'd been haunting his nightmares. It was the so-called Prosecutor who had tried to make a deal with him in jail years earlier. The same man who'd threatened Emily's life over the years. The same man who'd beat him senseless every chance he got. Chance bit back the bitter bile of revenge threatening to clog up his throat.

'Get in the boat, Donovan.' The Prosecutor nodded to the flashy speedboat pulled onto the wave-crashed beach. At the same time he waved his gun at Chance's belly.

'Make me.'

'Don't make me hurt you again, Donovan.'

The Prosecutor's voice reeked with authority as it had all those years. Only this time Chance wasn't securely confined or being surprised by an attack force. This time it appeared he and the Prosecutor were alone

216

and Chance wasn't going down. Not without one hell of a fight. He felt his own gun bite into the small of his back. A gentle reminder he wasn't defenseless anymore, but he knew he wouldn't be able to reach it in time.

From past experience he'd learned quickly his best defense was a good offense. The Prosecutor probably thought his gun would keep him in line so Chance figured he'd better prove him wrong. Now!

He launched himself headlong like a tornado into the surprised Prosecutor, knocking him off balance. The gun discharged harmlessly into the air as Chance's left foot flew outward and upward to nail the Prosecutor between the legs or in convict terms 'nailed him square where the sun doesn't shine.'

The man screamed in anguish and he doubled over giving Chance the perfect opportunity to knee him straight in the nose. Chance grimaced as he felt the man's nose crumble beneath the horrible blow. Crimson red streams shot from his nose spraying Chance's jeans and shirt. The Prosecutor dropped like a sack of potatoes and lay moaning on the sandy beach, clutching his face.

'Payback is a bitch, isn't it?' Chance shouted as red-hot anger slithered through him. He swallowed at the uncontrollable rage engulfing him and his eyes strayed to the Prosecutor's gun lying in the red grains of sand. It gleamed wickedly up at him, begging him to pick it up.

Chance hesitated. He knew without a doubt if he wrapped his hands around that gun, he might kill the bastard and he wasn't eager to get back behind bars.

Just then, an excruciating pain sliced into his back as someone sucker punched him in the kidney. Chance's legs were snatched right out from beneath him and he fell to his knees. Blinking wildly he tried to clear the pain fogging up his brain as realization zoomed over him that a second party had arrived on the scene. Before he could make a move to get up, a fierce blow sliced across his forehead and the barrel of a gun bit deep into his flesh.

Chance groaned from the searing pain and the beach reached up to meet his face. A split second later the cold barrel of a gun kissed his left temple and someone removed his gun from its hiding place at the small of his back.

Through the foggy haze of pain he could hear the Prosecutor swearing as someone asked him if he was all right. Chance didn't dare move his head to see who was talking for fear he'd get blown away, but the voice sure did sound familiar. He just couldn't place it.

One thing for sure, it didn't belong to Skip Cole.

'I said get in the boat,' the Prosecutor said.

'I said, make me,' Chance spat into the sand.

'Do as I say or this time I will go after your wife.'

Fury grabbed a hold of Chance. The thought of this man touching Emily made him nauseous and it gave him the required adrenaline to swing his leg into the Prosecutor's ankle. Once again the gun flew out of the Prosecutor's hand into the nearby sand.

'We have to get out of here!' the new man on the scene whispered in alarm. 'Someone's coming. I can't be identified.'

The Prosecutor cursed again and a moment later Chance heard the roar of a motorboat.

He made a move for the gun, which lay inches away from his face. The world tilted crazily, forcing him to close his eyes and remain as stiff as a corpse. A few moments later he heard footsteps sift through the sand and Emily's frantic voice hovered mere inches from his face.

'Chance! Talk to me! Please! You're scaring me.'

Her tormented voice cried through the

howling wind and he forced himself to open his eyes.

'Where are they?' he said through gritted teeth as the pain in his head intensified.

'They saw me coming and they took off in a boat.'

I can't be recognized, the second man had said in that familiar voice. A voice he couldn't place.

'One of them knew you,' Chance muttered. 'Said he didn't want to be recognized. That's why they ran. Did you get a good look at them?'

'No.' She looked around fearfully. 'Maybe we should get out of the open. Think you can stand?'

The last thing he wanted to do was move a muscle. Unfortunately she was right. They wouldn't be much safer back at the lighthouse, but there wasn't anywhere else to go.

With great effort and her help he managed to make it to his feet. The minute he did, the fierce wind almost knocked him over again. Her warm arm wrapped snugly around his waist and she lifted his arm over her shoulder and around her neck, gripping his hand tightly.

'Lean against me,' she instructed.

He allowed himself to put some weight

against her small frame. She sighed in frustration. 'More. I'm not a fragile China plate.'

He grinned despite his splitting headache and did as she instructed.

It was tough going. Between the wind beating against them, the rain dropping over them in buckets and the thunder cracking overhead, it was all he could do to grit his teeth against the shock waves sifting through his splitting head at his every step.

By the time Emily helped him into her bed, their bed, he amended, his headache and dizziness hadn't improved much. Heck, what was he complaining about? Over the past few years pain had been his middle name and this headache was nothing in comparison.

All he needed to do was sleep it off. Obviously she had other plans. He inhaled sharply as she began unbuttoning the top button of his jacket and he forced his eyes open.

'Don't!' The last thing he wanted was for her to see his chest.

'Your clothes are all wet and covered in blood.'

'Emily,' he warned sharply.

'I know you have scars, Chance. I felt them the other day when we . . . kissed,' she said softly as if she'd just read his mind. 'Please, don't be embarrassed.'

Oh, he was embarrassed. And scared. Terrified at what her reaction would be.

With ease she slid off his jacket and began to tackle his shirt buttons. He should reach out and grab her wrists to stop her from going any further. He should. Yet her touch felt so sweet against his skin and so gentle, a balm to his battered nerves. Besides he didn't think he'd be able to stop her even if his life depended on it. He was so tired.

So, he waited. Waited for the horror to cross her face, waited for the sharp gasp to escape her lips.

To his surprise, neither happened. Her beautiful face only softened into a soothing tenderness as she slipped his shirt over his shoulders. Then her gentle fingers were on those scars. Pressing and prodding or was she exploring?

'Tell me if anything hurts,' she said as she moved her hands up over his shoulders to the back of his neck, then down along his waist to his lower back.

That's when pain shot straight into his belly and he stifled a groan.

'Kidney transplant?'

Chance blinked, not quite sure if he'd heard her right.

'Some of your scars are surgical. I also saw

the pills in your duffel. Wasn't hard to figure out.'

He knew he should be angry at her for snooping in his things. Thankfully he only felt blessed relief that another one of his sweet lies was now out in the open.

'I'll get you something for your head.'

He didn't know how long she was gone, he must have fallen asleep or passed out. When she came back, she pressed something awfully cold against his cracking forehead.

'Easy,' he whispered. 'That hurts.'

'Good,' she said.

Chance was surprised to hear coldness underlying her otherwise concerned voice.

'Serves you right for running off without a backup.'

'What good would it have done if I'd told you?'

'I could have come with you.'

'Oh and they could have jumped both of us.'

'I don't think so. Didn't you say one of them didn't want to be recognized?'

She had a point.

'Besides,' she said, 'at least it would have been two against two.'

Despite his headache and the weariness claiming through his body, he found himself grinning. 'Ah, yes. I forgot about those muscles you bragged about at the dance.'

'Speaking of muscles, put yours to good use and hold this steak over your bump.'

Clumsily he lifted his hand and held the frozen meat to his aching forehead.

'Where else do you hurt?'

'Here,' he said softly and lifted his other hand to touch his lips with his finger.

She pinned a puzzled gaze onto his mouth.

'Right here,' he whispered again. 'Make me feel better.'

Realization crept into her face and her eyes suddenly sparkled.

'I know what you're doing,' she said smoothly.

'What's that?'

Slowly she leaned closer to him and stopped mere inches from his lips. Her warm breath cascaded across his mouth and he felt his lips part slightly in anticipation.

'You want me to keep you awake because you might have a concussion.'

'Is that what I'm doing?' Heck he hadn't even thought about that angle.

'Yes, because you might have been knocked out from the blow to your head.'

She searched his face and suddenly he knew what she was doing. 'And you're checking my pupils to see if they're both reacting normally.'

'You're catching on.'

'Everything in working order?'

'You tell me.'

Her lips parted and to his surprise she kissed him. Ever so gently, like a delicate brush of a butterfly's wings. Then she drew away and he groaned in protest as his headache returned with a vengeance.

'Hold the steak over your . . . bump.' Her eyes dropped to the bulge straining against his jeans. He looked down too. 'On your forehead,' she corrected, then said a little too cheerfully, 'Seems the rest of you is working properly too. I better get your pants off.'

'I like the sound of that,' he teased.

A hint of a pink blush streaked across her cheeks.

'I'm glad because that steak is tonight's dinner and it needs a good defrosting,' she said referring to her earlier comment about putting the steak over his bump . . . on his forehead.

Sense of humor. He'd almost forgotten that part of her character when she was under loads of stress. She sure was under stress because of him.

She didn't say anything as her trembling fingers worked at the brass stud and then she unzipped him. When she tried to take his pants off, the movement sent his head to spinning again. He closed his eyes, and leaned his head deeper into the pillows.

'Sorry, they're almost off,' she said.

Cool air hit his legs and that was the last thing he remembered before he drifted off to sleep.

11

The next few hours flew past in an anxious blur. Emily cleaned and disinfected the nasty cut on Chance's forehead and the scrapes on his raw knuckles. The frozen steak had done its job, keeping the swelling to a minimum, and was now sizzling slowly in the frying pan on top of the stove. Not that she was hungry. He, on the other hand, would need protein to recover from today's adventure with those two hooligans.

Dear God! Not again!

Chance screamed as strong, rough hands dragged him through the black, windowless door marked Execution Chamber.

Someone was already strapped into the electrocution chair and Chance immediately recognized Hunter, the inmate who'd agreed to help him get word to the outside that Steve McCullen was alive. Hunter's eyes brightened when he saw Chance.

'Donovan! Finally! Tell them I don't know squat!' Hunter cried.

Chance winced at the desperation in Hunter's voice.

'Hunter's telling the truth.' Chance shouted out the lie as the rough hands shoved him into a smaller, metal chair bolted to the floor directly in front of and ten feet away from Hunter.

Using a burst of adrenaline, Chance struggled against the leather restraints that were quickly and efficiently strapped over his wrists and ankles.

'Sweet Jesus,' he whispered to the three guards hovering around him. 'Don't do this.'

The guards, all dressed in military blue, moved away leaving him alone with the wide-eyed Hunter who struggled valiantly against his own restraints, which included an odd-looking steel band that held his head captive against the headrest of the electric chair. Strange electrodes were clamped on each of his legs, over his heart and upper arms.

'They're kidding right?' he squealed.

Chance didn't respond. What could he say? Sorry we got caught? It just didn't seem appropriate at the moment.

'They can't get away with this,' Hunter said angrily. 'This is a prison for Christ's sake!'

When the door to the Execution Chamber burst inward, Chance cringed as a man he recognized entered. Any hope he had managed to hang onto zipped away in a flash.

This man, 'The Prosecutor' Chance had nicknamed him, loved to torment Chance.

The Prosecutor didn't look at Chance or at his intended victim. He did, however, head directly for The Switch on the far wall that would send thousands of volts jolting through Hunter.

'Hey!' Hunter shouted at The Prosecutor as he tried to grab his attention. 'You can't do this. This is Texas, America! I have rights.'

The Prosecutor halted and Chance held his breath.

'This isn't America, son,' The Prosecutor said from under his black moustache. 'This is hell. You're going to pay for that man's mistake.' He nodded at Chance who winced when Hunter's tormented eyes pinned him.

'How many men have fried because of you, Donovan? Three? Four?' the Prosecutor asked.

Chance cursed beneath his breath.

The Prosecutor smiled and continued toward The Switch. When he reached it, he slowly wrapped his hand around the lever and once again turned to Chance. Hunter, who suddenly realized he'd be a fried tater in about a minute, began screaming for mercy.

Chance closed his eyes, forced his breathing to slow and prepared for the worst. Over the past few years he'd developed an interesting technique of self-survival. Most times it didn't work. Thankfully now it did.

He allowed his mind to blank out until he entered the world of billowing white cauliflower clouds drifting over a moody blue ocean with snow-capped waves. A rusty red sandy beach stretched out in front of him for as far as he could see. He sighed with pleasure as his hot bare feet sank into the cool, silky sand grains.

Heaven. Pure, sweet heaven.

He squinted into the sun's bright rays and relished the cool wind blasting his skin. The rhythmic crash of the snow-capped waves unrolling on the rippled beach drowned out his pounding heart and any other sounds he might hear.

Before he knew it, he was running. Running so fast he felt as if he were flying. Soaring with the virgin white seagulls. The air seemed fresh and crisp, heavy with an array of aromas. Pungent seaweed. The foul odor of rotting fish. The sweet smell of pine drifted from the nearby weather-stunted trees cradling the red shoreline.

And Emily. He smelled Emily. Fresh, clean and innocent. Where was she? Why wasn't she running beside him?

'Emily!' he shouted into the roaring wind.

No answer.

Another smell drifted through the air. A distasteful scent that didn't belong to this serene world. He tried to run faster, his only purpose to get away from the insistent smell. His legs grew heavy, his arms limp. He tried not to breathe, but the horrible odor had already clambered deep into his nostrils and settled snugly in his lungs.

That's when he recognized the sick stench.

Chance crashed back to reality. Back into the Execution Chamber, to the sizzling sound of burning flesh.

He squeezed his eyes tighter and willed his mind to leave this insanity. The clack of approaching footsteps on the smooth, cement floor refused to let him go. Someone stopped in front of him. He could hear The Prosecutor's nose whistle as he breathed, felt his intense stare burn into his face.

Chance knew without a doubt he was studying the welts and scars and burns. Welts, scars and burns this man had put there. Chance sure as heck didn't want to open his eyes and look into the man's evil charcoal-colored eyes, but he knew The Prosecutor wouldn't leave until he did.

Reluctantly, he opened his eyes and blinked at the smoky haze and at the dark figure smiling smugly down at him. Chance curled his hands into tight, angry knots.

God help him if he wasn't strapped into this chair, he'd crash his fists into The Prosecutor's face.

'You were warned not to talk to anyone, McCullen. You talk only to me. Only when you can tell me what you know. Is that understood?'

Chance nodded angrily.

'Say it!'

'Don't talk to anyone,' Chance said.

'Only to me.'

'Only to you.'

'So? Do you have any information you'd like to share?'

'No,' Chance replied coldly.

The Prosecutor inhaled wearily.

'If I did,' Chance said, 'I sure as hell wouldn't tell you!'

The Prosecutor cracked his knuckles lightly. When Chance spotted the glimmering brass knuckles, fear sliced into his every pore.

'These brass knuckles got a wonderful workout the last few times I used them on you, Donovan. Turned your handsome face into minced meat. I bet you get tons of stares from the guards.' The Prosecutor chuckled lightly. 'I suppose your wife would scream her bloody head off if she got a look at you now, wouldn't she?'

Chance remained silent. Anything he said now would only provoke The Prosecutor to hit him harder when he began swinging those fists.

'You might want to know the Boss instructed me not to ruin those new eyes or I might get into trouble again. Wouldn't want that.'

Chance didn't believe a word he said and continued to eye the brass knuckles warily, flinching every time those hands moved.

'Unfortunately for me, the Boss doesn't think you've recuperated enough from your last encounter with the brass knuckles. But . . . I do.'

Chance didn't get the opportunity to close his eyes as The Prosecutor suddenly moved away giving Chance full view of Hunter.

He cursed violently at the gray smoke curling up from various parts of Hunter's charred body. No one had to tell him the man who'd agreed to help him was dead.

'If you're not careful, Donovan. I'll go get your wife off that little island of hers, bring her here and she'll be the next one to sit in that chair. Wouldn't that be lovely?' When Chance didn't answer, The Prosecutor frowned. 'Hopefully my warning will stick this time around and we won't have to get *your wife involved. You have seventy-two hours to talk things over with Hunter here.'*

Chance shivered when The Prosecutor slammed the door shut behind him, leaving him alone with a stinking corpse for companionship.

'Chance! Wake up!'

Emily's soft yet insistent voice ripped into Chance's terror. Warm, gentle hands brushed across his cold, clammy chest, but the familiarity refused to soothe away the fear taking firm hold over his sweat-drenched body.

'You're dreaming. Open your eyes'

Her sharp command made him obey. Soft shadows drenched the dimly lit bedroom. Pain pounded his temples and a sense of urgency washed over him. He sucked in a shuddering breath in a desperate attempt to calm the icy grip of terror. When he smelled burning flesh, another jab of alarm ripped through him.

'Oh God! I can still smell it!'

'Easy, I burned the steak. You smell the steak.'

'No one is burning?' The question slipped out before he could stop himself.

Horror flashed in her eyes and a cold wave of embarrassment washed over him.

'No one is burning,' she said softy as she sat down beside him. 'It's okay. You're safe. You want to talk about it?'

He shook his head, realizing immediately the dizziness from the head wound had subsided. The sound of wind drifted to his ears. A flash of lightning splashed against the windows. The storm was here. They were safe. For now.

He exhaled with relief. He was home. In bed. With Emily!

She flicked on the light and he struggled to sit. The blanket that covered him drifted off his chest and came to rest low on his hips. He made a grab for the blanket and his heart skidded to a halt. Damned if he wasn't wearing any clothes. Heat blushed across his face and he suddenly wondered why the hell he was embarrassed about being in bed with his wife. He cleared his throat and pulled the blanket up over his waist.

Her face hovered close. He noticed the tendrils of her mussed hair feathered across her face. Soft pink lips were open slightly as she watched him. Checking his pupils again, no doubt.

'Breathe deep, Chance. In a minute you'll feel better.'

Heck, she thought he was still freaking out about the nightmare. *Au contraire.*

She frowned with concern. 'I think you need to talk about what just happened.'

'No. I'll be fine.'

'How's your headache?'

'Bit better.'

'Dizziness?'

'Pretty much gone.'

She sighed in relief, her warm breath floating across his chest making the muscles there tighten erotically. Her evocative woman scent swarmed over him and he noticed the enticing way her thin T-shirt was pulled tightly over her full breasts. He swallowed, hard, as a wave of desire swept through him and he turned his head upward to stare at the ceiling. He hoped to heaven she hadn't noticed his reaction to her.

'It wasn't a dream, was it? Something traumatic happened to you.'

He shouldn't say anything, especially now that he felt so vulnerable and so stupid.

'It was a memory,' he admitted. 'I'd rather not talk about it.'

'If not to me then at least to a professional.'

Chance scrubbed his hand over his face.

'I've already done the shrink bit, Emily. Now I'm at the 'deal with it' stage. I guess the smell . . . it must have brought back some things . . . '

She remained silent and when he turned to

look at her, he was surprised to see her smiling again.

'Back to your normal secretive self.'

Another flash of lightning illuminated the windows and a crack of thunder made him jump. He tensed as her warm fingers sprayed across his chest.

'It's okay. Only the storm,' she soothed.

He flinched as her fingers traced over his scars. Ugly scars. Scars from his past.

He'd made the doctors concentrate on repairing his mangled face. Hadn't given his chest much thought. Those scars had been low on his list of priorities and now he wished they were gone.

Yet earlier when her fingers had poked and prodded his chest as she'd tried to find broken bones, she hadn't looked at him as if he were repulsive. This time was different. He felt it immediately. He knew without a doubt those fingers spreading over his scars were exploring, her soft touch intimate. As intimate as a lover's touch.

He reached up and grabbed at her wrists, stopping her cold. Her eyes widened in surprise or maybe it was shock. He wanted to tell her to stop. It would be the right thing to do. He had no claim on her anymore. He'd given it up when he'd decided not to tell her he was still alive.

She wanted to kiss him. He could tell. She'd been wanting him from day one. He'd known it instinctively. He'd always been able to sense her body language, always known when she wanted him. She definitely wanted him now and the feeling was mutual.

He wanted to slip his arms around her waist, pull her sweet softness against him. Ached to feel her breasts flatten against his chest. Against those scars. Ugly scars.

'I think I'd better make you something to eat,' she whispered. Her breath was as ragged as his and it excited him, but he knew he had to let her go. So he did.

'I'm sorry,' he said. 'I . . . '

'I know. You have a headache,' she teased, but he saw the hurt of rejection in her eyes.

Before he could reach out to her, she'd slipped from the bed and padded out of their bedroom.

★　★　★

When Emily reached the kitchen, she whipped open the refrigerator door and literally stuck her head inside. Cool air washed against her hot, flushed cheeks and she allowed herself the luxury of breathing.

'This is nuts,' she whispered to the jar of applesauce staring back at her.

Something was very wrong with her. But very right between them. Something primal had been unleashed inside her. Sexually she wanted him. But it went deeper than mere attraction. There was a bond between them. It was almost as if . . . as if she should know Chance Donovan. Know him intimately.

God! Was she going crazy? Or had her body merely been without for so long she was willing to jump the bones of the first man who came along? A crude way of putting it, but wasn't that what was happening to her?

She shook her head in denial. She'd had Skip Cole hanging around her for the past year and she hadn't lusted after him. What was it about Chance that made her want to touch him? To boldly run her fingers along those frightful scars. Scars she hadn't even realized she'd been caressing. The heated look that had jumped into his terror-filled eyes when she'd placed her hand onto his chest had captured her attention.

She'd been so sure he wanted her to kiss him. In fact, so sure she'd been surprised, and not to mention hurt, when he'd stopped her hands before she'd had a chance to reach up and cup both sides of his face so she could kiss him.

She'd wanted to explore his body. To climb inside his head and find out what he was thinking. To kiss all his pain away. She wanted to vanquish the horrific dream he'd just had. No, not dream. A nightmare. Or memory as he'd put it.

What had happened to him? Why did he dream about burning flesh? Thankfully he'd admitted he'd sought professional help because it made her feel a wee bit better knowing he was dealing with whatever had happened in his past.

If the phone hadn't been disconnected, she'd be calling her brother-in-law right now demanding he tell her Chance's story. On the other hand, she could come right out and demand answers. He'd get angry and clam up tight just like he'd done right after their beautiful kiss the other day. The kiss that had been interrupted by the teenager.

There weren't any interruptions out here. Were there? Especially with a tremendous storm banging all around them.

The man preferred to keep his past a mystery, didn't he? She was beginning to think maybe she shouldn't blame him for keeping a secret. For God's sake the man's gut-wrenching screams alone had nearly made her faint with fear.

She'd been down in the tiny root cellar beneath the lighthouse searching for a Mason jar of homemade applesauce. When she'd come back upstairs, she discovered the steak burning and Chance screaming. For a few seconds she thought someone was trying to kill him.

When she'd managed to wake him, the look of horror in his eyes had almost broken her heart in two. When he'd asked her if someone was burning . . .

Good grief what had Chance endured? Who were those men who attacked him?

There was a more important duty on her agenda. The man needed food to stay healthy. Especially when they didn't have access to a doctor in case something went wrong with his transplanted kidney.

What could she feed him? Certainly not the steak. Perhaps something easy on his stomach. She knew exactly what she could make him. She grabbed the applesauce and shut the fridge door.

★   ★   ★

Twenty minutes later Emily was halfway to the bedroom when the bathroom door swung open and Chance stepped out, followed by a warm coil of mist. When she noticed he was wearing only a terry cloth towel, she almost dropped the tray she carried. It rode so low on his hips she could almost see . . .

He cleared his throat and she forced herself to look away trying her darndest to keep her face from flaming. It wasn't working. Heat seared through every part of her as she started to squeeze past him, trying not to show how flustered he made her feel.

Oh sweet heaven, how embarrassing.

'I see you're up.' Oh dear. Poor choice of words. 'You must be feeling better.'

'Much. The shower helped.' His voice sounded tight. Nervous? Just like her? It was a good sign, wasn't it?

'I noticed I slept much of the day and most of the night and . . . that smells good.' His cute brows crinkled in puzzlement. 'Is that milk rice? Oh man! Applesauce. You are a woman after my own heart.'

Sweet heat zipped through her nightgown as he neared her and took the tray.

'Let's eat in the kitchen.'

'Too cold in there,' Emily said quickly. The air was still stale with the smell of the burned steak. 'Let's go in the living room. The heater is on and it's nice and toasty.' Since you aren't wearing any clothes, she thought. Not that she wanted him to put on any.

She watched him, a little unnerved because of the large fist sized purple bruise marring his skin directly over his right kidney. By his slight limp, she knew he still hurt.

That didn't stop her from ogling him. Razor sharp tingles of awareness raked along her nerve endings as she inhaled his masculine scent. She could almost feel her fingers sift gently through his tousled baby shampoo-scented hair. She remembered the feel of his solid lean body pressed against her as he'd kissed her so passionately the other day on the peninsula.

Dear God, she could still taste the sweet coffee on his lips. As if sensing her thoughts, Chance looked up from where he sat on her couch. Piercing blue eyes made her breath back right up into her lungs. Blood roared through her ears, and pictures of seducing this man ran rampant in her head.

'Are you hungry, Emily?' He patted the couch beside him.

She swallowed hard as the muscles in his arms rippled with magnificent pride. Maybe he was planning on seducing her?

'We can share.' He held up the bowl of steaming milk rice. 'Dig in while it's still hot.'

Hot was the word. Air rushed into her lungs and she forced herself to move her legs. She must look awfully desperate, standing in the hallway, staring at him with her mouth hanging open in appreciation and her eyes shining with want.

'Actually I've already eaten,' she lied. She

took a seat in the club chair farthest away from him. With an amused smile on his lips, he began to eat.

She enjoyed watching him devour the food she'd prepared. Obviously he was starving. It was a very good sign. A few minutes later he glanced at her from his empty plate.

'Sorry,' he smiled.

'For what? Being hungry?'

She was surprised when the faintest tinge of pink swept across his cheeks. He must have taken her meaning the other way. Her insides trembled with excitement at the delicious thought.

She could feel the heat in his eyes as they caressed her body and drifted over her breasts. As if realizing what he'd just done, he ripped his eyes from her face, cleared his throat, grabbed a napkin from the tray and wiped his mouth.

'Would you like some more?' She was halfway out of her chair before he waved her to sit back down.

'I'm satisfied. Thanks for the grub. You're an excellent cook.'

'I like cooking and baking. I'm old fashioned that way.'

He nodded. That cute, amused smile of his wandered back to his lips. An awkward silence ensued.

'Chance? Who were those men on the beach?'

He froze and she noticed how his fists curled into tight balls. After a moment of silence he asked quietly, 'Did you recognize either of them?'

She frowned and shook her head.

'You sure? Because one of them said he didn't want to be seen because you'd recognize him.'

Uneasiness and anger bore into her belly at the thought that someone she knew would harm Chance. 'Are those the same men who put those scars on your body?'

'One of them is,' he said coolly.

'He's the one who was following you in town the other day?'

'That's him.' He kept his eyes glued to his empty plate.

She got up, walked over and sat down beside him. He looked up and she'd expected to see anger brewing inside his eyes because of her questions, instead she saw raw pain. She touched his arm and he flinched.

'Don't feel sorry for me, Emily. Please . . . don't.'

'You're too tough for me to ever feel sorry for you.'

He blinked in surprise.

'I saw how you fought that man. He was

down and out before I could even run two feet.'

'You saw that?' There wasn't a flicker of emotion on his face now. However his body had tensed into a tight coil. By the hard sound of his voice, he was upset.

'I almost killed that man. I would have if my gun hadn't been taken away. That man doesn't deserve to even set eyes on you, or utter your name, let alone threaten — ' He clammed up tight and ran a shaky hand through his damp hair.

'Must have been a doozy of a threat or you wouldn't be so upset. What did they say? Were they threatening me?'

'I don't want to go into this!' he shouted.

'I don't care what you want!'

'You better care what I want because I want you safe. I can't even protect you because they took my damn gun.'

'I have a damn gun!'

The anger slipped from his eyes.

'What?'

'The one on the beach. It's not yours, but I picked it — '

'Where is it?'

She shook her head, realizing she had herself a bargaining chip. 'Not unless you tell me what is going on. Why were those men beating on you?'

He grew still. Something in his eyes sent an icy shock wave of fear sliding through her veins.

'Do you want to end up dead?' he asked coldly. 'Because they'll kill you or worse to get to me.'

'Why would they even think you cared for me?'

'Dammit! Quit analyzing everything I say. Just tell me where the gun is.'

'To hell with the stupid gun. Why do you need one right now? So you can feel more confident? More of a man?'

'If you're not careful, Emily, I'll show you how much of a man I am.'

His soft-edged voice snaked around her and the raw, sensual look glowing in his eyes made her tremble with excitement. Fierce hunger fired those blue depths. The same hunger that throbbed inside her body. Suddenly she wanted him pressed against her. His warm lips on hers. She wanted him to make her forget they were stranded here with a couple of lunatics possibly lurking around outside.

'I'm sorry. I shouldn't have yelled at you. I know you just want to help.' His breath caressed her lips.

'I'd rather see you angry than mysterious. At least when you're mad you let things slip

. . . and I can sense how you truly feel
. . . about things.'

When one corner of his mouth inched
upward in amusement, her breath tightened
pleasantly in her chest.

'Things?'

'You know what I mean.'

Suddenly he stiffened and a shiver of fear
zipped along her nerves. He turned to look
out the bay window behind them.

'Do you hear that?' he asked.

Only the tick tock of the clock broke the
silence.

'I don't hear anything,' she replied.

'Exactly. The storm is dying down.'

'It's the eye.'

'Eye? Like in hurricane?'

'It was upgraded to one while you were
asleep.'

He swore softly beneath his breath. 'We
might luck out then. If they're out there, on
the island somewhere, now's the time they'll
make their move. Where's the gun?'

'In the bedroom. In the night table. My
side.'

He nodded and rose.

Her heart thundered wildly in her ears.
This time though it had nothing to do with
how dangerously low the towel rode on his
hips as he limped off to the bedroom.

On jittery legs and casting nervous glances at the dark window, she quickly gathered the tray.

So! The two creeps had threatened her. Very interesting. One of them knew her. They obviously knew Chance. But how?

Why would they even think he'd care enough about her to utter a threat? He'd only been here a few days. Hardly a reason for them to think he would give a rat's behind about her.

Yet, he did care about her. He must. Why else would he be so upset about their threat against her? She didn't doubt the sizzling attraction between them must have been apparent during the fair dance. Or maybe the two men had seen them together at Jake's Bar and Grill. That wasn't possible, the only one who saw them was Garrett Rustico and there wasn't an evil bone in that young man's body. It had to be someone at the fair and that pretty much included the whole main island.

12

Standing at rigid attention, Chance gazed out the living room window into the inky darkness. Dawn would be cracking soon and then maybe he could relax. He'd stood guard for more than two hours while fighting the dull throb pounding against his forehead.

Thankfully nothing had moved outside. Until now.

The breeze was once again picking up, wrestling madly with the stunted pine trees out back and gushes of rain blew against the window panes.

He caught glimpses of Emily's reflection in the glass as she occasionally passed the open kitchen door. She kept herself busy all this time. God bless her sweet heart.

When he remembered their earlier conversation, a sliver of uneasiness poked into his belly. Well, maybe it was more like his explosion about the gun. He glanced down at it lying on the arm of the sofa and chuckled softly. She'd told him she'd hidden it in the bedroom. In the night table. On *her* side.

Did she somehow already know the truth? Or was she simply saying her side because she'd been on that side of the bed?

Her heated looks gave him the impression she knew something was going on between them. If not at a conscious level, at least at a subconscious level.

'Is the coast clear?' Her hushed voice sifted across the living room.

He looked out the window, and gave the surroundings one final sweep. 'I think we can safely say they would have made their move by now. Wind's picked up again.'

Something soft bounced off the side of his neck and tumbled onto the floor. A pillow? He looked up to find her standing in the bedroom doorway, a touch of humor tipping up the sides of her lips. 'You looked bored. Thought I'd snap you out of it. Care for some coffee in about half an hour?'

He nodded, but the instant her back was turned he grabbed the pillow and heaved it. It caught her square between the shoulder blades and a squeal of surprise erupted from her. In a flash she leaned over and swooped up the pillow and turned around. Only to get nailed in the chest by the living room pillow he'd grabbed off the couch.

Her mouth dropped open in surprise. 'No fair.'

'Everything's fair in love and war.'

She muttered something beneath her

breath. Something he couldn't make out. Then she grabbed the other pillow at her feet. Both pillows were now clutched in her hands and held high over her head. She was moving. Fast. Toward him. He sucked in an excited breath and clambered behind the living room couch, using it for protection.

'No use hiding.' She chuckled. 'You will pay. Big time.'

She heaved one pillow at him. He ducked and it sailed harmlessly over his shoulder, but the other one smacked him right in the forehead.

'Ow!' he screamed and dropped to the floor behind the couch. Within an instant she had hopped over the sofa and was bending over him. He kept his eyes closed, his fingers curled tightly around one of the pillows.

'Oh my gosh, Chance. I'm so sorry. I didn't mean to hurt you,' she said.

He almost felt guilty for acting hurt. With a triumphant shout he brought the pillow up. She was faster. She blocked the shot and the pillow dropped from his grasp as she swung her body over his thighs and straddled him, pinning his wrists to the floor.

'Got you!' She laughed.

'No fair,' he muttered as her warmth seeped straight into his lower body.

'All is fair in love and war. You said it

yourself.' She threw him a suspiciously sweet smile and in a split second she released his wrists. Her arm came up with the pillow attached. His hand streaked out and captured her wrist.

'Caught you!' Chance laughed.

Their gazes locked. The victorious smile she'd toted died on her lips and turned somewhat uncertain. He knew what she was thinking. He'd captured her wrist the same way earlier when he'd lain in bed and she'd touched his scars. This time he didn't want to make the mistake of sending her away.

'If you wanted to be on top, all you had to do was ask,' he said quietly as he pulled on her wrist urging her downward, until her upper body lay on top of him. He could feel the hard peaks of her aroused nipples poke through her tight T-shirt against his chest. He watched in awe as her sweet pink lips swelled with passion.

'What are you doing?' she asked.

'I don't have a headache.' *Not anymore.*

Her breath fanned like feathers across his mouth and he knew she wanted him to kiss her. And he wanted to kiss her. Just one taste of those sweet lips. Who would it hurt?

★ ★ ★

Flames flared through Emily's entire body as she peered into Chance's seductive blue eyes. He said he didn't have a headache. His clue to allow her to take this wherever she wanted it to go?

She wanted it to go all right. All the way. She wanted a kiss. A taste of his hot, hungry lips. She lowered her head and when her lips brushed against his mouth, he moaned erotically. The sound sent a jolt of fire shooting through her insides. Then he was pressing hard against her, encouraging her to take the kiss deeper.

His tongue slipped past her lips and she reeled with joy as he took control. He tasted her, probed, explored and finally possessed her mouth.

Just then a loud beeping sound sifted through the air and Chance ripped his mouth from her trembling lips and buried his face into the column of her neck. 'What is that sound?'

She wanted to tell him it was her heart cracking against her chest and her pulse hammering against her throat where his face nestled. 'The cake.'

He heaved a shuddering sigh. 'You better get it.'

'You sure?'

She felt him nod against her neck and

254

regret flooded her. Of course. He was right. They couldn't do this. It wasn't proper behavior. Reluctantly she disentangled herself from him and on shaky legs headed into the kitchen to get the cake.

It took her more than half an hour to calm down and to work up the nerve to confront Chance. With a tray filled with coffee and generous slices of lemon cake she headed into the living room where she found him peering out the rain-spattered window.

'We need to talk,' she said as she settled the tray onto the table.

His gaze brightened when he saw the cake. 'You talk. I'll eat.'

She ignored the wickedly amusing grin he threw her way as he came around from behind the couch, sat down and reached for a slice of lemon cake.

'About us.'

His smile froze and his empty hand flew back to his side.

'Forgive me for being so bold. It is unlike me, but ever since you came into my life, I've sensed something between us.'

'It's called lust,' he said evenly.

'If it was lust, you would have made love to me by now.'

He didn't say anything.

'It's more than that. I can see it in your

eyes. The way you look at me with tenderness. Sometimes I can even see love, although you manage to hide it when you think I'm looking. I feel it in the way you touch me like when I burned my wrist with the teakettle. What's keeping us apart, Chance? Why are you pulling away from me? What are you afraid of?'

'Guys aren't afraid of anything,' he said calmly.

Yet when she sat down on the couch beside him, he shifted uneasily. His body heat screamed through her clothing and nestled erotically against her skin.

'I'm not the only one who feels this . . . connection, am I?'

'There's no connection, Emily. There can't ever be.'

Now she was getting somewhere. 'You can deny it all you want, Chance Donovan. We've got something special between us.'

He shook his head.

'Why are you fighting it? Fighting us?'

'Fine talk for a woman who's engaged.' His cold words made her wince.

'Is that it? Is that what's stopping you?'

'I'd say that sure is enough. It should be stopping you.'

There wasn't any accusation in his eyes, only fire and fear.

Fear of what? Fear she'd learn the truth? That he cared for her? Maybe even loved her? Why would that frighten him? He turned away from her so she couldn't see his eyes.

'My engagement can be canceled.'

'It can't.'

'Even if I told you I think I love you?'

He threw her a pleading look to stop, but she couldn't. She had crossed the line and wouldn't go back. 'I don't know why and I don't know how, because we've just met, but . . . I know this sounds silly, but we've got a magical connection.'

He ran a shaky hand through his hair yet remained silent.

'Let me in, Chance. I want to know you. Your past, your thoughts, all of you.'

'I can't,' he said tightly.

'Why not?'

'I don't want to hurt you,' he snapped angrily.

'Why would you hurt me?'

'Because . . . There are things you don't know about me. Things I don't want you to know.'

'So, you do feel this connection between us? This déjà vu.'

'I feel it.'

Emily exhaled in relief. 'I'm not going crazy after all.'

'It won't go any further than it already has. Go and get married and have your kids because there's a good chance I can't give you any.'

She inhaled sharply at Chance's words.

'What does that mean?'

'Exactly what I said. The anti-rejection drugs that are keeping me alive could be making me sterile,' he said flatly. 'It's time you put our . . . connection behind you and get on with your life because when the storm breaks, I'm taking the first chance outta here.'

Stunned at his outburst, she barely heard his footsteps as he headed for the door.

★   ★   ★

Chance was shivering and breathing heavily as he stepped into the cold lamp room of the lighthouse tower. Rain shot against the glass windows like bullets and he could barely hear the renewed thunder as it cracked overhead because his heartbeat was busily smashing in his ears.

When he'd told her he might be sterile, the look of hurt slashing across Emily's suddenly pale face had almost killed him. Sweet Jesus. He'd never intended to tell her the truth about him. Now at least she'd be able to put him behind her.

A soft sound from behind him captured his attention. He turned around just in time to catch a sharp slap smack across his left cheek.

'You sorry son of a bitch!' She stood in front of him, her chest heaving angrily, her lips clenched tightly together. She was mad. Fire spitting mad. He didn't remember ever seeing her so ticked off before. 'How shallow do you think I am?'

Her eyes were filled with unshed tears, but she valiantly fought them back. She always had been an emotional woman and he knew she was gathering all her courage to keep from crying.

'First of all, you've got no right to presume I want kids more than I want love. Second of all, you've got one hell of a lot of nerve saying what there is between us is only lust . . . and third of all whatever is in your past is in your past. It's history. If you don't want to tell me, it's fine. Just so you know there are other ways to have children. Adoption. Artificial insemination. You don't have to throw my love for children into my face just to get rid of me. I may be slow to pick up hints, but I'm not stupid. Fourth, we don't even know each other well enough to even consider having children.'

The tears spilled freely from her red-rimmed eyes and instinctively Chance reached out to comfort her. She slapped his hands away.

'Don't touch me!' she spat. 'Don't ever touch me out of pity.'

With that said she whirled around, slipped back into the stairwell and was swallowed up by the darkness, her footsteps echoing hollowly on the lighthouse stairwell.

She had it all wrong. She thought he didn't want her . . . but wasn't that what he wanted her to think?

He stared at his reflection in the gray rain-streaked window. A stranger's face. Shocking blue eyes he still hadn't gotten used to. Emily had. She'd looked right at his scars and hadn't even flinched. She'd peeled away his physical layers that made up his outside and she'd tried to look inside. What would she do if she knew about his emotional scars?

When he awoke from his nightmare, he'd seen the fear in her eyes. He knew he'd been screaming. Could she deal with being woken out of a sound sleep night after night?

How would she react if she found out her husband was still alive? He still had those drug charges they'd framed him with hanging over his head. If the authorities ever got wind he was alive, they'd throw him back into jail so fast it would make his head spin. How could he protect her then?

He needed to find that laptop and see what was on the disk. It was his only clue. If there wasn't anything worthwhile on it . . . then it was better to keep Emily believing he didn't want her.

★ ★ ★

When Chance came down from the lighthouse tower, he heard Emily moving around in the kitchen. Quietly he slipped into her room and began to search. After a long few minutes he'd come up with nothing. Dammit! Maybe it wasn't even here. Maybe she'd put it somewhere else while he'd been sleeping. Hands on hips, he scanned the room and honed in on the wedding portrait hanging on the wall. They'd talked about putting in a safe. Maybe . . .

In a few quick steps he was there. Heart hammering in his ears he yanked the portrait off the wall and grinned. A safe. With a computerized security code. It appeared it was his turn to try and figure out a password. A taste of his own medicine no less. It sure was a bitter pill to swallow. Payback certainly was a bitch.

He reached out to enter a password onto the lit keypad when the hall lights flickered and then went out. Power outage. He held his breath as he listened to the roar of the wind pounding the windowpanes. Uneasiness sparked his insides. Why didn't he hear Emily moving about in the other room?

He swore impatiently and waited until his eyes grew accustomed to the darkness. Then he flew into the kitchen. She was nowhere in sight.

'Emily!' Even before his echo returned to him he knew she wasn't in the house.

Could she have hiked back up the lighthouse tower to look for him? No, she was too ticked off at him. She must have gone outside. What the hell for? Unless . . . someone had taken her.

Panic made him yank open the kitchen door. Spears of howling wind and icy rain smacked painfully into his face as he stumbled across the slippery deck to the top of the stairs that descended along the rocky cliffs. When he couldn't see through the sheets of silvery rain, a horrible shudder coursed through him.

Damn! He couldn't go look for her. Not without the gun. Or a light. If he slipped and fell and broke his neck, he'd be useless to help Emily.

In a flash he retrieved the gun where he'd left it sitting on the sofa's armchair and then his mind raced frantically for any clue as to where he could find a flashlight or lantern. Suddenly an idea sprang to mind. God, he hoped it worked!

Stumbling back into the wild wind and using his hands to follow the deck railing, he blindly groped through the darkness. Hopefully he was going in the right direction. If not, then he'd most likely end up falling off the cliffs into the roaring surf, his drowned body carried out to sea.

A minute later the guardrail stopped and a storage shed loomed in front of him. Ripping open the wooden door, he stepped inside the musty room and ran his fingers along the splintery cedar. Years ago he'd placed a flashlight up here for emergencies and he hoped it was still here and that it worked.

His fingers wrapped around the cold handle of metal. He'd found it. It worked! He shone it around the murky shed to the generator in the far corner. A second later he yanked on the starter rope, praying it would work. To his surprise the old relic wheezed and puffed to life. A long second later obscene gas fumes permeated the air and the outside lights splashed through the silvery rain illuminating virtually everything in sight. Now all he had to do was find Emily!

Leaves and sand peppered his face as he followed the now dangerously slippery winding stairs. He shouted her name into the roaring wind, hoping for an answer. She could be anywhere. She could even have . . .

Chance clamped his jaws tightly. No, he wouldn't think about that. Emily was fine. She had to be.

When he stepped off the bottom stair, onto the slippery wharf, he immediately spotted Emily, her bright yellow raincoat a beacon of light. She sat on the picnic table, her back was hunched over, her hands cradling her face.

Anguish ripped at his guts. He'd been so mean to her earlier. God, he was a rotten s.o.b. To make her think he didn't care when he loved her so much it hurt.

'Emily?'

She turned at his voice, but her hands still covered her face.

'Chance!' she shouted into the fierce wind. 'I've got something in my eyes!'

He sighed with relief. 'Thank God!'

'That's rude!' she squealed. Hurt and disbelief quite evident in her voice.

'I thought — Never mind what I thought, give me your hands.'

He grabbed her outstretched hands, knitted them with his and pulled her off the table and against his chest, hugging her tightly. Her teeth were chattering a mile a minute and his fingers reached out to stroke her icy cheek. 'You're freezing!'

She didn't answer, but he felt her nod as she pressed her face into his chest.

Her eyes! She'd said she'd gotten something in her eyes. With all this debris flying around it could be anything. Too dangerous to check it out here.

'Hold onto me, tight!' he yelled.

Using his body as a shield against the wind, he guided her though the sheets of rain, and up the slippery steps. After what seemed like hours he spied the door to the lighthouse.

Yanking the door open, he pushed her inside and quickly followed.

He froze when he turned to face her. 'Sweet Jesus! Your skin is as red as a lobster!'

'At this moment I wish I were one dangling over a pot of boiling water.' Her eyes remained closed and her face scrunched up in pain. 'I'm so cold and my eyes are stinging.'

He jumped into action. Quickly he pried open one eyelid and gazed into her bloodshot eye and then he quickly looked into the other. He sighed with relief, 'Sand.'

'That's all?'

'That's all,' he reassured her, then anger boiled in his belly. 'What the hell were you doing out there?'

'I heard the shutter to the beach shed banging away and I didn't want it to rip loose. So I went down to close it and then the lights went out and the wind blew the sand into my eyes and I couldn't see . . . ' Her voice lowered to a sweet whisper. 'I knew you'd come.'

'This way,' he commanded gruffly, irritated that he hadn't been able to fool her one bit about his true feelings. On trembling legs, he led her to the sink where he turned on the faucet.

'Déjà vu.' She chuckled and Chance remembered the night he'd held her burned arm under this same faucet. How many nights ago had that been? Only a few. It seemed as if he'd lived here forever. As if he hadn't been gone for eight years.

Gently he guided her trembling cold hands under the water faucet and quickly washed them. 'Okay, I want you to bend forward, cup your hands under the water, open your eyes as much as you can and splash the water against your face.'

Silently she did as he asked and in a minute she opened her eyes and her stomach tightened at the intensity of raw fear flooding his face. Alarm rippled up her spine. 'What's wrong?'

'I thought . . . ' His voice cracked, clogged up with emotion.

'What? What did you think?' She already sensed what he'd been thinking. She hadn't told him she was going outside. He couldn't find her and . . . 'You thought something bad happened to me, didn't you?'

He nodded unable to speak.

She knew she shouldn't take advantage of his emotions in this way but . . . 'I thought you didn't care?'

He looked straight into her eyes and said, 'I love you.'

Emily blinked as those three beautiful words flittered like excited butterflies straight into her heart. 'You what?'

'You heard me.' His lips curled upward into a heart-cracking grin.

'Say it again.'

He moved closer. His hand reached up and curled his finger around a stray tendril of hair. 'I love you, Emily Montgomery McCullen. I've loved you from the minute I laid eyes on you.'

Those words, hauntingly familiar, made the eerie déjà vu warnings scream inside her brain. His pulsing nearness was more powerful and pushed aside those whispered warnings, forcing them into the deep recesses of her mind.

His erotic male scent, ocean fresh with a tinge of sea salt and pine, invaded her nostrils and her body reacted violently. Sensations of passion she'd forgotten she'd even had sizzled to life and unleashed into her abdomen. A wild heat made her insides melt with want for him, made her skin burn for the caress of his fingers against her body, made her need all of him.

Under her. Around her. On her. Inside her.

His eyes darkened to a new level of seductive awareness and instinctively she knew he sensed her desires. His fingers uncurled from her hair and moved downward, meeting his other hand as they settled on the lapels of her wet raincoat, which hung open.

'We'll have to get you out of all those wet clothes.' His whispered promise made her insides sparkle magnificently. Slowly, erotically, he moved the garment over her shoulders. He let it fall into a dripping heap on the kitchen floor. Suddenly the familiar flash of uncertainty claimed his eyes and she moaned inwardly. 'I haven't been with a woman in years. I'm afraid I might hurt you.'

She hadn't expected him to say something like that and was surprised and pleased at his tender concern for her. 'In that case, I might hurt you too. I haven't been with a man since Steve.'

Both surprise and relief claimed the

uncertainty in his blue eyes and gave her the encouragement to reach out. Gently she traced her fingertips over the white gauze she'd taped atop the gash on his forehead, ran her fingers feather light across his right temple, the gentle raise of his cheekbone, the shape of his slightly bristled jaw.

He inhaled sharply as her index finger wandered into the deep cleft of his chin. The pulse throbbed there in his neck.

'Emily . . . ' he warned softly.

'You like that do you?'

'Like isn't quite the word I had in mind.' His large hands cupped the sides of her hips and he pulled her against him, crushing her hands to his muscular chest.

She relished the powerful pressure of his body as he sank against her entire length. His magical eyes, mere inches from her own encouraged another round of intense heat to uncurl into her very core and she knew she was lost in this exotic dance of foreplay.

A flash of lightning brightened the kitchen and thunder cracked violently overhead, rattling the dishes in the cupboards and the floor beneath their feet.

'You seem to be getting used to loud noises,' she said softly.

'You seem to have a calming effect on me.'

'I don't think that's quite the word I had in

mind for it,' she teased as she pressed her abdomen against his exquisitely hard bulge. She cherished the sexy groan that escaped his lips and in a flash his mouth lowered to claim hers.

The eager pressure of his lips seared a path straight into her soul. Emily's mouth opened and she tasted his erotic power as his tongue explored, probed and stroked. His luscious lips drank greedily from her and her body swelled with fiery passion. Senses and needs shoved away all doubts, thoughts of caution and logic.

She arched her back and pressed into his hardness, her fingers trembled with a mind of their own as they quickly worked at unbuttoning the buttons on his shirt and then slid it over his shoulders until it got caught between them.

He abruptly broke the magical kiss and impatiently shrugged off his shirt. Then he began to unbutton her blouse, his fingers trembling with disuse at such an intimate task. Impatience urged her to help him and in a moment her blouse and bra joined his clothing on the floor.

She inhaled sharply as sweet heat shot into every nerve ending of her breasts as his fingers trailed a scorching blaze along the outside curves down to cup the undersides of her breasts. His large thumbs arced up to provocatively caress her sensitive nipples, which instantly hardened into sweetly painful rosebuds.

She knew this ecstasy. Had experienced it under Steve's confident hands. And she'd also known instinctively Chance was the man who could push aside Steve's ghost.

And then Chance's lips caressed hers again, his touches evoked a raging heat in her breasts and sent low soft moans up her throat into his moist mouth.

Her eager fingers found his chest. They smoothed themselves over taut muscles and explored the thick slabs of raised welts and puckered scars that crisscrossed his chest. His hot hands lowered from her burning breasts and slipped beneath the waistband of her track pants. Slowly, he peeled the pants and underwear down over her hips, down her legs and she quickly stepped out of them. All this without breaking their kiss.

Excitement rippled through her as his fingers intertwined with hers and he reluctantly broke off the kiss. His eyes were heated, full of desire and so full of sweet love she shivered from its fierce intensity. How could he love her so much? How could this have happened so quickly between them?

Questions for later. She pushed them back

271

from where they'd come. Back to where caution, common sense and the rest of her sanity lay.

'The bed,' he managed to say. 'Before my legs give out.'

Only a flicker of light from the open door followed them as he led her into the bedroom. It was enough for her to watch him slide his jeans and underwear down his long legs. Her heart cracked against her ribs and her eyes widened at the sheer size of him.

Just like Steve.

The teasing whisper slipped up from that dark cavern where she'd chased all her sane thoughts. She leaned back against the pillows and watched in stunned disbelief as he climbed upon the foot of the bed, his full arousal seeming to blossom even larger.

Heat from his body sliced against her skin as he hovered over her. His eyes darkened with passion until they were a fascinating deep midnight blue.

'I've waited so long,' he whispered.

She didn't have long to ponder what he meant as he positioned his knees outside her already spread legs, his hands came down beside her breasts. Careful not to let his seductive body touch her, he allowed his intense body heat to tease and torture her skin. He lowered his head and began a sultry trail of feather light kisses along her neck, across her collarbone, over her chest and to the sensitive valley between her breasts.

She arched toward him as his heated lips claimed one nipple, releasing a torrent of wild pleasure as he used his teeth to skillfully nip, nudge and suck her right nipple until it was once again a shivering mass of raw ecstasy.

When he started the pleasure-inducing strategy on her left breast, a tiny sensual sob broke from her throat. Showing her no mercy, his mouth left her passion-swelled nipple. She gasped when his muscular legs seared against her thighs, which automatically opened wider giving him full access.

A sensual smile played on his lips as he watched her with his now almost black eyes. 'Did I tell you how beautiful you are?'

'Save it for later,' she said breathlessly. She reached out and using her female powers grabbed his shoulders.

His breath quickened as her fingernails dug into his hard muscles.

'Bit of a hurry?' he teased, but she could tell by the way his jaw muscles twitched ecstatically, he held himself in check only so he could please her to the fullest.

'I've waited long enough,' she groaned.

It was all the encouragement he needed. In one insane, fiery rush, he entered her. At first the fit was so snug she thought she might not be able to accept him. Suddenly she remembered it had been this same way with Steve their first time.

'I love you,' he whispered soothingly in her ear as he slowly moved deeper, taking care not to hurt her. 'Just relax.'

She nodded and her body responded to his soothing voice. Soon his strong powerful arousal throbbed inside her, filling her with an unbelievable raging heat.

He allowed the rest of his body to claim her as he lowered his solid chest against hers. Her already aroused nipples reacted with over-powering erotic pleasure as they touched his chest scars. Slowly he began to move inside her, skillfully drawing himself almost all the way out.

Then her body convulsed as he pounded a fierce stroke, burying himself to the hilt. Her hips began to grind as she freed herself to the waves of blinding pleasure, crying out as she became lost in a storm of savagely sweet explosions. Wave after wave of overpowering pleasure washed her away into a carnal riptide of climaxes that seemed endless.

Somewhere in the dizzying ecstasy she heard Chance's somewhat familiar erotic groans escaping from deep inside his chest as he held onto her and continued to plunge furiously. He began to shudder violently and she knew he joined her in this all-consuming glorious world of blazing love.

13

Happy and totally satiated Emily snuggled closer to Chance, relishing the body heat curling against her skin. Using his muscular arm as a pillow, she lay her hand upon his heart and felt the steady tapping against her fingertips indicating he had finally fallen asleep.

All day they'd taken turns, finding different ways to please each other. Finally the sizzling passion between them had been quenched and their bodies exhausted, but it was only a matter of time before he woke up and reached for her again. She really should be trying to fall asleep and recharge her batteries. Yet she couldn't close her eyes.

A strange fear hovered at the back of her mind. An eerie premonition that if she fell asleep, this beautiful night would be over and reality would come crashing in all around her once again.

So, she lay awake, her eyes wide open as she listened to his soft breathing as it intermingled with the sounds of raindrops peppering the windows of her bedroom and the powerful roar of the waves crashing against the cliffs.

Eventually she turned into a more comfortable position and found herself relaxing as she stared at the rear wall and the area where her wedding portrait should be hanging. For some reason it wasn't there. Only the steel face of the fireproof safe she'd had installed stared back at her. She knew she should be alarmed at the disappearance of the portrait, but strangely enough she was happy to find Steve's green eyes hadn't been looking down on her as she'd made love with another man.

Her eyelids drooped and she fell asleep with a smile on her face.

★   ★   ★

Chance sighed with frustration as he stared at the laptop he'd stolen from Emily's safe. The password into the safe had been the first number he'd tried. His birthday. Too easy. He'd have to warn her about using personal information for a password. Somebody might guess it too easily. With shaky fingers he slid the disk out of the computer's drive and examined it carefully. This small object was the only thing he could think of as to what had destroyed their lives.

So? Why was he hesitating? Why wasn't he

slipping the disk back into the drive? Why wasn't he inputting the password and seeing what the disk contained?

He knew why. It was because the minute he began reading the contents, his theory that it contained helpful information about who had kidnapped and locked him away might just be a theory. Nothing more.

It would mean Emily had been needlessly exposed to danger by his coming back here. A hell of a way to thank her for allowing him back into her life.

He'd made love to Emily all day and into the night. He should be happy. She said she loved him, even though she didn't know his true identity. He should be floating on cloud nine because she trusted him enough to give him her heart and body.

Instead he'd screwed up. He hadn't accomplished his plan, which was to simply get inside the lighthouse tower, check if his laptop was still in the wall, take it and clear out. Instead he'd taken a detour into the kitchen and everything had changed.

He tapped the disk on the table. He could be opening up a can of worms if this disk actually contained something. It could endanger Emily even further.

The memory of when he'd given the disk to Skip sliced through his thoughts. He'd walked into Helena's office and found Skip searching through her desk drawers . . .

'Glad I caught you, buddy,' Steve said as he dumped his resignation onto Helena's desk.

Skip's head snapped up and he cursed violently.

'You better ease up on that coffee, Skip,' Steve said as he observed the paleness seep into his best friend's otherwise tanned face.

Skip shook his head, slid the drawer he'd been sniffing through closed and came around to sit on the edge of the desk. He smiled shakily. 'Helena's not here. Gone to lunch. I was trying to find a pen. You know me always losing my pens.'

'You should get yourself a laptop. They're pretty neat. Can carry them around wherever you want. It's like a heavy notebook without pens.'

'Pens are cheaper.' Skip chuckled. 'So what kind of business you got with Helena? Trying to get another deadline extended? Hey! I've been working on her to team us together again so we can work on another war story overseas.'

'Sorry, Skip. You were my next stop.'

'By the tone of your voice I take it I'm not going to like what you're going to say.'

'I've quit.'

Skip's mouth dropped open in shock. 'But why? I thought you loved investigative work? Is it money? Cause if it's money, I can beg Helena to give you more. She'll understand with you being newly married. You're going to want wee ones in the future. I know how much Emily wants kids.'

'Nothing to do with money, Skip. I just don't want to be away from my wife anymore.'

'I guess that makes sense.'

'You'll feel the same way when the right woman comes along.'

'I think not!' Skip threw Steve a horrified look. 'I'm not a one woman man. Never have been. Never will be.'

'Never say never, buddy. I said the exact same thing not too long ago and look what happened to me.'

Skip's eyes widened at the realization of the truthfulness in his words. 'What kind of work are you going to do? Maybe Helena can get you a desk job? We can still hang out.'

'We've already moved our things into the little lighthouse Emily's uncle left her. I'm heading back there tonight. Going to surprise her. She is expecting to be alone tonight.'

'You've quit as of today?' Skip asked.

'Resignation's on the desk for Helena when she comes back. I hope she won't blow her stack.'

'She will. You're moving too fast.'

'I know, but we're going to get started on the family right away.'

'Hence your rush to get out of here today.' Skip laughed.

'Oh! I almost forgot.' Steve slid the computer disk out of his jacket pocket. 'Here. Got it anonymously. Thought you might want to take a look at it. Might be hot stuff.'

Skip accepted the disk without even glancing at it. 'Are you going to come back and visit?'

'You can count on it. You know you're welcome out to Shipwreck Island any time. Emily enjoys your jokes.'

'Just my jokes?'

'Your company . . . I think.'

'Ha! Ha!' Skip smirked. 'You know what? You've picked an exceptional woman in Emily. I'm proud of you.' Skip eased himself off the desk. 'Prouder even when Uncle Skip can bounce babies on his knees.'

'You'll be the first to know when we succeed.' Steve fought the intense emotion sweeping over him whenever he thought of his wife. 'Emily's a gem, Skip. So sweet and innocent. I don't want her involved in my work.'

'I can understand, bud. In this line of work you never know whose toes you're stepping on until it is too late.'

'No more close calls. I think it'll be a big relief for Emily. I'd better get going. I still have to clean out the desk.' Steve stretched his hand out to Skip and they shook.

'I'll come out soon and see how it's going,' Skip said.

'Sounds like a plan. We'll leave it at that. Go on get back to looking for your pens before Helena gets back. You know how huffy she gets when someone's in her office alone.'

Skip smiled and threw Steve one more wave as he left Helena's office. It was the last time he saw Skip . . . until the fair.

That evening, Steve stepped onto Sweet Lies and was swarmed by the Coast Guard and other authorities. Life had never been the same.

Chance slid the computer disk into the laptop. Someone had to pay for ruining his and Emily's chance at a normal life together. With that thought squarely in his mind, he flipped on the computer and tapped in the password.

★   ★   ★

Emily awoke to coolness where Chance had lain beside her. He must be hungry again.

282

Probably making something to eat. Gathering strength so he could pick up where they'd left off.

She smiled and hugged herself tightly. She really didn't understand why this wonderful attraction existed between them. Or why she cared so deeply about him. Sexy Chance Donovan had finally admitted he cared about her too, even said he loved her. He'd certainly proved it. By making love to her so exquisitely, she knew in her heart it was true.

It had all happened so unbelievably fast. In a matter of days. It seemed too good to be true. She pushed the warm blankets aside and reached out for her robe hanging on the bedpost. Wrapping herself in its snugness, Emily bent down to pick up his wet jeans and blinked in surprise when a gold glittery item fell onto the carpet. His St. Christopher's medallion sparkled up at her. Scooping it up into her hand, she was about to place it into the pocket when she felt the tiny inscription tingle against her fingertips. Turning it over, her heart skidded to a halt.

★ ★ ★

Like a zombie, Emily padded barefoot into the empty living room and headed for the kitchen. She halted in the doorway when she spotted Chance. Cool grey early morning light seeped into the room, giving it a surreal quality. She could scarcely breathe as she watched him. His broad naked back to her, he sat at the intimate kitchen table for two.

He was quiet. Too quiet. Tenseness bunched up his shoulder muscles. There was that slight tilt to his head. She noted those golden highlights sprinkled with a dash of white in his sandy hair.

Spooky déjà vu feelings grabbed a hold of her again and she didn't like it. She didn't like it one bit. Heart hammering insanely in her ears she eased in behind him and peeked over his shoulder. Instantly she spotted Steve's laptop computer lying wide open. The screen was lit up and full of data. Obviously Chance had cracked the password.

'What's going on?' At the sound of her voice he whirled around. His face twisted in fear and anger.

Her stomach clenched as she noticed the color drain away from his face when he spied the gold medallion in her outstretched hand. He looked as if he might collapse right there in front of her. Quickly he stood and blocked her view of the contents flashing on the computer screen.

'Go back to bed, Emily,' he commanded harshly.

She quickly reined in her blossoming anger. He was more than scared, he was terrified. She could tell by the way he gripped the back of the chair, his knuckles white, his entire body trembling.

'Why do you have my husband's medallion?'

'I found it. In the shed.'

'You're lying.'

His eyes widened.

'I read the initials scratched in over top. C.D. for Chance Donovan. And TX? I'm assuming it means Texas since you mentioned during the Timber Sports Competition you were from Texas. Who are you?'

'Please, just go back to bed.'

For a heart-stopping moment she wanted to do exactly what he said. The terror sparking his eyes, the tightness in the way he clamped his jaws frightened her. Something in his face told her she was better off not knowing what Chance had found in Steve's computer files. Whatever it was, it had gotten him killed and now her life was in jeopardy and so was Chance's. 'Chance Donovan! Move aside!'

'I'm warning you, Emily. You don't want to see what's on the screen.'

'Like hell I don't!' She made a move toward the table, but he blocked her by raising his hands. She flinched in pain as he grabbed her shoulders. 'Get out of my way, Donovan.'

'Get a grip, Emily,' he said angrily.

'You get a grip! Don't you understand? I need to avenge my husband!'

'I don't want your help!'

She gasped as if she'd just been slapped. Horrific icy fingers tapped a violent warning along her spine and her knees threatened to buckle.

I have to avenge my husband, she'd said.

I don't want your help.

Once again déjà vu spilled over her as she remembered the slight tilt to Chance's head. She'd seen the endearing gesture a few times over the past few days.

What about the fair? The way he'd held her while they'd danced to her wedding song. How he seemed to know where to steer the boat. As if he knew where they were going. Other little things. How he liked his coffee. The way he looked at her with love in his eyes. The sizzling attraction between them from almost the minute they'd met. Yet he didn't look like Steve ... but there was always plastic surgery.

Oh God! She couldn't think about that angle. It would be too good to be true. Something else must be going on here.

Something sinister. 'Why did you break into my husband's laptop?'

'I was curious.'

'Who are you?'

'Leave it alone, Emily.'

'What's the password?'

He stiffened violently at the question and loosened his tight grip on her arms.

'I'm the only person close to Steve who could possibly crack the password. Here you walk into my life, a complete stranger and just like that — ' She snapped her fingers. 'You're in my husband's computer. Where's my husband? Is he the one who told you the password? Or . . . '

She watched him closely. There was something different about him. There was something in his eyes now that hadn't been there earlier when he'd made love to her.

He looked as if his innocence had been ripped away from him, as if . . . someone he loved had betrayed him. She sensed it had something to do with whatever was on the laptop.

The only person the information on the laptop would be important to would be . . .

'Steve . . . ' she whispered, feeling the strangeness of his name in her ears.

He let go of her arms and staggered backward as if he'd been shot.

Why wasn't he denying he wasn't Steve? Why did she suddenly believe with her whole heart the man standing in front of her, this virtual stranger who called himself Chance Donovan was her dead husband?

Questions exploded in her head. How could it be possible? He didn't even look like Steve. Except the night she'd found him in her bedroom looking for the can of Mace. He'd stood beside the wedding portrait. Their smiles had been so similar. What about the intense déjà vu warnings she had tried to ignore? And their connection . . .

The man so near and dear to her heart looked so different. Yet eerily familiar too. A stranger's face. A stranger's eyes. Yet she recognized the love in those eyes. 'How is it possible?'

'Emmie, please.' His rough voice had a desperate tone to it.

'Where have you been?' She reached up and he inhaled sharply when with horribly trembling fingers, she touched his lips and the deep cleft in his chin. A cleft that hadn't been there years earlier.

'You always said you loved men with clefts in their chin,' he said numbly.

She dropped her hand as if it were burned and clutched it to her heart.

She watched in shock as he eased his

unsteady fingers to his hairline by his temple and pushed back his hair. He traced a long finger along the faint scar she'd never noticed. Traced it until it disappeared behind his ear.

'Miracles of reconstructive surgery.' He shrugged.

At that split second Emily thought she'd somehow gone insane or maybe this was a nightmare.

She closed her eyes as a wave of lightheadedness whirled around her. She barely felt Steve's firm embrace curl around her waist as he led her to a kitchen chair. She practically fell into it.

He crouched in front of her and took her hands into his. 'Breathe. Deep.' She took a deep breath. The room continued to swirl wildly.

'That's it. Hold it. One. Two. Three. Four. Just like having a baby. Let it go.'

She exhaled and caught his grin, but only felt nausea uncoil into her stomach. 'I think I'm going to be sick.'

'You'll be fine. Inhale. That's it. Hold it in . . . Let it go.'

She followed his soothing voice for what seemed an eternity and finally the sickness clawing at her belly resided, only to be replaced by an intense uneasiness.

'Better?'

She nodded. Bravely she held back the dam of sharp tears threatening to unravel her.

'I guess I can't drop big news without expecting some sort of a fallout,' Steve said.

Worry lurked in his blue eyes. Blue eyes not green.

'This is unbelievable. A bad joke. A nightmare.'

Steve smiled and squeezed her hands in reassurance. 'The nightmare is over, Emily. I'm home.'

Heart pounding wildly against her chest, she found herself asking questions she wasn't prepared to hear. 'What happened to you? Where have you been?'

'I think maybe you need some time to digest everything.'

Indecision lurked in his eyes and she suddenly got the feeling if he didn't start answering her questions right now, he'd disappear. He made a move to stand but she gripped his hands refusing to let him go. 'Tell me everything. Tell me now.'

'Emily, there's things you shouldn't know.'

'I want to know the truth. All of it.'

'Do you?'

'Yes,' she lied. Maybe later. No. Now. Before he leaves. Or before she woke up from this dream.

'I don't know if you're going to want to hear it.'

'I need to know. So, I can somehow hold onto my sanity.' Her heart clenched as she recognized the intense pain, the haunted sadness in his eyes. 'Unless you'd rather not tell me. If it's too painful . . . '

His mouth was unsmiling now. Serious. Deadly serious. He looked down into her eyes a long time before he finally spoke, 'What do you want to know?'

'What happened to you? Your face. Your voice. All those scars. Your eyes . . . Where have you been?' Her voice trailed off as she looked into those stranger's eyes. Pain. Hurt. Anger. Other emotions she couldn't put a name to swirled like a brewing storm.

'Death Row,' he whispered it so low she wasn't sure she'd heard right.

'Death Row?' The two words resounded crazily in her head and she tried to clamp down on the fear clutching her heart.

He nodded and pulled his hands from her grasp. Taking the medallion, he hoisted himself into the other kitchen chair beside her. With trembling fingers he lay the medallion out in front of him on the table as if it were a piece of precious jewelry. Then he leaned his elbows on the table and ran his trembling hands over his face, shaking his head. A moment later he dropped his hands onto the table and clasped them tightly as if in prayer. Finally he spoke.

'I was on my way home to you.' His voice cracked and he cleared his throat. 'I'd just stepped onto *Sweet Lies* when the authorities swarmed the boat. They found drugs. They were planted.'

'I never doubted you. Not for a minute.'

He nodded grimly. 'They used the drug charges as a lever against me. A prosecutor presented me with a deal. He'd drop the drug charges if I told him what he wanted to know.'

'What did you know?'

'Nothing,' he spat harshly. 'I told him I didn't know anything and that deals should be made with my lawyer present. He left . . . after threatening you.'

'Me?'

'I would have told them anything Emily if I had known what they wanted. I would have done anything to protect you.' His voice turned cold, hard. 'He came back after awhile with some guards. They got carried away beating me up.' He winced. 'I ended up in a coma. They told me I was in it for six months. When I woke up, I had a new kidney, new eyes and a new identity.'

He emitted a strangled sort of laugh and

she reached out to curl an arm around his trembling shoulder.

'I thought I'd gone mad. I tried to tell people I wasn't Chance Donovan. They quickly transferred me to a prison infirmary. When I got better, to solitary. I think for awhile I went mad. I wouldn't answer any of their questions. They kept asking me where is it? Where is it? Where is what?'

His words were chilling and she wanted to ask him to stop, but she sensed he needed to spill all the hurt so he could begin to heal. He picked up the St. Christopher's medallion and rubbed it gently between his thumb and forefinger. A tiny smile lit up his lips.

'Finally they gave me back the medallion and I began to have hope. I was who I said I was. I started to look for a way out.'

She pressed a hand to her heart trying to calm the intense pounding as she tried to absorb what Steve was telling her. She couldn't make sense of it. Couldn't concentrate. Couldn't grab a hold of it. He was alive. He'd been held against his will in a prison! It didn't make sense. How could this happen?

'After a couple of years they started letting me out into the exercise yard. I managed to get a few convicts to believe me. It seemed everyone who tried to help me ended up dead.'

She shook her head in denial. Could he be crazy? Could she be crazy? 'Dead?'

Steve nodded. 'I couldn't believe it myself. Slowly I began to realize I'd been thrown into something real big. Whatever it was, it went deep. The private prison I'd been locked in had many eyes on me and it was obvious they weren't going to let me go.'

'You got out.'

'With the help of Michael . . . '

'The man in the grave you visited the other day.'

Steve nodded.

'It took me another couple of years to gain his trust. I had to be careful. God! It was like something out of a conspiracy movie. I was a nervous wreck. Didn't know who I could trust. Didn't know if I wanted another death on my head. Finally I managed to get to Michael. He was the top man. If you wanted something done like having another inmate killed, he was the man to arrange it. For a price. Said he'd take on my problem if I agreed to bury him over on Prince Edward Island. Wanted bachelor buttons and lupins on his grave. Wanted to know if I could arrange it when I got out.' He emitted a strangled laugh. 'When I got out? Can you believe it? The man sure had confidence in himself in getting me out.'

She shivered and pulled her robe tighter around her neck.

'I told him my problem. He said he'd heard about me. Rumors mostly. He didn't take the rumors seriously because he didn't believe in rumors. Only cold, hard facts. He eventually believed me.' Steve smiled. 'He believed I was Steve McCullen, investigate journalist. Not Chance Donovan, convicted inmate. I warned him not to tell anyone we were talking or he'd end up dead. He said he'd heard those rumors too. Since he didn't believe in rumors — '

'He decided to help you.'

'Big time. He smuggled out a note through the channels telling my whereabouts, but the note must have got lost somewhere. No one came to help.' Steve lifted the St. Christopher's medal from the table and turned it over. 'I scratched my convict initials and TX meaning Texas into the back of the medallion. I knew it was a long shot that anyone would even figure out what it meant. Michael managed to smuggle it out. We waited for weeks. No one came. By then my kidney was slowly starting to reject. Surprisingly the eyes didn't do too badly. They put me back into solitary again.'

'Oh, Steve.'

He cracked a grin. 'I wasn't a model prisoner.'

Then his face fell into a severe frown. 'Michael suspected I didn't have much time. I think he somehow fixed it so we were in the same exercise yard again. He picked a fight with an inmate who was three times his size. I think he wanted me to rush the wall and I was about to, then I saw him get killed and then I got shot.'

Emily touched the bullet hole above his heart. 'That's how you got this scar. I wondered. You were so touchy about your scars. I didn't have the heart to ask.'

He inhaled a shuddering breath and she noted something flicker in his eyes. Something that resembled fear. Why was he suddenly so terribly afraid?

'The prison officials transferred me to a private hospital . . . in another state. The hospital was under investigation at the time. It was in . . . Florida.'

Emily finally understood his fear.

'I was there,' she whispered and slowly drew away from him.

'Jo had called me. Told me they suspected the doctor who ran that hospital had something to do with your disappearance. I was there when it came out the hospital was being used to front an underground organ transplant business. They were harvesting organs from prisoners and other kidnapped people from across the country.' Betrayal swamped Emily as she became painfully aware of the timing. Red-hot anger began to build inside her. 'It happened a year ago, Steve. Obviously you were found and everyone neglected to tell me.'

'Why should I have contacted you?'

His cold question sent her mind reeling.

'So you could see what they had done to my face? To my mind? So you could feel sorry for me?' He shook his head. 'Thanks, but no thanks. Over the past year I've been in the hospitals more times than out. The kidney they forced into me rejected. Daniel was a perfect match and so he donated one of his to me. My face needed numerous surgeries and my temper . . . I was so angry, Emily. I was sick of life — '

'In sickness and in health, Steve. Those words were in our wedding vows. I guess you didn't take them as seriously as I did.'

'Till death do us part, Emily. You thought I was dead. I didn't want to interfere — '

'Didn't want to interfere? What do you think you're doing now?'

'I want you safe. I want you safe and happy.'

'Happy? Do I look happy?' she snapped angrily. 'Didn't you think I'd be happy to know my husband was alive? All these years I'd lie awake in my bed thinking about you. I used to dream about the things we'd planned for.'

'I told you there might not be any children.'

'I know. I remember, Steve. One of the side effects could be sterility. I told you there are other ways to have children.' He turned his face away from her and she felt a spear of anger shoot directly into her heart. 'That's why you didn't tell me you were alive?'

'That's one of the reasons.'

'Why did you come back to me now? Is it because I'm marrying Skip?'

'Yes. I wanted to protect you from him. He might be behind what happened to me.'

'Why are you pretending to be someone else? Were you ever planning on telling me who you really are?'

Steve shook his head.

'No?' The shock of his answer screamed along her nerves. An empty coldness grabbed a hold of her. 'Obviously I don't mean a thing to you.'

'Oh God, Emily. How can you say that? All I want to do is wake up every morning next to you. All I want is to see your beautiful smile every day. I've never stopped loving you.'

'You sure have a funny way of showing it. I've never stopped loving you either, Steve, but I can't let you walk into my life and rip my heart apart again.'

'What are you saying, Emily?'

'I'm saying you just can't show up here and expect to come into my bedroom and make love to me and then decide you have to leave because you don't want me to get hurt. You have to decide. Either you stay or you leave. If you leave, I don't want you to ever come back because I can't go through this again.'

'What do you want me to do, Emily?'

'I want you to come home, Steve, but you have to make up your own mind.'

'The past is in the past, Emily. Things can't be the same.'

She fought the burn of tears that welled up in her. She stood up and looked at him. His head was bowed. He didn't look up. Didn't say anything else. Didn't even acknowledge she was upset by his words.

'I guess I have your answer then.' She drew the robe tighter around her body as if it were a security blanket of armor. With as much dignity as she could muster, she walked out of her kitchen.

14

The swirling sickness in Emily's stomach had settled to a somewhat tolerable state, but a sense of mass confusion still hovered all around her. Chance Donovan was Steve McCullen. Her dead husband was alive.

To make matters worse everyone in the family knew, except her. The old saying was so true. The wife was always the last to know.

Betrayal and hurt ran rampant through her as with violently trembling fingers she frantically tried to make some headway knitting the booty with the baby wool she'd found in one of her drawers. Unfortunately her attention kept straying to Steve's jeans where she'd dropped them after finding the medallion. If she hadn't found it . . .

She shook her head in disgust. If she hadn't picked up the medallion and examined it, or if she hadn't caught him breaking into the laptop, she'd still be in the dark.

The delicate job of knitting just didn't hold up under her anger and she whipped the knitting needles, tiny booty and all across the bedroom. It landed square against Steve's bare chest and he managed to grab it before it fell to the floor.

'I guess I deserved that.' His gentle voice carried no hint of the anger that had been so evident between them when they'd fought hours earlier.

'Ever hear of knocking?'

'I did. I guess you were otherwise occupied.'

'Oh.' She clenched her hands tightly together so he wouldn't be able to see how much they were shaking.

'You okay?'

'Aren't I always?' she snapped. 'What did you expect? A raging lunatic throwing pots and pans at your head?'

'Just knitting needles.' The soft smile on his lips soothed away some of her anger. 'Can I come in?'

'It's your bedroom too. Oh, sorry, let me rephrase that. It used to be your bedroom. Seems to me you don't want it or me anymore.'

His sweet smile drifted away, replaced by an angry frown. Good! He deserved to be unhappy after everything he'd put her through. He walked into the room and held out a steaming mug. 'Chamomile. It'll help settle your stomach.'

'Thanks.' She accepted the mug, careful

not to touch his flesh.

The sight of his lean fingers evoked a fiery memory of how his gentle touch had traced seductively along the curves of her breasts, her stomach and . . . She closed her eyes and chased away the images. This was not the time to be thinking about sex. Or love. It was time for war.

Steve walked over to the window and peered out. She couldn't help but to stare at his partially nude body as she sipped the warm chamomile tea.

Now that she knew the truth, she noted again how heart-stoppingly familiar he seemed. She didn't know how she hadn't guessed his true identity on her own.

Sure, his face was different. His voice altered. His eyes were the wrong color. The rest of his body should have clued her in. She'd known Steve's body intimately. Touched him, everywhere. Kissed him, everywhere. Why hadn't she *known*? It wasn't as if she hadn't had many clues.

For instance the immediate sizzling connection between them, the endearing tilt to his head when puzzled or curious. What about his large hands? The shape of them. The way they'd gently cupped her waist when they'd danced together. It was now obvious he had requested *their* song that night at the fair. She'd melted in his arms just like she'd done in the past. What about the night she'd captured him in her room supposedly looking for the Mace? That night she'd first realized Chance's smile was so similar to Steve's.

'You must have had a good laugh,' she said. 'Get me into bed and when I'm sleeping, you have access to my safe and your laptop.'

'It's nothing like that.'

'I love you, Emily. I don't love you, Emily. I care for you. Oh! This one is my favorite, 'I might not be able to give you any children.' As if that would make me love you any less.'

'Emily, please. Don't do this.'

'Why not? I'm on a roll. Do you know how insulting it is for my own husband not to want to see me after he's been through whatever horrors he's endured?' She emitted a strangled laugh that made him wince. 'You still won't confide in me what happened to you to bring on those horrible nightmares.'

'I'm sorry you're still upset.' He turned to leave, but she dropped her cup and scrambled off the bed.

'Don't you dare walk away from me Chance Donovan or Steve McCullen or whatever you're calling yourself these days.'

His eyes filled with tormented anguish and all she wanted to do was forget her anger, take him in her arms and tell him she loved him. Yet she couldn't quite bring herself to give in. Not this easily.

'I realize I may have been too hasty walking away from our earlier conversation. You're absolutely right when you said the past is in the past. Things can't be the same,' Emily said.

A chill scrambled up her spine as raw fear suddenly flared in his eyes. He was afraid she was dumping him. Turning him loose without a fight. The man needed his confidence boosted when it came to her love for him. Pushing aside her raw anger, she raised her hand to touch his face. He inhaled sharply as she parted the fluffy hair covering his hairline. Electricity shot through her fingers as she lightly traced the faint white surgical line until it disappeared behind his ear.

'A stranger's face . . . ' she whispered thoughtfully. 'Yet beneath these physical changes, these scars, you're still the same man I fell in love with. All over again.'

He went completely still and she allowed her shaky fingers to lightly move over his stubbled jaw to rest in the dent in his chin.

'You obviously were holding out some sort of hope for us getting back together or you wouldn't have had them install a cleft in your chin.'

She could see the pulse hammer in his

throat, the uncertainty glowing in his eyes. Uncertainty about what? She'd just told him she loved him.

'I think we need to talk some more before you say anything else.' His voice sounded hoarse. She detected an underlying warning that made her believe he still hadn't told her everything.

Dizziness rocked her. My God! What else was there?

'When I was in prison, they did things to me no human being should have to endure, let alone explain to his wife.'

He watched her carefully, obviously expecting her to protest. She clamped down on the torrents of helplessness washing over her. 'Okay. I understand. You need space.'

'Some day I might be able to share, but not now. Maybe not ever.'

Her heart began to thump wildly as she realized the man was obviously setting down some ground rules. Ground rules for their marriage. It meant he was still interested in staying together!

'I have nightmares pretty much on a daily basis,' he continued. 'They come with the package. If you can't handle them, just say so and I'll walk.'

'I can handle it.' Even though her voice sounded confident she wasn't so sure she could. His tormented moans alone, when he dreamed, were unlike any human sound she'd ever heard. They frightened her. Gave her horrible feelings of helplessness not to mention the fierce hatred that had crawled into her heart. Hatred at the people responsible for separating them. At the loss of his confidence in their relationship.

'There's something else.' He held her gaze and she knew instinctively she had to agree to this next rule or else he'd walk, as he so eloquently put it.

'Go ahead.'

'My two brothers and their wives begged me to allow one of them to tell you I was alive. I just couldn't let them. I see I was wrong. I'm sorry for not telling you. Please don't hold my mistake against them.'

'Of course I won't. They're my family.'

'And I'm broke.'

'You look to be in fine shape to me.'

'I'm serious. I don't have any money. My operations . . . there are debts.'

'We'll manage. Don't worry. All married couples work off debts.'

'Something else I need to tell you,' he said. 'I'm clean. I've had all the tests done for diseases. I'm not carrying anything. In case you wondered . . . '

Once again Emily clamped down on the

fears at the horrible visions of what might have happened to him behind bars.

'One more thing. That is if you're up to the challenge?'

'Name it.'

'I'm going to need . . . ' His hand cupped her chin and her breath backed up in her lungs at his potent look.

His eyes were fired up with raw hunger. A hunger that made her blood boil, and her insides quivered with an achingly sweet need.

'I'm going to need the love of a good woman.' He tilted her face up and stared straight into her soul. 'A good woman. With strong muscles to keep me in line and to challenge me at next year's Timber Sports Contest at the fall fair.'

'I don't know if I can agree to that,' she teased. 'My muscles need daily workouts so they can stay strong and limber.'

'These workouts . . . ' His ragged breath caressed her lips and a delicious golden want uncurled throughout her belly. 'Are they a part of your set of ground rules?'

'Yes.' Her fingers slipped off his chin and both her hands reached up to curl around to the back of his neck. The solid wall of his hot body pressed against her and suddenly she wanted his mouth on hers.

'What are your other needs, Emily?'

He grinned and a wave of love shot straight into her heart.

'This.' She pulled his head down to her and brushed her mouth against his lips with a butterfly kiss. 'And this.'

She uncurled her hands from around his warm neck, ran her palms down the front of his muscular chest and stopped over his nipples. Then she pushed against him with all her might.

Suddenly he was falling. Right onto her bed. He bounced delightfully and the look of momentary shock on his face made her laugh wickedly.

Before he could move she stepped in between his parted legs. Long legs that dangled seductively over the mattress. She looked down and admired the enormous bulge blossoming against his skimpy briefs.

'Your underwear seems to be too small for you.' She grinned. 'We're going to have to get you out of them . . . until I can find you another pair.'

He blinked back up at her. His eyes were wide with passion, his sexy mouth upturned into a gorgeous smile. Obviously he was enjoying her playful mood and she had every right to be playful. Her husband was back. She wasn't going to waste another minute making war with him.

'Unfortunately . . . ' She leaned over and he sucked in a jerky breath as her fingers slipped under the elastic waistband. 'I don't have another pair.'

Slowly she peeled the cloth down his muscular thighs and she gasped as his erect manhood burst free. Her eyes widened at his size and she said shakily, 'Maybe you should drink some of that chamomile tea to calm yourself down.'

Suddenly he reached out and tugged her down on top of him. His naked flesh seared straight through her clothes and fondled her skin. Molten heat rushed into her abdomen where his arousal nestled.

'Workout time.' His voice was husky with desire. He slid his hands to her stomach and the ache inside her body grew stronger as he slid her track top up. She quickly took over and struggled out of it. Then his large hands were cupping her swollen breasts, his rough thumbs rubbing her aroused nipples.

A moan escaped her lips and he smiled up at her. 'You like?'

'No fair,' she said as she straddled his legs. 'I'm still laying down my ground rules.'

'Which are?'

'Breakfast in bed every other weekend.'

'Sounds reasonable.' His fingers seared against the sides of her breasts, making her inhale sharply as those fiery nerve endings sizzled to life.

'Oh damn. I'll tell you the rest later.'

'Thought you'd see it my way.' His hands reached up and curled around her shoulders, pulling the rest of her body down. Her bare breasts flattened against his solid chest and her mouth fastened over his. His lips were moist and firm and demanding. Just the way she liked him.

She kissed him hungrily and her blood boiled. Moist heat exploded between her legs, readying her for him. Her tongue searched for his and she found it, and she stroked his rough velvet and mated with it.

She was aware of his hands sliding over the small of her back to slip beneath the waistband of her pants. He pulled them down. She kicked them off and then he cupped her bottom. She sank down on top of him until he filled her. The ache she'd carried deep in her heart finally eased.

'Welcome home, Steve,' she whispered before his mouth claimed hers.

★ ★ ★

'Come on, tell me the password. I promise I won't go into the laptop without your permission,' Emily said.

Steve cradled her in his arms, not wanting to ever let her go. He knew he'd have to do it. Soon. The hurricane was dying down. Reality was dawning. Big time.

'Steve?'

He inhaled deeply at the curiosity in her voice. 'You promise not to even look at the computer or the disk?'

'I promise. I promise.'

'Okay. There was more than one password.'

She blinked in puzzlement and he chuckled.

'I encrypted one password on top of another. On both the disk and access to the laptop.'

'You mean I type in one password hit enter and then type in the second one and hit enter?

'If there were only two passwords.'

'There's more than two?'

He shrugged. 'Why make it easy when you can make it hard?'

'I can see that. How many? What are the words?'

He lifted his hand to his St. Christopher's necklace around his neck. Turning it over, he held it up so she could see the engraved inscription.

'No way!'

'I saw the medallion a few days before you

311

gave it to me. You shouldn't have left it in the drawer with our socks.'

She slapped his arm playfully. 'You call me a snoop.'

'I learned from the best.'

'To Steve. Your endearment always. Love Emily,' she said softly. 'Seven words? Seven passwords?'

'Actually three sentences. Three passwords. You happy now?'

'No. I won't be happy until you tell me what you found on the disk?'

'Emily, you promised.' He groaned.

'I promised I wouldn't break into the computer. I didn't promise anything about bugging you to tell me what's inside.'

★　★　★

'Oh my God, Steve.' Emily raised her surprised gaze from the computer screen and stared up at him.

Her full mouth turned down into a severe frown and his gut clenched at the sight. He wished he'd followed his instincts and thrown the disk into the ocean. She'd kept insisting on looking at the contents of the disk and against his better judgment, he'd caved in like an avalanche.

'You've got doctors, prison systems, police

precincts, homeless shelters, foster homes, and even charities. All linked to the underground transplant system in the States and Canada. Where did you get this information?'

'A little birdie dropped it on the doorstep.'

She exhaled sharply and shook her head. 'This isn't funny. We're sitting on a powder keg. Why haven't you turned it over to the police?'

'Because I don't want it exploding in our faces.'

'What do you mean?'

Sparkling, determined innocent eyes stared back at him. 'This information will slip me right back into the justice system.'

'You'll be on the right side this time.'

'Will I? Once the police figure out who I am, and believe me they will get wind of it, I'll be back behind bars so fast our heads will be spinning twenty years from now when I'm still on the inside. It was a lot of drugs planted on the boat, Emily. More than the few bags we found this time around.'

'All circumstantial evidence. No one saw you bring it on board. No one saw you buy it. No one saw anything.'

'People have been convicted on a lot less, Em.'

'We can't do nothing with it.'

'It's been doing nothing for the last eight

years. Why be in a hurry now?'

A pretty, puzzled little wrinkle appeared between her eyebrows. 'What's happened to you? Where's your spirit? Your drive to help others?'

'Died. Like your husband.'

'I'm beginning to think you're right.' She returned her attention to the screen.

The disappointment in her voice left him reeling. She thought he was a spineless coward. Dammit, he was a coward. He'd toyed with the idea of getting rid of this sizable bomb of information. Of never allowing it to get into the hands of the proper authorities, but if he destroyed it, how would that keep them safe?

Emily lifted her trembling hand and pointed to the familiar name on the screen. 'Oh my God!'

His throat knotted up. He hadn't realized she'd already gone this far into the files. He'd wanted to tell her about what he'd found, but hadn't had the heart to do it. He placed his hand on top of her fingers and squeezed gently. 'I know, Emily. I know.'

★ ★ ★

The next morning the hurricane had vanished leaving Steve and Emily on edge. While she kept herself busy in the kitchen preparing an early lunch, he resumed lookout in the lamp room of the lighthouse tower. He squinted at the November sunrays as he kept a sharp eye out for any movement while his thoughts whirled around him as if the hurricane was still around. Thoughts about how easily she had accepted him back into his life. How much he loved her and about the danger he'd now put her in and . . .

He stiffened as he detected movement in the water just off the point. A boat! It was zeroing in on Shipwreck Island. Heading straight for the lighthouse.

He grabbed the gun off the windowsill where he'd placed it and slapped it inside the waistband of his jeans. The gun's cold metal hugged the small of his back, giving him little reassurance that he could handle the upcoming situation.

When he returned his attention to the ocean, his mouth fell open in surprise. The boat bouncing along the large swells was none other than *Sweet Lies*.

★ ★ ★

When Steve barreled into the kitchen, Emily almost dropped the pot of spaghetti she'd just hauled off the stove. By the stern expression on his face she knew someone was coming.

'Showtime. Emily. Let's go!'

He ripped the pot from her grasp and stuffed it back onto the stove, grabbed her by the hand and led her into the living room just as a light noise came from the other side of the kitchen door.

'Behind the couch,' he ordered.

Her heart cracked like a jackhammer as he pushed her into the tight confines behind the couch. He shoved the can of Mace into her hand and a knife. Then he pressed her head down. 'Keep out of sight. No matter what.'

She nodded. When he left her, a sinking feeling grabbed hold of her belly.

*　*　*

Steve slid his body against the living room wall beside the doorway that led to the kitchen. His heart raced wildly and his breath escaped in noisy gasps. Too noisy. He clamped his mouth shut.

The click of the kitchen door opening made him shiver and his finger tightened dangerously on the trigger.

*　*　*

From her vantage point behind the couch, Emily strained her ears to listen to the footsteps in her kitchen. When the footsteps halted, adrenaline squirted into her veins. She could picture the intruder standing in front of the stove staring down at the steaming pot of spaghetti. Dead giveaway they were still here on the island.

A tiny click from the kitchen area sent a volley of shivers screaming up her spine. It almost sounded like the person had shut off the stove. Then again, it also sounded like someone had positioned a bullet into the barrel of a gun.

★   ★   ★

A gun poked its head through the living room doorway and Steve didn't hesitate. With icy smoothness he kissed his weapon against the intruder's temple. Skip Cole froze.

'I could pull the trigger right now, Cole,' Steve said. 'Might save me a lot of trouble.'

'I can see you still aren't an early morning person, buddy,' Skip said somewhat cheerfully.

Steve sucked in a shocked breath. The horrible feelings of betrayal and revenge he'd been carrying around all these years sprang to life and he tried to keep his insides from trembling, but he couldn't.

He'd been right all along. Skip knew him.

That meant he was behind everything. Steve's years of imprisonment, fear for Emily's safety, their separation and who knew how many others had suffered.

Red-hot rage made him want to pull the trigger, but something in Skip's soft eyes stopped him cold. He'd expected to see fear in those brown depths. Fear that Skip would get killed, but Steve saw only the familiar mischievous twinkle. It gave him the uneasy feeling he might be misreading this whole situation.

'Easy, buddy. I got your message from the boy. You wanted to see me,' Skip said.

'I want to kill you.'

'Just relax.'

'Hiring a kid to do your dirty work. That's low, Skip. Real low. To come back here in *Sweet Lies*. Real original.'

'I needed someone in a hurry. The kid was available. A local trawler recognized the boat as Emily's so I brought it back. I'm sorry I couldn't come earlier. There was a problem in town. I also had to wait until the hurricane passed. I was worried about you two.'

'I bet you were,' Steve sneered.

'I'm dropping my gun now. See?' Skip placed the weapon onto the floor and kicked it out of reach. He scanned the living room. 'I'm unarmed. Now where is Emily? Is she all right?'

'Such sweet concern from someone who wants to harm her.'

'You got it all wrong, Steve. I work for the U.S. Marshal Service.'

Steve blinked with amazement and he didn't miss the small gasp from Emily who had risen from her hiding place.

A glimmer of hope slithered against the rage and betrayal clawing through him. He clamped down on it and continued to stare at Skip trying to figure out why he should believe him. 'Prove it.'

'May I produce my ID?'

Steve waited until Emily handed him Skip's gun and he checked the clip before he nodded approval. He kept himself alert for any suspicious movements on Skip's part.

Skip kept his eyes on Steve as he carefully drew aside his suit coat. Skip's chocolate brown eyes remained steady, confident . . . friendly?

That glimmer of hope settled against the rage and betrayal and once again Steve clamped down on it. Hard.

Steve watched Skip produce a laminated ID folder from an inside pocket. He held it up for Steve and Emily to read.

'I had no idea,' Emily gasped.

Then Skip held up the Marshal's badge, but Steve wasn't ready to be fooled. 'Anyone can get an ID like that made up. How do I know it's for real?'

'You don't. You'll just have to trust me.'

'I don't think so,' Steve said tightly.

'After everything you've been through, I'm surprised you can trust someone. You keep the gun.'

Skip's gaze shifted to the other door in the corner of the living room. Steve sucked in a shocked gasp as he spotted two men dressed in black. They stood in the back doorway. Guns drawn. Pointed at both Emily and him.

'Everything's fine here,' Skip said. 'Both of you can wait in the boat.'

The two men nodded, shoved their guns in shoulder holsters and then quietly disappeared.

Steve slumped against the wall as his knees suddenly weakened in relief. 'I almost blew your goddamn head off.'

'You wouldn't have. You don't have the murderous gleam in your eye. Why don't we have a seat. Both of you. I'll explain everything.'

15

'You've been working undercover spying on Helena all these years?' Steve still couldn't quite believe what Skip had told them and he couldn't quite allow himself to lower the gun he still held in his hand as they both sat on the sofa in the living room.

'Yep,' Skip said. 'A disgruntled employee of hers who got fingered for extortion in a separate case tipped the Feds off. He told us Helena was using her newspaper journalists as a cover for smuggling drugs in from other countries. More recently we believe she's using sensitive information her journalists are digging up and bringing to her so she can blackmail certain people who can't afford to have their identities revealed in certain . . . compromising positions, and she's also connected to the underground transplant world.'

'Is that why you stuck to me like glue? Pretended to be friends with me? To see if I was one of her goons?'

'At first, yes.'

Steve frowned as that familiar feeling of betrayal reared its ugly head again.

'I have pretty good instincts about people,' Skip continued. 'I knew very quickly you weren't involved in her shady dealings. Hey! Cheer up! I wouldn't waste my great sense of humor on just anybody.'

'I thought you were behind everything.'

'Don't look so down, man. You give me too much credit, Steve. I'm not that powerful, but apparently Helena is. Her personal secretary tipped me off, she had some rather incriminating evidence against Helena.'

'Summer Roberts,' Emily said when she returned to the room.

Steve smiled as Skip's eyes widened with appreciation when he spotted the tray laden with a pot of steaming coffee and thick slabs of the lemon cake she'd baked yesterday.

'Summer Roberts called me shortly after . . . ' She hesitated for a moment then continued. 'Well, after Steve disappeared. We set up a lunch appointment. She said she had some information about why someone wanted him out of the way. But she never showed up for our appointment. I found out later she had disappeared without a trace.'

'Helena must have got to her,' Steve said as Emily deposited the goodies onto the table.

'As a matter of fact,' Skip replied, 'we staged her disappearance and put her into the

Witness Protection Program. She's the one who sent you the disk.'

Steve's mouth dropped open in shock.

'Unfortunately,' Skip continued, 'you handed the disk to me and I put it on Helena's desk right on top of your resignation letter. Then I went back to searching her office. When I left, I forgot the disk.'

'I never even read the contents,' Steve said as a horrible feeling sliced into him.

'I figured that one out. Why else would you give the disk to me? You would have gone straight to the authorities.'

'I was the one who begged him to give up that job and to move to the island,' Emily said in a strangled voice.

Steve looked up to see the guilt flashing in both Skip and Emily's eyes. He'd never wanted to see her suffer and now, no matter how hard he'd tried to protect her, she still was getting hurt. He placed a comforting hand on top of Emily's. 'Neither of you is at fault. How were you to know I had some sizzling information? Besides if there's anyone to blame it should be me. I should have checked it myself.'

'Speaking of sizzling information,' Skip said, 'where is the disk?'

When Emily made a move to retrieve it

from the laptop they'd stashed in the bedroom safe, Steve squeezed her hand in warning.

'Still don't trust me.' Skip nodded slowly. 'I can understand that.'

'What makes you think I still have the disk?'

'The one you gave me was a copy.'

Fear tingled up Steve's spine. 'How do you know that?'

'Summer told me the disk she sent to you was black. You gave me a grey one. When I remembered you had given me the disk and I'd left it in Helena's office, I went back but the disk and Helena were gone. I didn't think anything else about it until Summer went to the cops a couple of days later. One of my contacts inside the police force tipped me off she had info about Helena and about you going missing. By the time I could talk to her . . . ' Skip sighed heavily.

'My husband had already fallen into Helena's clutches,' Emily whispered hoarsely.

Skip nodded affirmation.

'You still haven't answered my question,' Steve said to Skip.

'Why do I want your disk?'

'That's right. Summer's a trained receptionist. She knows the value of making backup disks. Why not use hers?'

'Unfortunately her original and backups were stolen from her home safe. Hence why she's still in the Witness Protection Program.'

'Couldn't Summer give you names, dates, whatever, to send you to the appropriate criminals?' Emily asked.

'Summer has given us everything she can remember. Unfortunately Helena has shut down most of her operations. People disappeared. Others ended up dead or simply wouldn't talk to us. The woman must have some bad blackmail stuff on some of these people because the ones we were able to convict refused to testify against her or use their sentences as bargaining chips to help themselves.' Skip sipped the hot coffee gingerly. 'After all these years we don't even know if the information on the disk is still good, but I'd like to take a look at it anyway.'

'Oh, it's still good,' Emily blurted.

Skip cocked an inquiring eyebrow at her.

'There's been trouble,' she admitted.

'The kind that left Steve with the bandage on his forehead?'

Steve decided it was his turn to jump into the conversation. 'I know the name of one of the men who held me prisoner. He's a lawman from the States. There isn't anything I can do to go after him legally until my name is cleared.'

'I'm afraid you won't be able to go after him at all.'

'What do you mean?'

'He's dead.'

An icy shiver slipped into Steve's body. 'Dead? How do you know who the hell I'm talking about?'

'I'll fill you in, but let me get something that I left on the kitchen table. Then I'll answer more of your questions.'

★ ★ ★

Emily watched the severe frown cross Steve's face as Skip rose and left the room. 'Are you all right?'

'I don't know.'

'Skip wouldn't have told his men to leave if he wasn't on the up and up, would he?'

Steve smiled faintly. 'I'm not sure.'

When Skip wandered back into the room with a newspaper clutched in his hand, they both jumped.

'Good thing you're sitting.'

Skip smiled down at them, but Emily detected no smile in his eyes as he placed the newspaper on the coffee table. Beside her Steve cursed.

Alarm screamed through her as his face went chalk white. She looked at the newspaper and at the picture of a dark-haired man with a well-groomed mustache. Bold headlines screamed at her. *Prominent U.S. Prosecutor Found Murdered off North Cape.*

'Who is he?' Emily asked.

'The Prosecutor,' Steve said in a strangled voice.

'The Prosecutor?' Emily asked.

'He's the man who tried to make a deal with me regarding the drug charges when this whole nightmare started.' Steve inhaled a shuddering breath before continuing. 'He was one of the men on the beach the other day. The same man who was following me in town. Who killed him?'

'At first I thought it was you.'

'There's no way you can pin this on him,' Emily snapped at Skip. 'I saw two men beating up my husband on the beach. When they left, they were both alive and healthy and my husband was a bloody mess.'

'Easy, Emily. I said at first I suspected Steve. The autopsy showed he took an ice pick into the base of his neck. It's a trademark of Helena's.'

'Then you don't believe Steve did it?'

'No.'

'I wish I had,' Steve said.

Emily gasped at the violence in his statement. By the way his fists were clenched and the hatred clouding his face, she knew he said the truth. Silently she thanked the Lord someone else had gotten to this prosecutor first.

'Did I tell you it was Helena's idea I ask Emily to marry me?'

Skip's voice broke into her thoughts. Skip was trying to change the subject in an effort to give Steve some time to absorb the news about the prosecutor's death.

'Of course, I thought it was a good idea.' Skip grinned.

'You'd be stupid to think otherwise,' Steve said. By the way his eyes twinkled she suspected he was beginning to mellow and trust Skip.

'I'm going to ignore that remark,' Skip replied then returned his attention on her. 'As I was saying before I was so rudely interrupted, I figured it was a good idea. It gave me a reason to stick close to you. Keep an eye on you until Steve here came to his senses and decided to come back home.'

'How did you know I was alive?' The distrust was back again and Steve's eyes turned ice cold. She didn't miss his grip tightening around the butt of the pistol he held in his lap.

'Easy, buddy,' Skip said. 'I've only known a few months myself. I wanted to come and visit you, except your brothers told me it wasn't a good idea with all your surgeries and all.'

Emily winced as Steve cursed.

'How the hell do my brothers work into all this?'

'Aside from their busy married lives they do have jobs, Steve. I got the inside scoop from Mathew, the one who used to be an undercover cop. He's got quite a few connections. Found out I was undercover investigating Helena and told me about you being alive. At least your brothers trust me.' Skip let the sentence dangle in the air.

Emily held her breath as she waited for Steve's reaction.

'What happens if I hand over the disk to you?' Steve said.

'I take it to my people who will have Summer authenticate it. If there's something credible on the disk, we follow it up and see if we can't get Helena.'

'Wait a minute,' Emily said quickly. 'What happens to Steve? He still has the drug charges hanging over his head. When the police find out he's not dead, they'll haul him right back to jail.'

Skip smacked his lips and put down his coffee mug. He leaned both his hands on the table and his eyes narrowed with excitement.

'I've been thinking on that one.' He looked at Steve, who once again tensed up like a coiled cobra. 'I won't tell the Feds a thing. At least not yet. They're only interested in the disk and don't give a rat's behind about you, so you'll have to do this on your own. You up to it?'

Steve nodded. 'Let's hear it.'

★ ★ ★

The gentle sway of *Sweet Lies* rocking against the ocean swells did nothing to comfort Emily as she stood at the helm peering down to the bow area where Steve and Skip were engaged in an intense discussion on how to bring down Helena and her empire.

If something happened to Steve . . . Emily shivered at the memory of the magnitude of emptiness she'd experienced when she'd been told Steve was dead. Now he was home and she was whole again. They were together. Why did he want to casually throw it away?

A tear streamed down her cheek and she angrily swiped it away. To top everything off, the woman she had trusted all these years was the one behind this whole nightmare. It was too much to take. She felt like screaming or better yet having it out with Helena. One on one.

She didn't hear Skip come up behind her until he spoke.

'I'll take the helm, Emily. You go and be with Steve.'

'For how long?' she snapped. 'Until Helena kills him?'

'We've gone over the plan numerous times, Emily. Chances of something going wrong are small.'

'There is a chance. That's already too big a risk for me to take.' She angrily swiped away another tear that dared run down her cheek.

'It's up to Steve, Emily. He's the one who has to live with the consequences if he doesn't try to clear his name.'

'He won't live if he fails, Skip.'

He smiled tenderly, reached out and gently wiped away another stray tear. 'Maybe you should tell Steve how you feel?'

'Apparently he doesn't care. He made the decision on his own. Didn't even bother to ask me, did he?'

'I guess we got caught up in the excitement about all the stuff on the disk.'

'Just like old times. Right, Skip? Chasing adrenaline rush after rush.' He avoided her gaze and her heart plummeted with guilt. 'I'm sorry. I didn't mean to snap at you. It's Steve I'm mad at, not you.'

'No harm done. Now, go and talk to him.

I'll take the helm.'

'I'll talk to him later. I don't want to put you or your men through all the yelling when we come to blows.'

'Or the making up part?' Amusement etched his voice.

She didn't reply and a moment later she heard his footsteps echo down the steps to the deck. She squinted against the glare off the water as she returned her attention to the looming silhouette of Prince Edward Island.

There would be no making up after this fight. Not if Steve went ahead with his plans to go after Helena tomorrow. Because if he did, she'd leave him.

★ ★ ★

After catching a charter plane from Prince Edward Island to New York, Skip secured hotel rooms for the three of them.

Emily had been quiet all the way over and Steve figured she was tired and scared and probably still very confused. She'd had a lot to digest in a very short time and he was amazed at how well she'd taken the news he was alive. He ached to go back upstairs to reassure her everything would work out, yet at the moment getting Helena was top priority.

Skip grilled Steve until his nerves were frayed and then Skip grilled him some more. When Skip was finished, he nodded approval, leaned back against his chair and with a severe frown on his face proceeded to thoughtfully rub his thumb up and down the moist film on his beer bottle.

Instinctively Steve knew Skip wanted to say something he wouldn't like and was figuring out a delicate way of saying it. He began to feel a sinking sensation build in the pit of his stomach.

Finally Skip spoke. 'You sure about tomorrow?'

'What do you mean? Am I sure? Of course I'm sure. Unless . . . ' That sick feeling in his gut twisted into a tight knot. 'You want out?'

'It's not me I'm worried about.'

'Don't worry about me. I'm in. All the way.'

'What about Emily?' Skip asked quietly.

'What about Emily?'

'You still love her?'

Steve was taken aback by Skip's question. 'I can't go five feet away from her without missing her. Does that answer your question?'

'Have you asked her what she thinks about you going up against Helena tomorrow?'

'She understands.'

'Does she?'

Steve shoved his beer bottle away from him. The smell of it suddenly made his stomach heave or maybe it was the realization Emily might not understand why he wanted to go up against Helena.

'She's pretty upset about this whole thing,' Skip said softly.

'She told you this?'

'On the boat.'

'How come she didn't tell me?'

'Probably because you didn't ask her how she felt.'

'I figured she understood my need to get my identity back. To prove my innocence.'

'Maybe she just needs your reassurance you'll be around for her in the future, buddy.'

'We both know there aren't any guarantees.'

'Which brings me back to my question. Are you sure you want to do this? If not then tell me now. I'll go in myself and try it.'

'This is my fight, Skip. Besides, Helena might get suspicious if you show up with the disk. You might blow your cover. You're going to need it if something happens to me.'

'It's your call.' Skip leaned forward, placed his elbows on the table and clasped his beer bottle with both hands. His eyes narrowed into serious slits and he lowered his voice so Steve could barely hear above the music echoing through the bar.

'Before I forget. The man you fingered in the Canadian Coast Guard was found dead in his car outside his home a couple of nights ago.'

'An ice pick to the base of his neck?' Steve whispered.

Skip nodded. 'Looks like Helena is burning all her bridges behind her. Just make sure she doesn't burn you, Steve.'

'I'll try my best.'

'You do better than your best,' Skip said seriously. 'Is there anything else we need to go over?'

'Not unless you want to. I just want to get some sleep.'

Skip smiled. 'Go on. Get out of here. I'll pick up the tab.'

'And that little redhead over there?' Steve suggested with a smile as he threw a sideways glance to a nearby table. A redhead had her baby blue eyes glued on Skip.

'Looks like she needs a broad shoulder to cry on, don't you think?'

'Haven't changed have you?' Steve chuckled as he pushed out his chair.

'I'm a sucker for redheads. You know that.'

'I'd better let you get on with your business then.'

'Not business, my dear boy.' Skip chuckled

as he saluted the redhead with his bottle of beer. 'Pleasure. Pure. Sweet. Pleasure.'

'My mistake. I'll let you get on with your . . . pleasure. Good night.'

'Nighty-night. See you in the a.m.'

When Steve reached the elevators, he turned around to check on Skip. Sure enough the petite redhead hadn't wasted any time in securing the seat Steve had occupied only moments earlier. Both were already engaged in a conversation.

'The man hasn't lost his touch.' Steve shook his head and stepped into the open elevator.

★   ★   ★

Steve quietly slid the key into the lock, opened the door and slipped inside the hotel room. It was dark. And quiet. Thank God. He was way too tired to argue with Emily tonight.

Checking first to make sure the door was locked, he then turned around and froze. Through the darkness he spotted movement and smelled her sexy scent. A light flicked on and he found her standing beside their queen-size bed. Her arms were folded tightly around the stuffed red lobster and one foot tapped impatiently on the carpeted floor. His heart began to pound in his ears at the grim determined frown plastered on her pale face.

'Thought you'd be asleep by now,' he said as he dropped the key onto the television set.

'So you could avoid a fight with me? Not a chance.'

'I don't want to fight with you, Emily.'

'Then don't. Don't go tomorrow. Let Skip do it. Let him bring down Helena and her empire. It's his job.'

'You know I can't do that. It's my name that needs to be cleared.'

Her angry frown cracked and Steve glimpsed the devastating fear she'd been hiding. For the first time he knew exactly how frightened she was for his safety. The truth left him reeling, and he ached to comfort her.

In a couple of quick strides, he drew to her side. Emily jumped away from him like a hyper jack-in-the-box and threw the red lobster at him. It bounced harmlessly off his shoulder and dropped to the ground.

'Déjà vu,' he whispered, trying to tease her into a better mood. It didn't work. The determined look in her eyes hardened and her dead steady voice stopped him cold.

'You run off tomorrow chasing after another one of your adrenaline rushes like you did in the old days, you can forget about me being here if you come back.'

He inhaled a steadying breath. 'I didn't know you felt this strongly.'

'If you'd bothered to ask, maybe you would have saved us a lot of anguish.'

'If I don't go tomorrow, I won't be able to live as Steve McCullen.'

'I don't care what name you use. I just want you safe.'

'I want you safe too. I want you safe in my arms, forever.'

'You sure have a strange way of showing it. Especially if you don't come back.'

At the tinge of a tremble in her otherwise strong voice, he felt his resolve slip away. 'Okay, you win. If you don't want me to go, I won't. You're the best thing that's ever happened to me and I don't want to lose you.'

Relief sparkled in her eyes at his words and her shoulders slumped slightly, however it did nothing to dispel the disappointment slithering through him. Disappointment that he'd been so close to finally getting a chance to reclaim his own name. To be able to lead a somewhat normal life with the woman he loved more than anyone else in the world.

'I'll go down and tell Skip right now. I'll tell him everything's off. I'll be right back.' On somewhat shaky legs he turned and headed for the door. He'd been so close. So damn close and to not even have a chance at trying . . .

He exhaled wearily. Emily was right. He might not make it back to her and their future would go up in smoke. Again. He was about to slip out the door when her soft hand curled over his right shoulder and she pulled him back inside the room.

'I'm so sorry. I shouldn't have told you what to do.'

When he turned to face her, he blinked in surprise as her strong facade crumbled. Her lower lip trembled and tears bubbled up in her eyes. Thick lashes lowered as she lifted his hand and placed it directly upon her warm nightgown, directly over her heart. Judging by the way it pounded violently against his palm she was terrified. She threw him a wobbly smile he figured was meant to cheer him up. It didn't.

'What kind of a woman am I? Instead of supporting my husband when he needs me the most, I'm thinking only about myself. I know you're scared too. I can see it in your eyes.' He inhaled sharply as she then placed her other hand over his heart. 'I can feel it here too. We're both scared. Terrified. I have to tell you that every minute that goes by I feel as if I'm going to wake up and you'll just have been a beautiful dream.'

A hard knot formed in his throat.

'I'm letting my fears control me, control us,' she continued. Her voice now a soft whisper. 'You do what you need to do tomorrow. Just make sure you come back because I'll be waiting.'

He drew her into his arms and before she could say anything else he lowered his head as that familiar obsession swooped over him. The same uneasiness he'd felt that afternoon on the beach years ago, on the day before their world had fallen apart, slid into his body. Was it a premonition? When he tasted chocolate, his thoughts drew back to Emily and he chuckled. She always nibbled on chocolate or drank hot chocolate when she was nervous.

She stiffened and abruptly broke the kiss. 'Why are you laughing?'

'You taste good.'

'This makes you happy?' She smiled and brushed her passion-swelled lips urgently against his.

'Extremely. You smell good too. Clean and fresh.'

'Took a long hot shower while you were out.'

'Sounds heavenly.'

Her eyes twinkled with mischief and her smile turned secretive. The sensual sight sent his heart to pounding and heated blood headed straight south. 'What are you up to, Emily?'

'You'll find out.' Fresh urgency zipped along every nerve ending as she took his hand in hers and led him into the bathroom. Warm mist greeted him. 'We haven't showered together in over eight years. You think it's about time we reacquainted ourselves?'

When she pressed her luscious body against him, his throat went dry and his senses went into overload.

He reached out to curl his arms around her waist, but she grabbed both his hands and pressed them to his sides.

'Let me take care of something first,' she said as her breasts flattened against his chest and her hot hands slipped beneath his sweater and T-shirt. He shivered in anticipation as her fingers skimmed along his naked waist around to his back.

'We won't be needing this.' In one quick move she slid his gun from its resting place against the small of his back and lowered it to the toilet seat. Her sultry hazel eyes showed both love and bits of fear as she stared into his eyes. 'Or this.'

Her tender hands popped the brass button on his jeans and he heard the zipper lowering, as well as his heart thundering wildly in his ears. Quick as a lick, she yanked both his jeans and underwear past his hips and below, allowing his full arousal to spring free and he knew he was in for one interesting and heavenly night.

16

The light knock at the door came very early the next morning when Steve was in the shower and Emily paced a path into the hotel carpet as she worriedly nibbled on her knuckles. Adrenaline seared like a bolt of lightning through her veins at the intruding sound. She didn't make a move to answer it. She could only stare at the door and wish Skip would just go away. Maybe he would leave if he thought they weren't here? Maybe her stubborn husband would change his mind if he thought Skip had left without him?

'Maybe you should get that?' Steve's strangled whisper erupted from the open doorway of the bathroom.

'I can't.'

'If you don't want me to go, I won't.'

Emily could see the disappointment flicker in his eyes again just like it had last night when she demanded he not go after Helena. 'Go get ready. I'll let him in.'

'You sure?'

Another round of taps echoed through the room. Steve didn't move. His eyes were stormy and her heart thundered in her ears and cracked against her ribs. For a moment he looked as if he might not go and then the confidence spilled back into his face and he nodded slowly, then disappeared into the bathroom. Aware that her legs were about to give out, she forced herself to answer the door. Skip stood in the hallway, his hand poised to knock again. He seemed startled to see her.

'Thought you might have changed your minds,' he said softly.

'Come on in. He'll be right out.'

'It's okay. I'll stay out here and wait. Give you two time to say a proper goodbye.'

'There won't be any goodbyes,' Steve said from behind her as he struggled into his T-shirt. 'Because I'm coming back.'

Her heart fluttered wildly and the sharp sting of tears spiraled into her eyes. She turned to face Skip, who suddenly looked very uncomfortable. 'Skip, you have to take care of him. Please. Make sure he comes back.'

'I'll make sure he stays safe,' he said and threw her a wobbly smile that made her feel worse.

Behind her, she heard a sharp click as Steve checked the clip in the gun.

'I got a hold of your brothers. They're on their way,' Skip called over her shoulder. He turned to Emily and that wobbly smile was back on his face again. 'They're bringing their wives along . . . '

Just in case. The words went unspoken, but she knew it was for her sake . . . in case she needed them. In case something happened to Steve. When his warm hands curled over her shoulder, she just about jumped out of her skin. He turned her around to face him. His hair was still wet but he'd combed it straight back off his forehead. He looked good this way. Real good. And he smelled real good too. A delicious scent of strawberries curled around her and she realized he'd used her shampoo. Perhaps as a way to keep her with him? She started to shake at the thought that he might not be coming back and this might be their final goodbye.

Horrific sadness welled in her and she forced herself to blink back the hot tears and made herself meet his intense gaze. His warm breath caressed her face as he spoke. 'Don't open the door to anyone but Skip or my brothers or Sara and Jo. Okay?'

She nodded weakly noting instantly he hadn't mentioned himself.

His head lowered. The instant his warm, gentle lips touched hers, her brain shorted out and her fears vanished as every pleasure center in her body sizzled to life. If she hadn't wrapped her arms around his neck, she was mighty sure she would have fallen. And then he was easing away from her. His eyes dark, full of passion.

'I'll be back,' he whispered, his voice full of promise.

Then he was gone. Leaving her with the sound of the door locking and an intense fear uncoiling like a cobra inside her.

She bit her bottom lip to prevent herself from crying, but it didn't work. The tears fell like two hot springs down her cheeks.

A moment later a knock erupted at the door and her heart soared. Steve had changed his mind! He'd come back!

Wiping away her tears, she rushed to the door, quickly unlocked it and flung it open. Her heart stopped. It wasn't Steve at all.

'Hi!' She managed a quick smile. 'What are you doing here?'

Her smile vanished and a finger of ice stroked a warning through her brain a split second before her visitor pulled out a gun and aimed it straight at her midsection.

★ ★ ★

When he heard the familiar high heels clicking toward Helena's office, Steve straightened in the plush office chair and forced himself to inhale a steady breath. The door swung inward. If Helena was surprised to see him sitting behind her desk, she didn't show it. She merely breezed inside as if she knew all along she had company. She dropped her purse onto the desk in front of him and smiled. A creepy shiver of what Steve could only figure out was fear slithered a chill warning up his spine.

'Why, Mister Donovan. What an unexpected pleasure,' she said cheerfully.

'Cut the crap, Helena.'

'Oh dear. Something's upset you,' she said, totally unoffended by his bold reply. 'I hope you aren't too upset because I had to leave early the other day after Emily's fitting. I had an appointment. How about we get together today? For lunch? We can discuss plans for your future.'

'How about we discuss plans for your future, Helena? Like how are you going to match your hair color with the orange overalls you'll be wearing in prison.'

She blinked rapidly for a second, then recovered quickly. 'My you certainly are touchy. What is it that I can do for you, darling?'

'More like what I can do for you, Helena. I'm going to give you a couple of metal

347

bracelets and crucify you. And that's just for starters.'

'Dear boy, what are you babbling about?'

'I have evidence against you, Helena,' he said. He wanted to shake her up, but nothing changed in her demeanor. The woman was unshakable. A goddamn rock. 'Information that is being leaked to the press as we speak.'

'Ah, I see. You want money for your silence. I'll write you a check.' She reached for her purse, but he grabbed it out of her hand, and placed it back on the table.

'Aren't you afraid your security cameras will catch you bribing me?'

'Darling,' she said gently. 'My people mind their own business. Something you should have done years ago.'

'Oh, sweet heavens, Helena. Don't tell me you're the one who planted those drugs on my boat? Oh, wait! I already figured that out, didn't I? I had plenty of time in prison.'

She didn't say anything, but Steve didn't miss her quick glance at the purse sitting on the desk in front of her.

'Dead giveaway, Helena.' In a flash he reached out and snapped up the purse and sifted through the contents. 'Lipstick, compact, appointment book . . . '

'Please, there is no need for you pawing

through my personal belongings, Mr. Donovan. You are being entirely too rude.'

He ignored her snappy remark and threw her an amused grin. 'Oh look! A gun?'

He withdrew the deadly weapon from it's hiding place in a side pocket and relieved it of all the bullets before placing it back into her purse. 'Shame on you, Helena.'

'A woman can't be too careful these days. It isn't like the old days when you could trust someone with a mere handshake or by their word.'

'Funny you should mention that, Helena. Didn't you give me your word over the phone years ago when I used my one telephone call to ask you to send me a lawyer? Didn't you give me your word you'd get me out of there?'

Her smile wavered ever so slightly and she reached up to brush away an imaginary stray strand of her neatly coiffured hair.

'Ouch, a sore spot?' he said coolly.

'You can't prove anything, Steve.'

'We have some things to discuss, Helena. Top of the list is something rather . . . personal.'

'What are you insinuating?'

'Revenge,' he said coldly.

'How enticing,' she replied. It surprised him to see how she seemed to cheer right up.

'And exactly how do you propose to exact your revenge?'

'Why don't you grab yourself a fresh cup of coffee over there. Stay awhile. I'll explain everything in detail.'

'Well, if I must stay and be entertained. Would you like a cup?'

Steve nodded. 'Please.'

He watched anxiously as she headed over to the bar where he'd prepared the coffee and left it warming on a hot plate.

'As I remember correctly you prefer cream and three teaspoons of sugar?'

'You flatter me with your memory,' Steve said dryly.

A moment later she walked over toward him and with both steaming cups in hand threw him another cheerful smile. 'Don't even think about throwing it in my face, Helena.'

She chuckled. 'You insult me, Mr. McCullen. I would never do such a hideous thing to a guest.'

When she placed his mug down in front of him, he relaxed. She continued to stand as she sipped her coffee. He didn't touch his.

'Now, what do you have in mind?' she said sweetly. 'Torture? A knife to the heart?'

'Something a little different, but I'll tell you

in a bit. First, we need to have a heart to heart.'

'How pleasant. Would you mind if I have a seat?'

'Please do. Only keep your hands where I can see them.'

'You don't trust me? How insulting.'

'Cut the act, Helena. I have the disk. The original. I've seen it all.'

A curiously satisfied smile slipped across Helena's red painted lips. 'I knew you did.'

He leaned forward in the chair and placed his hands on the desk. 'Only one problem, Helena. You see, I only saw the contents for the first time yesterday.'

'What?'

'That's right. You think I'd be stupid enough to give away the only disk if I'd known what was on it? I would have gone straight to the cops.'

'I expected you to be more loyal, Steven. I gather you brought the original along with you this morning?'

'And if I said I did?'

'Then I would tell you I might be interested in taking a look at it.'

'Why would you be interested? You've already stolen the original from Summer's safe and all her backups. You have the disk that was left on your desk. You already know what is on it. Unless . . . there's something on the disk you haven't been able to cover up? Too many people to kill?'

Her face paled. 'How much money do you want?'

'For the last and very incriminating copy? It might take me some time to think up a proper sum.' When she frowned, he allowed himself a smug smile.

'You were my best journalist, Steven. And a very dear friend. I assure you, what happened to you wasn't personal.'

'Purely business? Isn't that right? You planted the drugs on my boat using a man in the Canadian Coast Guard who conveniently knew where the drugs would be. You used the same man again a few days ago when you tried to get away with the same thing. He failed and you killed him.'

'I did no such thing!'

'So, you hired someone else to do the dirty work. Am I right? It had to be someone knowledgeable. Someone who could stick an ice pick to the base of the skull. Doesn't leave too much blood at the scene.'

'I prefer my employees to keep things neat and tidy.'

'You used the planted drugs to get me into jail,' he continued. 'Where your other hired man, the prosecutor goon, could work out a deal with me, right?'

'It was a brilliant plan on such short notice,' she admitted with a self-righteous smile that eroded away at his concentration.

'I spill my guts and reveal what I know and they drop the drug charges. Unfortunately for you I didn't cave. So your goons beat me up. Too bad they lost control. They certainly weren't neat and tidy on this job. Very messy. When they were through with me, I couldn't talk for some time. I ended up almost dead.'

'You would have died, had I not intervened, Steven.'

Her hushed response brought an uncomfortable uneasiness shooting through him and he immediately spied a gleam of excitement in her eyes. Automatically he straightened to attention. She was up to something. The touch of nervousness had vanished from her, replaced by pure confidence.

'Unfortunately I needed you alive so I could question you about the disk. In order to save your life and allow you to see again, a youngster had to be sacrificed.'

'Let's get back on track, Helena,' he warned. His insides began to tremble. This was information he didn't want to hear.

Immense delight snapped across her face. 'You don't know the identity of your donor, do you, dear?'

'Shut up, Helena.'

'A young boy. A dear sweet, innocent, young boy.' Her voice was soft, gentle.

Steve found it extremely difficult to tune her out. He knew he should ignore her, but if she was behind the murder of a child, he needed to dig up that information. 'You're lying.'

'On the contrary. When you were beaten, your eyes were severely damaged — '

'More like they were popped out like grapes by your personal goon squad,' he said. He tried to keep a lid on the rising anger churning in his heart.

'Nonetheless, I felt you would be more . . . co-operative if you had a new set of eyes, along with a new kidney.'

'So, you did what? Killed a kid for parts?'

'Must you be so indelicate, Steven? That was a job for an acquaintance of mine.'

'And that made it okay?'

'You are living a virtually normal life aren't you? And you do have a new pair of eyes. Thanks to my genius acquaintance and his state of the art techniques. Nonetheless I don't hear you complaining.'

'Helena!' a familiar voice said from the doorway.

Immediately Steve recognized the voice of the man who'd pistol-whipped him on the beach. His head snapped around and he spotted Doctor Baker standing in the doorway. And someone stood beside him.

Emily! When he spotted the gun jabbed into her side, adrenaline squirted like wildfire through Steve's veins. His mind urged him to scramble from his chair and knock the deadly weapon from Baker's trembling fingers, yet he remained seated. Any movement from him would encourage Baker to pull the trigger.

'Brought you a special present, Helena.' Baker smirked.

'Well!' Helena's confident gaze swung to Doc Baker. 'Looks like we have company. What a delight! Please, do come in. Join the party.'

Baker gave Emily a rough shove into the room.

'Mr. Donovan, we meet again,' Doc Baker said quietly.

'The handyman with the ice pick.' Steve said.

He held his breath as Baker cocked his gun and aimed it at Emily's head. 'I'm quite handy with a gun too. I trust this time you won't lose control like you did on the beach?'

Choking back a sob, Emily threw Steve a look that said she was sorry.

'Did you find it?' Helena ambled over to Baker.

'Got it.'

Baker withdrew the gun from Emily's head and Steve sighed a breath of relief. His relief was short lived when Baker held up the briefcase containing his laptop. 'It was in Cole's hotel room. The original disk is inside the A drive,' Doctor Baker said. 'Damn computer sure is heavy. Thankfully they don't make them like this anymore.'

'You're a bastard!' Emily said furiously. 'And you, Helena! You are a horrid person. I trusted you.'

'Oh, Emily, stop your melodramatics.' Helena retrieved the case from Doctor Baker and lifted it onto the desk. She flipped the case open and a moment later lifted out the disk. She stared at it in awe. 'Just as I suspected. Same brand of disk my once trusted assistant used.'

'Why did you make Steve disappear?' Emily's soft question ripped at Steve's insides.

'I didn't know for sure what he knew, Emily. I found his resignation on my desk and a very incriminating disk. I had to stop him before anything was leaked and I needed him alive on the chance he could give us the whereabouts of the disk. But now you both know too much. I can't be sympathetic simply because I love the two of you.'

'Love?' Steve spat. 'You don't even know the meaning of the word, Helena.'

He should go for his gun stashed inside his boot. All he needed to do was cross his legs to get at it, but first he needed to call in the reinforcements. 'Helena, dear. Haven't you forgotten something?'

Her head snapped up and she threw him a bewildered look.

'Our little discussion we had earlier?'

Her perfectly manicured eyebrows crinkled into a puzzled frown.

'The matter about revenge?' he said smoothly.

She visibly relaxed. 'My dear boy, you simply have no opportunity for revenge.'

'Ah yes, I do.' He smiled. Leaning back in his chair, he casually propped his elbows behind his head and tried hard to portray he didn't have a care in the world. 'You see, Helena. I told you my revenge is purely for selfish reasons. I want to watch you die in person.'

'What's he talking about?' Doc Baker broke in.

'Not to worry, Steven is only toying with us.'

'Am I? There was a nice batch of rat poison in your office kitchen. In the cupboard, way up top. Behind the paper plates.'

Helena smiled shakily.

'By chance did you find the coffee tasting a bit . . . different?'

That was one of the phrase's Skip and he had agreed upon when Steve decided it was time to pull out. He braced himself for Skip's appearance. Nothing happened.

'What are you saying, Steven? You poisoned my coffee? You honestly think I'd believe you would poison me?'

'Prison sure does change a man.'

'Does it?' There wasn't an ounce of softness left in her voice. Her gaze drifted to her half-full coffee mug.

'About now you should be experiencing the beginning of mild abdominal cramping.' Steve crossed his legs and slowly began to slide his hands across the desk toward him. Where the hell was Skip?

'Helena,' Doc Baker said, 'if what he's saying is true, we have to get you to the hospital.'

She studied Steve with her icy stare and he stopped moving his hands. 'You seriously think I would come here without a plan, Helena? By the way, is that a dusting of perspiration beading your brow?'

He fastened his gaze on Doc Baker. 'Doc, don't you think she's getting a little pale?'

Doc Baker licked his lips nervously.

'Helena? How are you feeling?'

'Oh for heaven's sake. I feel fine. Doctor, please check and see if Steven is unarmed.'

Dammit! He needed to stall Baker. 'How'd you hook up with Helena, doc? She blackmail you into helping her kill people? Or are you in it for the money?'

'A doctor's salary isn't what it used to be.'

'So you kill people with ice picks to earn your salary?'

'Gotta make a living.'

Steve tensed as the doctor grabbed Emily by her arm and stuck the gun into her ribs.

'I assume you didn't come unarmed. Place your weapon on the table or else — '

There was a loud crash as the door swung inward. Skip Cole casually strolled in, gun in hand. 'Mind if I join the party?'

Steve didn't wait. The blood drained from his body as he yelled to Emily to take cover. At the same time his hand dug into his boot. His fingers snatched up the cold, deadly weapon.

From the corner of his eye he spotted Baker. One hand clutched Emily's wrist as she desperately kicked at him with her feet and in the other hand a gun was raising toward her head. Steve launched himself off his chair and fired quickly. He managed to get off a couple of shots before landing heavily on his side, his breath knocked painfully from his lungs.

For a split second a deadly silence and the acrid smell of gunpowder hung in the air. He aimed his gun at Doc Baker who stood clutching his wounded arm. Emily held a gun on him, her eyes wide with fright. Quickly Steve swung his weapon on Skip, who had his arms wrapped around a struggling Helena's waist.

'Easy man! I'm on your side!' Skip shouted when he spotted the gun on him.

'What the hell took you so long?' Steve shouted back.

'We didn't take into consideration how long it would take to get from the security room to here.' Skip was still shouting.

'What's all the yelling about?' Daniel chuckled.

When he spied his two older brothers flanking the open office door, Steve sighed in relief. Both had their guns drawn.

'It's over, Helena,' Matt said. 'The only party you're going to will last a lifetime.'

'We got everything on the security cameras,' Daniel, the lawyer, said happily. 'And since you admitted you knew you were being filmed, your confession will hold up in court.'

'You really don't look too good, Helena.'

Skip chuckled. 'Don't you think you would have preferred the rat poison?'

'You're fired!' Helena snapped at Skip.

He withdrew his identification from his vest pocket and flashed it in front of her pale face. 'Looks like the joke's on you after all, Helena. You can't fire me. I don't even work for you. I work for Uncle Sam. Take them away, guys.'

He cast a smile at Steve and Emily. 'Let's leave these two to get reacquainted. Although I do believe they've already gotten to that point.'

He winked at Steve and then suddenly he and Emily were alone. From across the room, she looked over at him.

'You okay?' she asked.

'Better than okay.' He grinned. He rolled onto his stomach and then got up on one knee.

'You're not hurt, are you?' She said as she came over and crouched down in front of him. Intense worry marred her pretty face.

'I'm fine.'

'Here, let me help you up.'

'No.' He waved her hand away. 'Just stand up.'

She frowned and reluctantly stood.

He reached into his back pocket and pulled out the item he needed. He lifted the lid and held out a tiny velvet black box so she could see the diamond engagement ring he'd bought yesterday. He'd dragged a reluctant Skip to a nearby jewelry store before they'd headed back to the bar last night to talk over today's plans.

Taking a deep breath he said, 'Will you marry me?'

She gasped in surprise and Steve's heart filled with love.

'But we're already married,' she said.

'That's not quite the answer I'm looking for.'

'You're serious?'

'I can always take the ring back.'

'No!'

'No, you don't want to marry me?'

'Don't take the ring back.' She examined the sparkling diamond. 'It's so beautiful.'

'Just like you.' With suddenly trembling fingers, he managed to wrangle the ring out of the much too tiny velvet box. He took her left hand in his and slipped the ring onto the appropriate finger.

'Perfect fit,' she said softly.

He climbed to his feet and was nearly bowled over when she literally threw herself at him. Curling her welcome arms around his neck, she hoisted her legs around his waist. Automatically his hands cupped her rounded buttocks in an effort to hold her in place. Her sexy scent just about drove him insane with desire for her. One by one his muscles contracted with delight as her warm body heat seeped through clothes and nestled lovingly against his skin.

'A perfect fit,' she said again.

'Just like us.' Steve stared into her clear hazel eyes and saw hope and love and tiny bits of fear. She reached out and smoothed a finger over the face of the medallion peeking out from between his open shirt collar.

'St. Christopher gives safety to travelers,' she said softly. 'It worked for you.'

'Took a while but yes, it worked.'

'And what about Helena? Do you think she'll leave us alone?'

'Hey! You're forgetting I have two big brothers who'll look out for us.'

Emily laughed and Steve caught his breath at the sight of those gorgeous dimples popping out in her flushed cheeks.

'Don't worry. Daniel's a pretty good lawyer. He'll find ways to keep her wrapped in the court system for a few years. She won't have any time for us. Besides, I know the owner of this cozy little lighthouse on a secluded island tucked away in Canada. No one hardly ever drops in unexpectedly. And it's a great place for kids to run around on. There's only one problem.'

'What?'

'We can't start anything until you answer my question.'

His heart soared as she cupped her silky hands to both sides of his face.

'Yes, I'll marry you.'

Before he could shout a happy yowl, she captured his mouth in an erotic kiss that left him totally breathless. And the happiest man on the face of the earth.

Epilogue

3 months later . . .

At approximately ten minutes after one o'clock in the afternoon Steve stood at the altar anxiously waiting for his bride to walk down the aisle. On one side of him his dad stood as best man. On the other side of him the preacher continued to throw nervous glances at his watch.

The wedding was supposed to have started ten minutes ago, but it appeared something was holding up the women. They were probably putting the last minute touches on their makeup. It was quite windy outside and with yesterday's major snowstorm Steve had worried the wedding might have to be postponed. The snowplows, however, had managed to plow a path directly to the quaint, white church they'd picked just outside of Charlottetown, Prince Edward Island.

Here they were. All the people he loved so dearly.

Emily and his sisters-in-law had worked hard organizing the big event. The church looked fantastic. The sanctuary was decorated in breathtaking bunches of sweetheart pink and delicate purple lilacs. At the end of each pew huge garlands of sharp purple lupins were intermingled with a scattering of light powder blue bachelor buttons and one yellow rose. Their fragrance filled the air with a heady perfume he found extremely pleasant.

Matt and Daniel and Skip stood in the vestibule of the church. All were decked out in light grey tuxedos with black bow ties, hair slicked in place. They sure looked dapper.

All the men were casting quick nervous glances his way. Then back down to the end of the aisle where he spotted his sister-in-law, Jo, casting her own nervous glances toward the side of the church where the bridesmaids and bride were supposed to have emerged from ten minutes ago.

He had to admit, Jo glowed in the lovely pale yellow matron-of-honor's dress. She held an overflowing bouquet of sharp purple lilacs over her abdomen, but it couldn't hide her rounded pregnancy.

Both Sara's and Jo's dresses had to be taken out several times over the past few weeks. Through it all, Emily had remained calm. Just like she'd remained calm and cool headed as she'd leafed through all those dozens of wedding brochures, magazines and tons of other bridal items strewn around the lighthouse.

When Jo walked up the carpeted aisle alone, his nervousness picked up big time. She threw him what he figured was a reassuring smile, but by the way Daniel was frowning as she whispered in his ear, Steve knew something was wrong.

* * *

'Steve! It's bad luck for the groom to see the bride before the wedding,' Sara's insistent voice said from out in the hall.

'We're already married. It doesn't count.'

Emily cringed as Steve's loud voice boomed through the lady's room.

'Emily? Where are you?'

A split second later, the door to her stall creaked open and she looked up to into his worried face. She couldn't help but throw him a wobbly smile from her perch on the floor in front of the toilet.

'My God! You look pale! You've picked up the flu, haven't you? I knew it. You've been looking green around the gills for the past week.'

She couldn't help but laugh at his way with words. 'Steve, what are you doing here?'

'I'm taking you home. You need to get into

bed right away and get lots of fluids into you and some proper food.'

Her stomach heaved gently. 'Please, don't mention food.'

She thought he'd get the hint. He didn't.

'You look so sexy with your head in the toilet.'

'I'm not sick,' she snapped at his teasing remark.

'Okay. The flu. In a few days you'll feel better. We can have the wedding in the summer. A June wedding. Like our first one.'

'This dress won't fit in June, Steve.'

'Sure it will.' He grinned his gorgeous grin and she had the sudden urge to run her fingers through his smooth hair, ruffle it and make it look messy as if he'd just climbed out of bed.

'Remember our workouts?' he said softly. 'They'll keep you in shape.'

'Well, those workouts worked.'

She waited for recognition to light up his face. Nothing happened.

'Of course, they worked. That's why you look so damned good in the wedding dress. You have good-looking muscles too. Here let me help you up.'

Emily sighed in frustration. He still wasn't getting it! The man was impossible! He helped her up and led her out of the bathroom stall. She'd wanted to tell him about her pregnancy on their honeymoon in Hawaii. Over a romantic dinner set for three. By golly if the man didn't pick up the hint with the extra plate on the table, she was going to leave him.

Just then Sara popped her head into the room.

'Can we come in? J.D. needs to have his diaper changed.'

Steve brushed past Emily and reached out to take the squirming, pudgy angel.

'Hi, J.D.' He held the baby high in the air. J.D. giggled furiously as he looked down at Steve with huge emerald green eyes.

'You're getting so big, little fellow.'

'You feeling better?' Sara asked as she slid the baby's diaper bag onto the counter beside Emily.

'Much, thanks.'

In the background, Steve made loud engine noises as with outstretched arms he whirled J.D. around as if he were a lightweight plane. After a moment of play, Steve returned the giggling baby to his mother.

Then he looked over at Emily, and she noticed something different in the depths of his blue eyes. She wasn't sure what it was, but it brought tears into her own eyes. Hormones. She'd heard pregnant women got very emotional over nothing.

Steve rubbed a hand over his face and cursed lightly under his breath. 'I wanted to tell you something during our honeymoon, but I'd better tell you, now.'

He reached into J.D.'s diaper bag and dragged out a diaper.

'Here.' He handed it to her and thumbed a tear from her cheek. 'Perhaps you should practice on J.D. before summer comes.'

'You already know?'

'I found the baby name book under your pillow, and I peeked over your shoulder a few times when you were on the Internet. Saw the baby furniture sites you were on, and . . . ' His face was now only inches away from hers and she could see the glitter of tears in his eyes. 'I found the early pregnancy test wrapper when it conveniently fell out of the garbage bag the other day. Like I said you've been looking green around the gills too.'

'So much for the healthy glow a pregnant woman is supposed to have,' Emily said.

'You're always beautiful to me,' he whispered softly.

She raised her gaze to his and finally recognized the look in his eyes. Disbelief.

'I never thought I could love you any more than I already do, but I do. You've made me the happiest man, Em. Beyond my wildest dreams.'

Tears streamed down her cheeks.

'Do you think you can get married, now?' Mathew chuckled from behind her.

'You can show her how much you love her on the honeymoon.' Daniel's amused voice echoed through the bathroom.

Emily and Steve turned around to find Mathew, Daniel, Jo and a whole passel of faces with huge smiles peeking through the now wide open bathroom doorway.

Steve gently kissed her on the cheek and brushed away more of the tears.

'Duty calls,' he whispered. Then he threw both hands in the air and headed for his brothers. 'Give me high-five, bros. I'm joining the ranks of fatherhood.'

Cheers and slaps reverberated throughout the bathroom and Emily knew without a doubt she was the happiest woman in the world.

We do hope that you have enjoyed reading this large print book.

Did you know that all of our titles are available for purchase?

We publish a wide range of high quality large print books including:
Romances, Mysteries, Classics
General Fiction
Non Fiction and Westerns

Special interest titles available in large print are:
The Little Oxford Dictionary
Music Book
Song Book
Hymn Book
Service Book

Also available from us courtesy of Oxford University Press:
Young Readers' Dictionary
(large print edition)
Young Readers' Thesaurus
(large print edition)

For further information or a free brochure, please contact us at:
Ulverscroft Large Print Books Ltd.,
The Green, Bradgate Road, Anstey,
Leicester, LE7 7FU, England.
Tel: (00 44) **0116 236 4325**
Fax: (00 44) **0116 234 0205**

Other titles published by
The House of Ulverscroft:

PEPPERMINT CREEK INN

Jan Springer

Sara and her husband Jack, an ex-cop, had bought a log cabin in the Canadian wilderness and had worked hard to turn it into a successful inn. However, their happy life at Peppermint Creek Inn ends tragically when someone creeps up to their isolated home and shoots Jack in the head. Crippled by survivor's guilt, Sara remains alone at the inn — until, one stormy night, a desperate and injured fugitive forces his way into her home and straight into her wounded heart. Is he the man of her dreams? Or her worst nightmare?

AS BIG AS THE SKY

Jan Springer

Five years ago, Jocelyn Brady had acted as lawyer for the prosecution in the trial of Dr. Seth Martin, who was accused of murdering little Johnnie Garrett and removing his eyes and heart for transplant. Jocelyn had lost the case, but knew that it had been fixed. Now the defense lawyer, Daniel McCullen, is himself in the clutches of the vile doctor, who wants his lungs for a wealthy client. Daniel is lying unconscious on a hospital bed — scheduled for termination — and Jocelyn knows she must rescue him . . .

DANGEROUS DECEPTION

Lisa Andrews

Emma gazed at the photograph. It showed a man — the man now sitting opposite her — with a blonde, sophisticated woman. The woman's face was the exact image of Emma's own. They could have been twins! The man said that he and his fiancée had broken off their engagement. Now he needed to travel to Spain, so that his grandfather, who did not have long to live, could meet his fiancée. He said he would pay Emma to act the part of his fiancée. Emma despised the man for his money and herself for even considering his offer. 'Do you always get what you want?' she flashed. He answered softly, 'Everyone has a price.'

TOO LATE FOR LOVE

Lisa Andrews

When Gemma Davenport hears that Blake Adams is going to buy her glass company, her heart sinks. Ten years ago they had a passionate affair which left Gemma broken-hearted and with a permanent reminder of Blake. As soon as she sees him again, it is clear that Blake is enjoying every moment of the take-over. He makes it apparent that he has never forgiven her for what he sees as her 'betrayal' in marrying another man. Gemma is soon wondering (and hoping?) if Blake is so intent on getting his own back that he's trying to rekindle their once 'fatal attraction' . . .